fire bird

Celebrating 35 Years of
Penguin Random House India

PRAISE FOR PERUMAL MURUGAN

Pyre

'Powerful and compelling'—International Booker Prize Committee

'*Pyre* is beautifully done, with flashbacks to the lovers' meeting in a soda shop, second thoughts as Saroja finds herself thinking fondly of the confinement of her old home and a further elopement to evade what prejudice threatens to bring down on them. The title promises a dramatic conclusion, and the book delivers'—*Guardian*

'A book marked with the same quality of luminous integrity and beauty seen in *Maadhorubaagan* (*One Part Woman*). What a world of hidden treasure is being unveiled by this writer and his sensitive translator . . . In reading someone like Murugan, there is always a sense of wonderment and mourning at the resonances lost in not reading in Tamil, but Aniruddhan translates with a fine ear that beautifully preserves the music of the original . . . I have yet to read an Indian author who writes of love as beautifully as Murugan does . . . the love between man and wife glows with a sweet, strong passion that draws you into its folds like the drowsy buzzing of bees on a heady summer afternoon . . . the tenderness pours off the pages like golden honey . . . This is Murugan's rich Kongu land, which he has mined so deeply and well. It's a barren, sun-scorched and unforgiving land but it comes blazingly alive in the writer's eloquent voice . . . To classify Perumal Murugan's books as *vattaara ilakkiyam* or sub-regional literature would be tragic, because he succeeds in universalising Kongu Nadu to such a degree that place and person fall away and all that remains is a hard and glittering gem of a story'—*The Hindu*

'Murugan's *Pyre* is haunted by its title—a word that appears nowhere in the novel, but contributes to the growing sense of dread and desperation that shadows it . . . [A] very readable English version by Vasudevan . . . In addition to drawing the reader into Murugan's Tamil-language environment, Vasudevan also signals the subtle differences in dialect, distinguishing Saroja's speech from Kumaresan's.

The translation succeeds in reminding the reader of the work's non-Western, multilingual setting, without compromising the fluency of the narrative'—*New York Times Book Review*

'A novel with a title like *Pyre* is unlikely to have a happy ending. Nevertheless, the journey towards this inevitable outcome delivers a disturbing insight into human bigotry and brutality whose application extends far beyond the novel's treatment of inter-caste marriage in contemporary Tamil Nadu . . . The translation from the original Tamil relies on simple English and the occasional American idiom yet comprehensively captures the claustrophobic atmosphere in which the lovers exist'—*Asian Review of Books*

'The prose is deceptively simple and sparse. And yet it has the effect of hitting you hard like the blazing sun, the parched land, the rock and the thorny karuvelum shrubs . . . Perumal Murugan, a poet and a scholar, knows how to handle masterful imagery and human emotions. Especially when he delves into the emotional space of his women characters, be it a coarse, unloving mother-in-law or the soft, sparrow-like, bewildered new bride . . . It is a sensitive translation done with great care. There is not a single word that jars, and the narrative is more tightly woven . . . It will haunt the reader for a long time'—*Indian Express*

'Murugan gives us a tight narrative, a memorable love story, and a truly unforgettable ending'—*Chicago Review of Books*

'An acclaimed writer in his native India, Murugan skilfully contrasts the young couple's innocence with the increasingly caustic attacks on their marital union. His spare prose mesmerizes, and Vasudevan's translation of the original Tamil conveys both meaning and needed context for Western English readers. India's casteism is on full display, but what makes this novel so powerful is how Murugan shows that intolerance, cruelty and bigotry are universal traits of humankind, even while tailored to the peculiarity of each society. Universal too, are the love, kindness and familial bonds that exist between individuals who have the sensitivity to look beyond societal custom and coercion . . . A haunting story of forbidden love set in southern India that illustrates the cruel consequences of societal intolerance'—*Kirkus Reviews* (starred review)

'Murugan delivers a powerful fable of star-crossed lovers and societal intolerance . . . Murugan describes rural life in piercing detail, making the everyday toil and inner lives of humble people the backdrop to the unfolding drama of escalating threats from Kumaresan's relatives and neighbours. The simple, elegant prose of Vasudevan's translation ranges from poetic to suspenseful as the hopeful innocence of young love bristles against tradition and Saroja faces increasing danger from the villagers . . . Murugan deserves worldwide recognition'—*Publishers Weekly* (starred review)

'[A] sensitive, richly textured translation . . . Murugan writes with cinematic power, and the final images of *Pyre* will sear your heart'—*Business Standard*

'It is one of those books that will forever haunt one, especially the dramatically chilling end. It is seminal reading. It is stories that like this that bring out the rich diversity of Indian literature'—Jaya Bhattacharji Rose

One Part Woman

'Murugan's unsurpassed ability to capture Tamil speech lays bare the complex organism of the society he adeptly portrays . . .'—Meena Kandasamy, *Guardian*

'The life of an innocent couple, who are led to believe that the expectations of the system define their pursuit of happiness forms Perumal Murugan's captivating story of love and desire. With his brilliant artistry, he captures the ups and downs of their lives. Works such as these have the power to subject contemporary value systems to intense introspection, it is for the same reason they are met with resistance. This work of art by Perumal Murugan can be acclaimed as modern mythology for its unusual access to cultural memories of the land and language, and the extraordinary courage with which it is dealt'—Vivek Shanbhag, author of *Ghachar Ghochar*

'It is rare to come across a writer who enjoys such intimacy with a land and those who live in close contact with it. *One Part Woman* is so rooted in the soil of tradition that its rebellion against it is all the more unexpected and moving'—Amitava Kumar, author of *Immigrant, Montana*

'Perumal Murugan's Tamil is vivid and terse, an instrument he uses with great care and precision to cut through the dense meshes of rural Tamil social life. The result, in this novel, is a brutally elegant examination of caste, family and sex in South India'—Anuk Arudpragasam, author of *The Story of a Brief Marriage*

'It's poignant, funny and painful and will expose readers of English to a region and class they likely haven't seen represented in literature . . . Murugan has an ear for the gentle absurdities of marriage as well as sympathy for his characters' woes'—*Kirkus Reviews*

'Murugan works his themes with a light hand; they always emanate from his characters, who are endowed with enough contradiction and mystery to keep from devolving into mouthpieces . . . I'm hoping for a whole shelf of books from this writer'—*New York Times*

'Beautiful . . . Plunges readers into Tamil culture through a story of love within a caste system undergoing British colonization in the early nineteenth century . . . Murugan's touching, harrowing love story captures the toll that infertility has on a marriage in a world where having a child is the greatest measure of one's worth'—*Publishers Weekly* (starred review)

'Perumal Murugan brings a playful, fable-like quality to his tale of traditional values and their subversion'—*Vanity Fair*

'Intimate and affecting . . . Throughout the novel, Murugan pits the individual against the group. How far you willing to go, he asks, in order to belong? . . . The true pleasure of this book lies in his adept explorations of male and female relationships, and in his unmistakable affection for people who find themselves pitted against the world'—*New York Times Book Review*

'Translated by Aniruddhan Vasudevan, this novel from the globally bestselling Murugan will give fans of South Asian fiction a new perspective and fans of excellent historical fiction a new read'—*Literary Hub*

'Perumal Murugan's *One Part Woman* contains the sweetest, most substantial portrait of an Indian marriage in recent fiction. A touching and original novel'—Karan Mahajan, author of *The Association of Small Bombs*

'A superb book in which tenderness, love and desire kindle each other into a conflagration of sexual rapture'—Bapsi Sidhwa, author of *Water*

'Perumal Murugan opens up the layers of desire, longing, loss and fulfilment in a relationship with extraordinary sensitivity and surgical precision'—Ambai, author of *In a Forest, A Deer*

'Perumal Murugan turns an intimate and crystalline gaze on a married couple in interior Tamil Nadu. It is a gaze that lays bare the intricacies of their story, culminating in a heart-wrenching denouement that allows no room for apathy . . . *One Part Woman* is a powerful and insightful rendering of an entire milieu which is certainly still in existence. [Murugan] handles myriad complexities with an enviable sophistication, creating an evocative, even haunting, work . . . Murugan's writing is taut and suspenseful . . . Aniruddhan Vasudevan's translation deserves mention—the language is crisp, retaining local flavour without jarring, and often lyrical'—*The Hindu Business Line*

'This is a novel of many layers; of richly textured relationships; of raw and resonant dialogues and characters . . . Perumal Murugan's voice is distinct; it is the voice of writing in the Indian languages rich in characters, dialogues and locales that are unerringly drawn and intensely evocative. As the novel moves towards its inevitable climax, tragic yet redemptive, the reader shares in the anguish of the characters caught in a fate beyond their control. It is because a superb writer has drawn us adroitly into the lives of those far removed from our acquaintance'—*Indian Express*

'Murugan imbues the simple story of a young couple, deeply in love and anxious to have a child, with the complexities of convention, obligation and, ultimately, conviction . . . An engaging story'—*Time Out* (India)

'Versatile, sensitive to history and conscious of his responsibilities as a writer, Murugan [. . .] the most accomplished of his generation of Tamil writers'—*Caravan*

A Lonely Harvest and Trial by Silence

'In both the books, Perumal, the consummate storyteller, is in top form and makes the reader come face to face with questions of morality, fairness, faithfulness, family, grief and hope time and again. He has the ability to speak of intimacy, lust and love with equal sincerity and ease. A generous and free writer, he shares his uncanny understanding of human nature'—*News Minute*

Resolve

'*Resolve* is an extended meditation on the politics of marriage in India'—Scroll.in

'Translated with an elegance that reflects Murugan's deep understanding of the unbreakable links between farmers and their land, Resolve is a searing indictment of the skewed gender equations in India'—*Financial Express*

'*Resolve* is a typical Perumal Murugan story that beautifully brings out typical problems faced by rural societies. Translated from the original *Kanganam*, Aniruddhan Vasudevan's translation works beautifully . . .'—*The Hindu Business Line*

'Replete with marriage brokers, horoscopes and rejections as is signature to the tradition of Indian arranged marriages, this seemingly comical book is a treasure waiting to be discovered by a reader'—*Telegraph*

Current Show

'*Current Show* will force you to pause and ponder on the impermanence of our experiences. It will make you involuntarily sending up a prayer in gratefulness. Pick up this book on a day when you feel that you've been dealt a bad hand'—Anjana Balakrishnan, News Minute

Seasons of the Palm

The writing is filled with grace and compassion and bears a fable-like quality'—Quint

Rising Heat

'With news about the climate crisis and environment taking centre stage in the last few years, this moving book is still as relevant today as it was when it first released in 1991. Through this novel, Murugan makes the readers question the human cost and true value of never-ending development in the name of progress and urbanisation'—*Times of India*

fire bird

PERUMAL MURUGAN

Translated from the Tamil by Janani Kannan

PENGUIN

An imprint of Penguin Random House

HAMISH HAMILTON

USA | Canada | UK | Ireland | Australia
New Zealand | India | South Africa | China | Singapore

Hamish Hamilton is part of the Penguin Random House group of companies
whose addresses can be found at global.penguinrandomhouse.com

Published by Penguin Random House India Pvt. Ltd
4th Floor, Capital Tower 1, MG Road,
Gurugram 122 002, Haryana, India

First published in Tamil by Kalachuvadu Publications 2012
First published in English in Hamish Hamilton by Penguin Random House India 2023

Copyright © Perumal Murugan 2012
English Translation © Janani Kannan 2023

10 9 8 7 6 5 4 3 2

ISBN 9780670089604

Typeset in Adobe Caslon Pro by Manipal Technologies Limited, Manipal
Printed at Thomson Press India Ltd, New Delhi

www.penguin.co.in

1

The ox tied to the right side of the yoke dropped dung and lay on the ground.

This has never occured before. The oxen always pull on with their heads lifted and mouths frothing no matter how long they are driven. Never have they excreted in defiance. Even with heavier loads, they somehow manage on without showing strain. The cart is practically empty now. It isn't not very hot either. What can it be?

The ox on the right always led the way for the ox on the left. It was ambling down the cart road at a relaxed, unhurried pace when suddenly the ox turned around as if startled by something and stared skyward with its eyes bulging out. It then collapsed to the ground and lay down. The ox on the left did not lie down but lowered its neck trying to yield to the pull.

In an instant, Kuppan leapt out of the cart and rushed to hold the yoke down to stop the rope from tightening around the ox's neck. A minute's delay and the rope could choke the ox to death. The cart had spun with the ox and was stopped across the mud path. Muthannan got off the cart, walked around to the ox on the right and released it from the yoke. By now, the other ox's eyes were bulging with fear too. Muthannan untied the left ox too and pushed the cart out of the way to the side of the path. He gently patted and stroked the whole length of the leading ox's body, trying to calm it down. It recognized his touch and his strokes and, as if to acknowledge it, seemed to shiver less. A large pile of dung lay on the ground by the ox. He stroked its horns as he made his way to its face. He gently lifted its front, caressed it, placed his cheek upon the ox's and whispered to it, as if sharing a secret. 'What happened?'

Muthannan gently tugged on the rope and nudged it to stand up. 'Mmm . . .' The ox tried but its forelimbs remained buckled. He tugged again. This time, it stood up, although barely. Not just its legs but its whole body was shaking. He patted the ox again as though he was brushing the dust off its body. That seemed to help the ox regain its composure. He then loosely secured the free end of the rope to a spoke in the wheel, and rummaged under the middle bar of the cart for a packet containing *thiruneer*, holy ash. He couldn't find it. Peruma had made four or five little packets of the thiruneer that she had brought back from their family deity Kooliyayi's temple a long time ago, to send along with them on their journey. She had carefully tucked them under the front, middle and back bars. She had smeared some on the oxen's foreheads and had handed some to Kuppan and Muthannan as well. Muthu had closed his eyes to invoke Kooliyayi's blessings as he smeared the ash across his forehead.

He went back to the spot on the cart path where the ox dropped dung and searched for the packet.

A cart path made of ash. Surely, this track must have existed for years. Crushed over and over again under the pressure of countless passing wheels, the dirt on the track had turned bright white, much like the thiruneer itself. He squinted his eyes and spotted the paper packet amidst the whiteness. The packet was torn and nearly all of its contents had spilled out. Along with the torn packet and its contents, he scooped up the ashen dirt beneath and walked back to the ox. The dirt dazzled like flour in his hands. He smeared some on the ox's forehead and sprinkled some all over its body. He smeared some on his own forehead too.

Kuppan was holding the other ox as it grazed along the edges of the track. Muthu brought back the now mollified leading ox and tied it back to the cart. It was a strong beast but he could tie it to a blade of grass for—as if bound by a promise—it would neither try to break free nor run away. The bodies of both the oxen gleamed in good health. Whether Muthu and Kuppan had enough to eat or not, they never compromised on the feed for the oxen. When they spotted a suitable location, they always stopped to let the oxen graze and drink water to their contentment before resuming the journey. 'How can we prosper if these poor animals starve?' Muthu would say.

More than ten days had passed since they had left their village. They wandered relentlessly through numerous villages, taking numerous paths. They had come to experience a whole range of roads, from ones that were broad and abundantly shaded by large canopies of tamarind trees to vine-covered tracks through forests made only by the imprints of wheels. '*Saami*, are there really so many kinds of paths in this world?' Kuppan wondered in astonishment all along the way. *Nowhere else had the oxen been frightened or behaved strangely in this way. It was usually enough for them to pause at a grassy spot to graze freely until their stomachs were full. They pulled the cart all day long after that.*

Perhaps, since cattle could see ghosts, they were startled by a ghost or a spirit? There wasn't the slightest hint of a spectre in the wind either. Muthannan inspected the area. Like a garland of chrysanthemums flung carelessly, the road meandered into the unknown for as far as his eyes could see. Flanking the path on both sides were barren fields with traces of the harvested finger millet and little millet crops. In the intense heat of the summer, the lands lay caked and dry. The sun was at its zenith.

Maybe the oxen aren't able to endure the heat. What hardship does a man driving a cart seated comfortably on it endure? It is but the oxen pulling the cart in that merciless heat that brave it. Perhaps we should have stopped in some shade and let the beasts rest. But these are the same oxen that breezed over hills of any elevation back when they took on chartered jobs carrying loads of heavy bags for delivery. Surely, they cannot have any trouble pulling an empty cart on a dirt path? With all these thoughts, Muthu turned eastward. In that moment, his face shone with clarity and brilliance.

'Kuppanna, the oxen have shown us the location! This is where we are going to live! Look towards the east. Look at that knoll where our Karattur Mansaami lives. Our God, Ayyan, who never lets us out of his sight, has not forsaken us this time either. That is why our mother Kooliyayi has come in the form of these oxen to tell us to halt here. If not, why would the thiruneer spill here?'

'Did the thiruneer spill here, saami?'

'Yes, Kuppanna, did you not see? The paper packet somehow fell here and our mother Kooli's thiruneer became one with this soil. It is that mixture that I have smeared on myself and sprinkled on the ox. If that's our mother's command, how can we disobey her?'

'If that is the case, then you are right, saami. This *is* our spot.'

With goosebumps all over his body, Muthannan faced eastward and prostrated on the ground. From where they stood, a healthy man running at a steady pace could reach the foot of the knoll within the time it would take to chew on a betel nut. The knoll was more like a large clump of mud that was covered with trees. It was not very tall—only about as tall as four palm trees stacked atop each other. On top of the knoll stood a temple, shaped like a woven basket turned upside down. How Muthu knew that the temple was for Mansaami, Kuppan could not figure out.

'Saami, are you sure this is a temple for Mansaami?'

'Yes, Kuppanna. Only if you step out of your village and travel around would you know all this. Not if you stay glued to the farm. A temple on a hill with a flat top will always belong to our God. Look over here, there are trees sheltering the hill. This is our Mansaami's temple for sure. If a place doesn't have the shade of a few trees, our Ayyan will not live there, Kuppa.'

Muthu's voice was filled with excitement. His body was covered in white dust but he was oblivious to it. Kuppan saw a vigour on Muthu's face that he hadn't seen before. Here was the fruit of their ten-day-long search! They pulled the cart off the road and under a neem tree providing expansive shade on a farmland by the road. Kuppan unpacked the pots and pans and began to set up to cook under the neem tree. Muthu picked out three similar-sized stones from among the plenty found all along the sides of the track. He brought them to Kuppan to help prop the vessel above the ground and make a stove. *Kuppan will take care of the rest.* Muthu lay down on over his towel spread out the shaded sloping roots of the neem tree. The gentle unevenness of the roots that he could feel through the towel soothed his sore back.

2

Muthannan did not have the heart to leave his village. However, an infuriated Peruma had moved into her parents' house with the children and had declared that she would come back to him only if they relocated to another village. With no other option left, the man readied his cart and set out accompanied by Kuppan, his father-in-law's farmhand. Every person he knew recommended a different village. His father-in-law suggested Maatoor; he knew of it from their weekly market on Saturdays. He talked to him about the largely agricultural villages around there and said, 'Our people form the majority in these places. They will be of help when in need, *maaple*. One is respected only when one is among his own, bear that in mind.' Although Muthu nodded in agreement, he did not want to move there. Neither did Peruma; she wanted to live at a safe distance away from all their relatives.

When they reached Karattur, he found himself unclear on which road to take. It was true that he used to drive there every day to deliver loads on hire. But back then, he was never uncertain of his destination. The hirers decided which depot he needed to pick up the load from and gave him a chit with the name of the village on it. For a man with a plan, there is but one path. For one with none, limitless options open up. A myriad roads appeared in front of him. Curving in and out, they each seemed to flutter their lashes to lure him into an embrace. Muthu stopped at the base of a hill with a temple on the top and prayed with all his heart. *All I ask for is the ability to decide which path to take.* After that, his mind was cleared of any doubts. He decided to take the road that ran along the foothills. *If I embraced the feet of God, isn't he bound to show the way?*

Kuppan was an older man with barely any exposure to the outside world. Still, Muthu would have found it difficult to manage without Kuppan. He referred to him as Kuppannan, something he learned from the depot owner during the few days that he worked there. No matter who it was or how old they were, the owner always referred to them as *annan*, or elder brother, and never used the derogatory *da*. Most considered the labourers unimportant, but not the owner. 'Refer to them as annan, Muthu, and you can get any work done.' That habit had stayed with Muthu as well. 'Saami, please call me da. I feel strange when you refer to me as annan, please,' Kuppan had protested, initially. But Muthu wasn't going to listen to him. 'You are older than me, aren't you, Kuppanna?' Kuppan found it odd at first; eventually, he not only got used to it, but the affectionate honorific made him happy too. Once they left their village, everything was new to Kuppan. Muthu, on the other hand, was familiar with the neighbouring villages from his days of chartered deliveries.

The road along the foothill ran due east, passing by the larger towns of Mandoor and Kuratoor. Past the Kuratoor *mitaadhar*'s house that now appeared sullen. This house, or 'the palace', as people referred to it, was once bustling with men, machines, horses and ox-drawn carts. Every Tamil month of Maasi, during Karattur's chariot festival, food was served around the clock in the long, open corridors along the exterior of the house. The stoves were not turned off for nearly a fortnight. People arrived in throngs day and night, and ate to their fill. Muthu had come here once or twice when he was a little boy, with his eldest brother. The mere sight of the dazzling bright grains of paddy rice that sparkled like dew drops, served in little heaps on leaves, was alluring. Crowds gathered just to eat that rice to their heart's content. At times, they had to wait in line between rope barricades before they could be seated to eat.

At the back of the house, in a pandal that covered almost half an acre, they served food to the needy. Needless to say, that got crowded too. The people who came to eat there usually went on their own to the section they belonged to. However, once, the time that Muthu visited, someone who should have gone to the backyard pandal decided to sit in the front instead. Just as he settled down and began to sprinkle water on his leaf to clean it, someone identified him and called him out. '*Dei*, aren't you Meenur Vatthan's grandson?' A face still too young to shave looked up and blinked vacantly. The person supervising the food distribution came rushing over, scolded him and directed him to the pandal at the back of the house. Hearing someone mention that the rice served in the front corridors was finer than the rice served in the backyard pandal, this lad had craved to taste the difference. The incident died down after only a small rumble because the supervisor said, 'Don't raise a hue and cry over it. There will always be a case or two like this. Make this any bigger and the mitaadhar may stop serving food altogether. Look around and see for yourself how many that have never eaten paddy rice ever before are eating their fill here.'

On the days the great temple chariot was pulled through the streets of Karattur, the road to Kuratoor would be jampacked with vehicles. People from other villages who set out to see the chariot would also plan to stop for at least one meal at the Karattur mitaadhar's palace. Food was served generously on areca leaves. Only rice and saaru were served. As the leaves became empty, they served more. But food could not be taken away. The sight of sated folks lying stretched out in the shade of the tamarind trees lining the road was still fresh in Muthu's mind. The palace was completely empty right now. All the relatives of the mitaadhar had moved to big cities in the north. No one went to the palace because they believed it was haunted. The palace was taken over by bats.

As soon as they crossed Karattur, the road forked into two. The road to the right went to Nangoor, the other to Rattoor. Muthu paused at that spot, unsure of which way to go. He then loosened the harness a little—he would go where the oxen went. The oxen took the road to Rattoor without any hesitation. And he accepted that. *If we take this road, we will go to Raattoor and reach the foothills of Selli hills. If we go west, we will join the road to Saethoor.* Muthu had been on this road only once or twice before, that too at night. *So what, I can always ask around for directions.* Dense tamarind trees lined the way. So dense that their branches touched each other across the path, like hands joined together. 'Saami, why are they all trees that ghosts reside on?' said Kuppan. Muthu laughed. 'Are ghosts bigger than man, Kuppanna?'

'It is true, saami. When I was young, I was quite energetic and was part of a gang of about four or five lads from the *valavu*, the labourers' quarters, where we lived. We were so brave, so bold we believed we could take on anything. So audacious we were. I had a grandfather named Chinna. He never stayed home; he would go to all the markets in all the villages. He would seat himself across the market entrance, on a sack spread under a large tamarind tree like this one, and cobble footwear. When one market ended, he went to the next. That was his livelihood. He refused to work on the farms. He stopped by the village once in a while. When he did, he spent about ten days with his wife and children, gave them the money he had, and left again. There wasn't a political gathering that he hadn't been to, either. Especially if it was Periyar speaking or Annadurai—they were his favourites. When he came to the village, he used to tell us one story after another . . .'

When it was decided that Kuppan would accompany Muthu, Muthu's brother-in-law said to him, 'You will never be in need of something to listen to, *mama*. A song here, a story there, that is Kuppan for you. You have nothing to worry about. Kuppan will take good care of you.' Muthu sensed Kuppan's rising fervour to continue on with the story. He nodded actively as if to encourage him. 'I too always wanted to listen to Periyar speak. Your grandfather was a lucky man,' he said.

'Yes, saami. You know that *mandapam* with forty columns in front of that temple in the lowland? That's where those meetings supposedly took place. Ostensibly, the priests shut the doors and did not open them until the gathering was over. After he would finish his speech, he would say, "If you have any questions for me, ask boldly".

Once, my grandfather asked him, "Saami, you keep a beard . . . are you a man of God?"

He replied, "A man of God keeps a beard and so does a lazy man. I am just a lazy man." And then he asked about my grandfather.

After my grandfather finished, Periyar asked him, "I go around saying there is no God. How can you address me as 'saami'? Like you, I am just human too."

"But you are God to the likes of me," said my grandfather. Periyar stroked his beard and laughed. "Nonsense!" It was only because he constantly said so that we also grew up not believing in gods or ghosts. Despite that, a tragedy found its way to us, saami.'

The cart rolled along slowly. Muthu never rushed his beasts unnecessarily. He held the handle of the whip in his hand but only crackled it in the air. He was listening to and smiling at Kuppan's story, over the crunching sounds from the wheels. But when Kuppan paused with a heavy sigh, he felt uncomfortable. He sensed that he was going to open a pot brimming with despair and needed some time to brace himself to bear its pungent odour. He loosened his grip on the oxen and turned around to face Kuppan. Kuppan was softly scratching his greying beard that seemed to be clinging to his face. His eyes appeared distant and empty. Muthu decided to change the topic.

'Have you heard him speak, Kuppanna?'

'No, saami . . . it has been several years since I travelled outside the village. The millet fields and corn fields are the only places I go to. Occasionally, I shepherd the cows and goats to the little mud hill in our village. That's all. I've folded my life to fit only the farm, saami.'

'If it is a good place then one can fit oneself to live there for a lifetime, Kuppanna. It is in search of such a place that I am going through all this trouble.'

'What can a place do by itself, saami? It is the people from whom a place gets its character. If you have the love and support of the people around you, any place will be agreeable. You can abandon all care and live in contentment.'

To Muthu, Kuppan's words were heavily loaded. *Everyone has so many troubles that they keep bottled up within them. I'll make him open up another time*, he thought to himself and made a gesture as if to drive his oxen faster. He folded his tongue to make a 'ttha' sound and touched the backs of the beasts with the grip of the whip gently. The oxen hastened their pace.

3

A journey towards an undetermined destination. This will culminate at the place that gives the most confidence for survival.

The cart rolled on patiently. It stopped at the outskirts of every village, sometimes turning suddenly onto cart tracks branching off from the main road and leading into villages. After roaming through the villages, the cart would emerge back onto the main road from a different connecting point. As the oxen grazed on the dense grass by the roadway, Kuppan cooked up some kali. Peruma had covered the top of a wicker basket with a sari after filling it all the way to the top with millet flour, and tied it up with another piece of cloth to keep it from spilling. No one knew when she found the time to grind all the flour, yet there it was, enough to last them for another ten days!

The kali Kuppan made was so smooth that it simply slid down the throat. To go with it, he mashed up some edible greens he somehow managed to find either by the fringes of farms or in the shade of the trees by the roadside, wherever they stopped to cook. It was the period of respite after harvest. The moisture from the late winter month of Maasi had drawn out the cheery green faces of grasses and other flora. There was still time for the rains. Panguni, the month after, may bring in the occasional, unexpected drizzle. After that was Chittirai with all the heat. Then, with the advent of Vaikasi and its first spells of rain, farmlands everywhere would turn verdant. *Hopefully, we'd find a place by then. That would be good. If not, there was always the bag of dried broad beans left to be eaten. But no, we cannot roam about for that long, we have to find a place to settle down within a month's time.*

What a perfect pairing broad beans and kali make! Muthu jokingly told Kuppan while eating, 'Kuppanna, don't you go about telling everyone that "The landlord ate with relish" every morsel of the food that you made. You must say instead that it was I who made the tasty food.' Kuppan laughed and agreed. Kali had but one taste. All one had to do was make sure it didn't develop lumps while cooking to keep it smooth enough to put some in the middle of one's tongue and swallow it clean. It was the saaru served alongside the kali that imparted flavour to the preparation. Kuppan resourcefully changed around the taste every day. 'Is it you who cooks for Thangaa?' Muthu asked. 'Yes, I do, *nga*. I have my mother's knack for cooking. Thangaa doesn't have it in her. If I want to eat tasty food, I just make it myself,' Kuppan elaborated.

While Kuppan tended to their food, Muthannan went into the villages to gather information. To find out if there was 'any land available for sale?' Initially, he felt awkward asking such a direct question. Especially because those who

toiled on their lands for a living considered it inauspicious
to be asked if they would sell their land. Some would even
get ready to pick a fight with him. 'You want us to sell what
we have and loiter from village to village with a begging
bowl?' He later evolved subtler means to find out—if there
was a shop in the village, he would hang around there and
bring up the topic casually in conversation with locals. Or,
if he ran into older men, he would ask them politely if they
knew of any pieces of land that were expected to go up
for sale, and other such ways. In some villages, he did not
have to go very far—the washerman's house was the first to
welcome him at the outskirts. Clothes hung from endless
clotheslines over pasture lands as donkeys grazed about.
How could there be a village secret without the washerman
knowing about it? A chat with him would usually be enough
to decide whether or not to pursue that village.

He went along if someone offered to show him an
available piece of land. In every village he went to, he was
always eyed with suspicion at first. Hearing his polite way
of speaking would help the locals build some trust in him.
They usually came forward to show him their land only
after first consulting with a few people in their village. The
first thing they asked him was his caste. But that alone
didn't suffice; he had to tell them his sect, the village he
came from, the deity of the temple his family prayed to
and all that before they trusted him enough to engage in
a conversation with him. Muthu and Kuppan had come
all the way to Raattoor and seen many a plot of land but
none had felt right as yet. If the land was good, there wasn't
enough of it. If there was more available, the price was

much higher. Moreover, because he was from a different place, they quoted an even higher price for him. Everything cost an arm and a leg. Mutthannan was seeking to buy for a fraction of what was usually asked of him.

Going inwards from Guruvoor led them to hilly farms. The prices people quoted to them there were on the lower side but there was very little access to water, with no potential to better the situation on their own. It was only Maasi and yet they saw women carrying pots and walking towards the wells looking for water. *Should they take on this new burden trying to escape another?* Still, Muthu stayed an entire day in that place and visited the available plots. Even though it was close to his village, he felt he needed to consider the option. But nothing worked out. In a place called Kalloor, he saw shacks all around the fields. Everyone there was a farmer. They spent that night at the choultry.

Muthu parked the cart in front of the choultry. Two vadhanarayana trees stood at the entrance, their leaves covering the front yard like a layer of sandalwood paste. He tied the oxen to the trees. He was confident in his decision to stay the night there. He could tell that, after the seven o' clock horn, a handful of people would come to sleep there too. Once Kuppan got busy setting up the stove to prepare dinner, Muthu decided to make good of the opportunity to get him to talk. *Only work can lighten the burden of grief. No matter who it is, they will always yield when they are fully engaged in a task.*

'Kuppanna, when you were talking about your grandfather yesterday . . . you mentioned that a tragedy befell you . . . what happened? I wanted to ask you about it then, but I got distracted.'

The sun had set; the last rays reflected dimly across the sky. Kuppan got the fire started for the stove and turned towards Muthu with a smile spread across his face. Even though there was a faint hint of sadness in it, Muthu felt that he was going to be able to talk about it now without much struggle.

'That was nothing, saami . . . it was an injudicious thing I did in my sprightly young days. Even now, the mere thought of it sends shivers down my spine. You know of those vagrant fortune-tellers, saami? One of them came to our village when I was fifteen or sixteen years old. I used to roam around in a group with four or five fellows all the time then. We used to profess that there was no God or devil and other such things, echoing my grandfather. It was during that time that this fortune-teller started visiting our village. Whenever he came, he made sure to halt for ten days. The temple in our valavu was his spot. He wasn't allowed inside the temple of your community. At exactly twelve at night, he would go to the cemetery. He would pray to his Goddess Jakkammal there and then leave the cemetery to go into any one of the valavus around. He would stop in front of each and every house, sound his *udukkai*, a small handheld drum, and portend the future. "The goddess of wealth, Mahalakshmi, lives in this house . . . Mahalakshmi lives here. Whatever you touch will sparkle. Whatever you do will be successful." Or, "Pthu . . . pthu . . . the goddess of ill luck, Moodevi, has entered this house . . . Moodevi has found her way in. Evil has taken hold of this place. If you

are not cautious, everything will be destroyed, everything."
Even a dog would hide from him if it saw him approach.
Because if it barked at him, he would cast a dreadful spell
and seal the dog's jaw shut. Over the next day or two, he
would go back to at least four or five of the houses where he
had predicted misfortune would befall, and would manage
to get them to donate a bunch of items, including chicken
and clothes, in return for prescribing remedial measures—
that was his ruse. A wicked desire to play a prank on him
overcame us.'

The pot boiled audibly. He removed the dish he had
used to cover the pot and steam spread out everywhere.
He quietened the fire, slowly added the flour that he had
measured and began stirring the pot.

'Did you beat him or rough him up? They used to
say that if you ran into him while he was out on his
soothsaying routine, he would curse you with something
evil. When I was a little boy, I woke my mother up one
night to take me outside to urinate. Suddenly, I heard the
sound of the udukkai and a bellow of "Jai Jakkamma!"
I didn't even check to see where he was. I raced back
inside our house and hid under the blanket. My mother
kept calling out to me, but I didn't come out. The urine
I was trying to desperately hold in, made its way out, and
I unwittingly wet the cot. Everyone teased me after that
incident—they called me "chicken-hearted", "bedwetter"
and all that, Kuppanna.' Muthu laughed aloud as he
narrated his story.

Kuppan stirred the kali with two palm stalks that
he was using as ladles. In the dark, the embers alone

smouldered brightly. He used two more palm stalks as tongs to hold the pot in place as he stirred the kali continuously—if he faltered even a little bit, it would turn lumpy. Until he finished cooking it, he didn't say anything. He then poured into the kali the water he had heated in the dish he had used as a cover for the pot, and increased the heat. Just a little longer before the kali would be perfectly cooked.

He then continued, 'At that time, we knew no fear. There is reason to believe that a gang such as ours had no heart. One of the fellows pointed out that if the fortune-teller went into the cemetery in the middle of the night, then he must feel absolutely no fear at all. I challenged him saying that he surely must have *some* fear—there is no man without fear. So we decided to test both our theories and hatched a plan, you see . . . and that was to scare him when he was on his way back into the village after his rituals in the cemetery. Remember how the road we travelled on appeared dark even in broad daylight because of the tamarind tree canopies? The road through our village was like that too. Each of us climbed a tree and hid ourselves well in there. It was frightening to even hide in those trees by ourselves. It was only after taking a swig of arrack each that we were emboldened to take our spots. Each of us had two mud pots with us—we had collected the broken and discarded ones we had found lying around the village. We were six people in all and had positioned ourselves atop every other tree.

'The man was on his way back from the cemetery in the dim moonlight. When he approached the first tree, I made a grunting sound and dropped the two mud pots. They fell on the road and splattered everywhere—a couple of shards may even have hit his legs. He stood petrified for a minute. I could tell, sitting atop the tree, that he was shivering. Then he pulled himself together. "Mmm . . . Jai Jakkamma!" he chanted loudly. I hid myself. The crows on the tree flew away, cawing. He hastened his pace. When he crossed the next tree, the next fellow dropped his mud pots just like I did. This happened at six spots. The man chanted Jakkamma's name the whole way through. Whether he was walking or running, we couldn't tell. But he didn't go into the village that night after that, you see. He went directly to our temple . . .'

He stirred the kali a few times again and took the pot off the stove. He adjusted slightly the stones that made up the stove to support the dish holding the water. Into the water, he dropped the amaranth greens he had picked, de-stemmed and cleaned, earlier that day.

'He couldn't have gone fortune-telling that night. He must have gone to sleep at the temple, petrified and crushed. No man can be fearless, Kuppana . . .'

Muthu handed him a peeled onion and some green chillies as he chatted on. Adding onions made the greens more fragrant and flavourful—grind them together and the saaru would be licked clean off the plates. Whenever the phrase 'Stop or the plate is going to disappear' was uttered in jest, one could safely assume that a saaru made from amaranth greens was the reason. Amaranth greens were rare. In Kallur, someone had planted groundnuts in a portion of their land. Kuppan somehow managed to spot the open, palm-like amaranth greens growing sporadically, amidst the light green leaves of the groundnut crop. These greens were quite like the stars in the sky in the way they twinkled and drew your attention. Kuppan had requested the farmer's permission and collected them carefully.

His eyes became slits as he tried to see through the smoke and finished cooking. Not a drop of oil was used to cook the greens. Yet, they smelled as though they were being cooked in butter.

'Now I know, saami . . . but back then, I didn't. Once the man had gone towards the temple, we were all jubilant. We had managed to frighten the man who the whole village was frightened of. We drank more arrack, went home and went off to sleep. Because we had stayed up so late and had some to drink, we didn't wake up even when the sky turned bright. The murmurs running through the whole valavu reached our ears much later—we got up and walked over to the temple, only to find the fortune-teller lying there lifeless. Not just that night—he wasn't going to predict the fortune ever again . . . He had chanted Jakkamma's name loudly when the pots fell around him, but within, he must have been so terrified that it literally killed him. Who could have known that our prank could result in something so dreadful? From then on, I stopped spending time with those lads; I don't spend much time in the valavu either. That fortune-teller must have been about thirty. Wonder how big his family of dependents was. My heart is still distraught at wrongfully taking a life. Where can I go to wash away this sin? It is this incident that has completely crushed me, saami. No matter how you look at it, that was a murder, saami . . . a murder carried out by six boys. I have since curtailed my entertainment and don't go anywhere. It is only for the sake of my master's daughter that I agreed to accompany you.'

'*Pch.* Is that how it ended? We sometimes do things hoping for one outcome and it ends with a very different one. But what can we do? We have to call it fate and move forward. As a child, I was so spoiled by my family. Until I was ten, my feet seldom touched the ground—someone always carried me on their shoulders. I wasn't exposed to any discomfort; I was the apple of everyone's eye. I thought that was how my entire life was going to be. But look what happened to me. That's how things are, Kuppanna. Even after so many years, you are still tormented by that memory. You are truly a good person . . . What did you then end up doing with him?'

'That is the other part of the trauma, saami. No one knew where that good man hailed from. His kind splits their time between living at home and wandering about. We looked around for other fortune-tellers in the area but didn't find any. After two days of searching, we buried him in our village cemetery. To date, we know nothing about that man—his name, place of origin, relatives, nothing. Year after year, when other fortune-tellers would come by, we would enquire about that man's details, but we still haven't found out anything. His family probably believes that he is still alive somewhere, you see . . .'

Kuppan mashed up the greens into a paste using the ladle. They hadn't brought a churner along; Muthu wanted to keep their load to a minimum. Of all the things that

Peruma had packed, he had picked only a few to take with him. It is the women who need a lot of utensils to cook and fill their houses with. Enjoying the aroma, he served himself some kali and greens when two people arrived at the choultry. 'Come and have some kali with us, anna,' Muthu invited them. 'We just had a bite to eat. You please eat,' they replied and started to chit-chat with him. In a corner, meanwhile, Kuppan sat pushing the kali around on his plate, oblivious to the words being spoken around him.

4

The cart trudged along with a sense of discontentment and in want of more options. Added to this was the angst that a suitable place may not be found at all. But Muthu knew he could not return empty-handed: Peruma would destroy him with just a glance. When she made up her mind about something, there was no changing it. 'Take me and my children to a place far away. If not, in place of this sacred thread hanging from my neck, there will be a noose,' she had warned and not said a word more after that, just to drive home her point. It could be a neglected, rock-strewn piece of land that not even a fly would bother with, but he had to find it and make a farm out of it before he returned to her.

They left Kalloor early in the morning and didn't stop anywhere. The lands in that region were very similar; the earth was red, but devoid of water, unfortunately. Far and few were the wells, and that too with water levels barely enough to quench a bird's thirst. All along the way, the two witnessed people carrying pots and looking for wells. There wasn't enough even to drink. They saw women flock around wells and draw water standing atop irrigation apparatuses. The labour-class women were gathered at the base, begging the ones atop it, 'Please have some compassion for us too, saami.' *Let's not fall into the mouth of a tiger trying to escape a ghost*, thought Muthu, and he drove his cart on without stopping. By the time the sun rose above his forehead, they had already entered Raattoor. Kuppan had not said much since the time he had finished narrating his fortune-teller story. If he was asked something, he responded only in monosyllables. *It must have been, what, about forty years since that incident took place? Could something that happened so long ago still trouble a man so much?* They needed to stop somewhere to get water for the oxen before it got hotter. They needed to feed them something too.

Only after driving a fair distance into Raattoor did he notice that there were other carts on the road. Carts with covered carriages moved along slowly with fodder tied to the top of the carriages. Carts drawn by two oxen carried women with large baskets to the market and raced against each other. The goats and goat-kids on some of the carts bleated non-stop. Many people were walking towards the market as well, carrying baskets on their heads and holding ropes tied around the necks of goats in their hands. Seeing the happiness on all their faces made Muthu not only forget his woes, but also feel excited. But Kuppan did not seem to have noticed any of it. His face carried the stoic expression of a solitary reaper in an open field. Muthu decided to drag him to partake of the liveliness surrounding them.

'Looks like it is market day here today, Kuppanna. Say, what day is it?' he asked him.

'Saami . . . I don't track days. The sun rises in the east every day and sets in the west. Night falls. Then the sun rises again. That's all I know, saami. What am I going to do knowing what day it is? You appear to be happy today. Therefore, we will assume that today is "happy day",' said Kuppan. Unable to control himself, Muthu burst out laughing.

'How can you be like this, Kuppanna, you are so indifferent! Somehow, seeing this market crowd is making me feel energized,' chirped Muthu. He then mentally calculated that it was the third day since they had left their village. They had cooked chicken at home on Sunday morning. Muthu had loaded the cart after drinking some chicken saaru. Peruma had then packed rice and meat saaru for lunch for the two of them. To ward off the ghosts that the meat stew was bound to attract, she had tied together some neem leaves and charcoal from the stove and placed them in the lunch basket as well. *Sunday and Monday— that's two nights of staying out. Today must be Tuesday. So just like Karattur, Raattoor's market was on Tuesdays too.* Muthu followed a two-bullock cart in front of him into a large open ground outside the market. Quite a number of bullock carts were parked there.

On one side of the ground, women were pouring water into two wide-mouthed vessels each. As Muthu walked his oxen in that direction, the women came running towards him. 'Please come over here, saami,' they flocked around him, each of them, almost dragging him by his hand. 'This pot has cotton seed, bran, all mixed in already. Just one rupee per beast,' they hawked in unison. It was mostly the

Pannaar women who engaged in the business of selling fodder water in markets. They wore nose pins in both nostrils and their saris reached only till their knees. These women appeared to be dressed the same way. He looked at a middle-aged woman and said, 'You must mix in plenty of bran and cotton seeds, okay?'

'We will add as much as is appropriate for the animal, saami . . . why would anyone cheat these poor creatures?' she replied. Once it was clear that he had chosen her, the rest of the women scattered to look around for other customers.

The earthen vessels were generous in size. She added only half a *padi* of cotton seed and maybe about half a winnow of bran. No matter how much he coerced her to add more, she wouldn't budge. 'Cannot, saami . . . don't you know how expensive cotton seed is? And does bran just show up like that, you tell me?' she reasoned. Finally, he promised to pay her an extra rupee and had her add another half a measure of cotton seed and a half a winnow more of bran. By then, the oxen had begun to draw towards the fodder mixture. Seeing all this, Kuppannan came running towards them. 'Stay close to the cart, Kuppanna. This is where the scoundrels lurk. If we let down our guard even a little, they will simply vanish with our oxen, tether and all,' cautioned Muthu and sent him back to the cart. 'Do hold on to your *komanam*, tightly too, saami . . .' the woman quipped with a laugh, referring to his loincloth. Muthu smiled politely but decided to refrain from any more conversation with her. He watched his oxen instead.

Both the oxen dipped their snouts deep into the water to eat the bran first, chewing it well, before drinking the water. When they were halfway through, the woman walked over to pour more water into their vessels from another pot nearby, but Muthu stopped her. He was well aware of these connivances—if she added more water to their pots, the taste of the mixture would change and the oxen would stop feeding. She would save on water and the remaining cotton seed and bran. He let her add the rest of the water only after they had finished all the water and feed in the vessel. The oxen gulped down a mouthful of plain water and stopped drinking. He paid her the three rupees he had promised and took the oxen back to the cart. He tied them one on each side of the yoke and looked around the open ground.

There were four or five shops selling bales of leaves along the wall that divided the open ground from the market. 'A bundle for a quarter, a quarter!' Muthu went up to the sellers. Usually, the men who sold leaf bales were tree climbers. They would go to various farms, negotiate a price in exchange of trimming the leaves, and then sell them at the market. They usually did the job during the off season for climbing. Many days had passed since the oxen had had fresh leaves to eat, so Muthu decided to feed them some. The leaves were neither too tender nor overripe—they were perfect. The tree climbers were smart about cutting the leaves at the right stage so they would be sold immediately. All the bundles were of the same size, as if deliberately tied up that way. He bought eight bales for two rupees. Each bundle was only two mouthfuls for the

oxen. He fed them two bundles each. Kuppan loaded the
rest onto the cart.

'This is the first time, saami, that I'm seeing a market
like this. Look, even water has a price.'

'Kuppanna, not only water for the animals, but for
humans too. They sell a glass of water for a paisa each.
Anything will be sold at a price if there is a demand for
it. What will the people who come here to sell or buy do
when they get thirsty? Go into the market and you will
find ten, fifteen women standing with pots and tumblers
selling water. Alright, we've arranged to fill the oxen's
stomachs. Now, how about finding something that will
fill the men's?'

Kuppan chuckled at the way Muthu rubbed his stomach
as he said that. 'Of course, we have the kali soaked in water,
saami,' he replied.

'Let's keep that for later, it would make for a soothing
drink in the heat of the afternoon. There are usually puttu
shops in a market like this. Let's each eat four puttus,
Kuppanna. The stew they serve with the puttu is so tasty,
you'll want to drink it before they've even finished serving,'
said Muthu as he scanned around for a puttu shop. He
spotted one in the open ground itself. It was made out
of fabric sheets erected like a stall. Muthu walked over,
carrying a plate. Each puttu cost a quarter and was as big
as two palms spread out. He paid for eight and took four
puttus onto his plate. He then went back to the cart and
sent Kuppan with his plate to take the rest. Just as Muthu
had said, the saaru was so tasty that they licked their
utensils clean.

'It was during the chariot festival that I last had puttu, saami . . . we don't have the means to make rice, much less puttu. Today, I'm getting to eat this because of your generosity,' said Kuppan repeatedly as he ate. They took turns getting more saaru until they could eat no more. It had been two days since they had filled their stomachs with gratifying food. Muthu also bought two paccas of puffed rice and peanuts, and a few kacchayams or fried rice, banana and jaggery as snacks for later, from a shop located right at the entrance to the market.

He struck up conversations with other cart drivers there at the ground to chalk out his next move. A few goat sellers were also roaming around. Transactions in the business of selling goats usually wound up before the sun was fully up. After concluding their business, the sellers moved quietly towards the puttu shop to count the money they had made. Muthu read their faces and picked out a few he could speak with about finding land that met his needs. Some advised him to go towards Sellikundru and others directed him towards Saethur.

Muthu readied his cart to head out, still confused.

5

An old goat merchant said to him in the midst of slurping saaru loudly at the puttu shop, 'Land around Sellikundru is available for less. With little effort, you can mend the soil and grow cassava. Takes only a year. Once you plant it, your work will be done. All you have to do after that is stroll around your farm once a day, like a king. It is in high demand these days. Businessmen from Malayur negotiate the yield of an entire farm and take all of it. Many are moving northwards from here too for that reason. But the plots will not have any of the paperwork in order. After you buy the land, you will have to spend a little more to get the documents straightened out.'

'Land will be inexpensive if you go towards Saethur too,' said another merchant. 'You will see land everywhere. Just that no one there really puts in any effort into them. Any land there will need to first be corrected. But you are a farmer. You can make even a rock yield a crop, I'm sure. Go there. Four or five years of hardship but then you will be all set. You can grow cassava with some effort. You can even rotate some cotton and groundnuts. Hell, you can even sow paddy. The water there is sweet as sugarcane. I have travelled extensively in that area in search of goats. The soil there is wonderful,' he said with conviction.

Regardless of the direction, Muthu thought, they still had quite a distance to travel.

He was not keen on farming on the hills. He had been to Sellikundru only once when he had a load of cotton to drop off at Nallur. After he had dropped it off, he had been asked to wait an entire day till the return load of rice was arranged. Kannaiyan, the other cart driver, had invited him to look at some cattle in Sellikundru. They had taken the road that connected Nallur to Thuruvur, until they had reached the Pottoor Hill. They then parked the cart in an orchard at the foothill and climbed up the hill. It was winter then—the cold was unbearable even during midday. He was wearing only a *veshti*, a thin cloth covering him from waist down, and a towel over his bare torso. Had it been night time, they would have shivered to death. It occurred to them that they were inadequately dressed only after noticing that even the locals had covered themselves from head to toe. But because they had come so far, they went on to look at some cattle in a handful of villages. All the cattle were of the Sindhu variety. Their bodies were shrunken and their horns seemed thinner, proportionate to their bodies. They stood licking their snot, with tired faces. These cattle were best-suited to plough the lands on the curves of the slopes. If they were made to work on expansive areas, they couldn't last a stretch. Eventually, as if to account for all their efforts, the two of them bought a jackfruit each and made their way down before the sun went down.

*Any land meant for farming should be open and outspread.
One should be able to stand at one end and see everything going
on all over the farm. When cattle are let out to graze, they should
always be observable so that they don't fall prey to wild dogs
and foxes. The only way to understand what sort of livelihood
one can eke out there is by living there. With the land being
so uneven, was it really even feasible to farm on the slopes?
Moreover, given the cold weather, I can't just walk around the
farm whenever I want to. It will be hard to acclimatize the
children to it too. If something untoward were to happen to
any one of them, I just will not be able to face Peruma.* He
didn't share any of these thoughts that filled his mind with
Kuppan. The cart simply turned towards Saethur.

'Saami . . . why were you so anxious at the market? Can
people be that bad? Looks like staying put in a farm turned
out to be a good thing for me.'

'Kuppanna . . . if you carry even a wee bit of money on
you, you should be very careful when going to a market or
a chariot festival. We may think they are chatting with us
normally or simply staring at us, but they could be casting
a spell or pulling a trick on us. And before we know it, they
will hypnotize us and loot everything we have.'

'I know nothing about all this, saami. It is Thangaa
who takes care of going to the market, buying new clothes,
all that. What needs do I have other than two pieces of
komanam? Moreover, every year, the landlord's family
gives me two veshtis and towels, one for Pongal and one for
the chariot festival. Even those I don't get to wear, nga. It
is only because I am travelling with you now that I've been
wearing vesthi for these past three days, you see.'

Muthu had noticed how Kuppan felt no attachment to the piece of cloth around his waist. He fidgeted with it all day, oscillating between folding it around his knees and leaving it to fall straight to cover his ankles. He often removed the tuck around his waist to redo it. Because it was summer, whenever they stopped to rest, he removed his vesthi and slept in his komanam, gazing at the sky as he lay on the cart. No matter how much Muthu told him to, Kuppan never put a towel on his shoulder. 'If I put a towel on my shoulder when I'm with you, what would become of your status?'

Muthu got used to wearing a veshti only after he started running loads for hire. Before that, he too wore only a komanam. Till he was seven or eight years old, he wandered about even without that. 'Look at him, still roaming around dangling his bell,' Amma had remarked before she got him into the habit of wearing a komanam. She changed his komanam every day. When she did, she bunched her fingers, touched his penis with her fingertips and kissed it. 'Wonder who the lucky girl is going to be,' she would comment and laugh. Muthu had not understood what she meant then.

Once, about the time he started getting a moustache fuzz above his lips, his *athai*'s husband visited them from Nachchur. 'Come here da, maaple,' he said fondly. Muthu went to him affectionately. 'Look at the way you've worn your komanam,' he said and pulled it off in a flash. There were more than ten people around. Muthu ran to his mother crying and hid behind her. 'Mama wants to see your penis, dear. Only then he'll give his daughter in marriage to you,' she said to pacify him. But Muthu couldn't handle the embarrassment. He didn't visit that athai for a long time after that. Following that incident, Periannan taught him how to wear the komanam properly. 'Take the tail end on the back over the *aranakayiru*, the thread worn around the waist. Bring the rest from underneath, between your legs, and tuck it inwards on the front—that's it. If anyone tries to pull it out, it will tighten but never come out.' From then on, that's how Muthu wore his komanam. He had found it hard to get used to wearing a veshti too. But now, it didn't bother him at all.

'Kuppanna, only if you venture out will you understand earnings and expenditure. Do you know how much we spent in the market today? Water and feed for the oxen cost three rupees. The leaf bundles were two rupees. The puttu cost two rupees. The puffed rice and the kachhayams cost one and half rupees. In all, we spent eight and half rupees. I can't believe that I spent so much. We should not spend our money like this anymore, Kuppanna, otherwise we will have spent all the money we have saved for the land, just on food.'

Kuppanna didn't say anything but he couldn't hold back his laughter. With great difficulty, he controlled himself and laughed without making any sound. He even looked upwards to try and hide the expression on his face. Muthu, who was riding the cart, shot a sideways glance at him and caught a glimpse of him laughing. What did that laugh mean?

'Are you laughing because I'm being such a miser, Kuppanna? Not just you, everybody thinks that farmers are all misers. Tell me, what is it?'

'You are not a miser, saami . . . you are simply being responsible, unlike us. Otherwise, how would you be able to survive? But, that wasn't why I laughed . . . I got reminded of a landlord from my village. That's why I laughed.'

'What about him, Kuppanna?'

'I will narrate the incident the way it happened. You mustn't read between the lines . . .'

'You have been with me for three days now, don't you know me already? I will not read between the lines, no matter what it is you tell me. I am going through all this struggle only because I want to be far away from that kind of underhandedness. Your words give me a boost of energy, so do go on.'

Muthu slowed down the cart and got ready for Kuppanna's story. Since the roads were flat, the oxen were pacing leisurely. Somewhere in the background, the faint sound of the misaligned wheel could be heard, rubbing against the pin as it rotated. Even though Kuppan started off hesitantly, he gained momentum as the story progressed.

'Do you know a person named Mosaiyan from our village, saami? He owns the land to the west of our landlord's. The two sheds there—one with a flat roof and the other with a thatched roof—are both his. When he was young and had gone on a rabbit hunt, once, he had apparently left as soon as he caught the first rabbit, dashing straight to his home. Everyone thought that he had run away because he was frightened. But by the time the rest of the hunting party returned, he had given the rabbit to his mother, made her clean it and fry it, eaten it and even taken a nap, leaving nothing but an empty pot

for the rest. That's how he got that name, Mosaiyan, the
rabbit man, you see. His nature hasn't changed at all since
his youth, you see.

'It was Rangan from my valavu who took care of his
farm. Year after year, he had to practically extort his yearly
dues from him. Where else could he go for money other
than to the family he worked for? Not a single year did
he receive the measure of grains he was promised. How
can the man survive if he doesn't get paid? Doesn't he too
need to eat at least twice a day? Especially when he has
to toil in the fields. Now, let's take you in comparison.
You don't eat anything without sharing with me. In fact,
I can even say that you fill my stomach before you fill
your own. But that landlord was not like that. *He* was a
miser, you see.'

Kuppan tried to read Muthu's face to figure out how
engaged he was in his story. He knew how to stretch or
shorten the rest of the story based on that. He saw that
Muthu's eagerness to listen showed all over his face.

'Some people are like that, Kuppanna. They seem to
think that they are going to take everything with them after
they die. How can you not pay a man who is at your service
night and day?'

'Yes, you see, saami . . . on top of that, that year, he
told Rangan not to do any work at the farm. He told him
that he, his wife, sons and daughters were all going to take
care of the farm by themselves. Whenever there was a lot
of work, he would call him over for his assistance. But for
the rest of the time, he would refuse his help. What could
poor Ranga do? He couldn't go to any other farm—the

ones who were in-charge there, wouldn't allow him in. One year, the landlord didn't even have him make a pair of slippers for him. You see, he is the kind that walks around carrying his footwear in his hands, lest they wear out. Each pair would last him four or five years. He didn't give Ranga his annual allocation of grains either. Ranga tried over and over again to get his payment before he finally gave up. He then decided that the livelihood wasn't working out for him and that even if it meant living off alms from others, he would not go back to his landlord to demand his dues again.'

'Then what did he do to survive?'

'Don't you ask about that saami . . . he was roaming about here and there herding his two goat kids and a buffalo calf. When other farms needed labourers, he went in exchange for daily wages. His two sons herded goats at our landlord's farm. A couple of years went by this way. Then one year, the rabbit man's daughter was to be married. For the ritual in the wedding ceremony when the father of the bride has to gift new footwear to the bride and groom, that's when the man remembered Ranga, you see. He even came to our quarters, looking for him. "Make the footwear for the wedding. It has to be really good. I will pay you, whatever the wages," he said and handed him a stick with the measurement of their feet marked on it. Ranga agreed without protest.'

'*Aaha* . . . ! He must have been expecting this. So, did he make the footwear? Did he show up on the day of the wedding or not?' Muthu asked, unable to control his curiosity. Kuppan continued with a hint of a smile.

'How can he continue living in the village if he didn't show up at the wedding? He made exceptional footwear for both the bride and groom, and took them along with him. During the ritual, he stood in front of the landlord, placed the footwear near the feet of the couple and had them touch it. Traditionally, after this is when he would spread out his towel to symbolically ask for the landlord's acknowledgement in the form of money. But Rangan refused to spread out his towel. There was a huge crowd at the wedding. People from both the families' villages were present and added up to a rather large number. Everyone was surprised that a farm in-charge refused to spread his towel before the landlord. But Rangan stated categorically, "Saami, I'm giving these slippers to my saami's daughter for free. I want not a paisa in return." Everyone wondered why a man such as he would give something for free to his landlord. That's when word spread that the landlord wasn't paying him his annual dues.

'The village leaders and other important people declared that if the farm in-charge had not been paid, he was under no obligation to take part in wedding rituals. But since Rangan had abided by custom and taken part in the ritual despite not getting paid, they said the slippers he had made would be considered a gift. The landlord nearly died of embarrassment. He hung his head low, feeling humiliated in front of everybody. He had not at all expected such behaviour from this poor man. Later, after consulting with others, Rangan told him he would accept the money for the footwear if he got three years' worth of dues along with it. How could the landlord refuse him in the middle of a wedding gathering? He quietly handed him three years' worth of his dues. It was only after that when Rangan accepted the money for the footwear. What's more—the landlord told Rangan that he could collect his dues every year, going forward, regardless of whether he actually worked at the farm or not.'

Muthu could not hold back his laughter. '*Ade appa!*', he exclaimed, 'Just so you know, I'm not that kind of a person. I unsuspectingly calculated my expenditure out loud before you and you put me in the same category as that rabbit man!'

'Not at all, saami. For some reason, the memories came to mind. You also insisted on knowing the story, so that's all,' said Kuppan humbly. Every time Muthu thought of Mosaiyan, he smiled. 'How did Rangan actually utter the words "the footwear are a gift"?' he would ask Kuppan often and laugh every time.

The two of them travelled the distance by occupying themselves with such stories. Even though Kuppan had never left his village, he had many things to talk about. It isn't quite true that only people who travel are knowledgeable. Doesn't a worm in garbage keep digging deeper to find what lies at the bottom? Kuppan was like that too. Listening to him talk made Muthu momentarily forget his desperate situation and feel cheerful. Any concern about food was resolved easily as well, thanks to him. Kuppan saved some kali from the night and kept it soaked in water. The kali usually dissolved in the water, stirred by the jolts of the cart. Sometimes they got some curd or buttermilk to mix with the kali, but even the plain preparation was pretty tasty. It felt cool as it descended into their stomachs in the mornings. They had it in the afternoon as well. On occasion, if they found a puttu shop, they ate puttu. On such occasions, as Muthannan grappled with the idea of spending money on food, he remembered the rabbit man. Although he reassured himself with Kuppan's words, that 'rabbit fellow was a miser, I'm simply being responsible,' he could not use the money kept aside to buy land, to feed himself. He had taken on an extraordinary amount of trouble to ensure that that money was left intact.

When it was time for the sun to set, he stopped the cart in the closest village. He didn't ride after the skies began to grow dark. If anyone asked him where the cart was headed, he said they were going to pick up a load of hay. Muthu was very particular about his cart and oxen, too. He was content only when he was in control. Rarely did he give the reins to Kuppanna. Even when he did, he couldn't let go—'Don't rush the oxen, Kuppanna', 'Don't pull on their necks', 'You are being too kind letting the reins hang so loose'—the commentary was endless.

Back in the village, Kuppan was in-charge of the landlord's cart. It was he who always drove the cart, whether it was for fetching sand from the dam, disposing of waste or transporting grains. But he had never driven the cart on a road like this where a bus or a lorry would pass by occasionally. At such times when a vehicle went by, Muthu leapt forward and snatched the reins from his hands in panic. On single-lane tar roads, he stopped the cart by the side of the road to make way for buses. Whenever Muthu reacted this way, a barely perceptible smile appeared on

Kuppan's face, unbeknownst to Muthu. But he never said anything to him.

In any village they stopped at, they found a choultry, a temple or some public place to park the cart and Muthu made Kuppan sleep there for security. Usually, there were at least four or five people who spent the night in the choultry. He didn't have to worry about finding help if he needed it. Muthu would then go into the heart of the village where the locals lived and on the pretext of finding out about saleable plots of land available in the area, he would find a house to stay in. He didn't mind spending the night even in a cowshed on a broken plinth, being bitten by mosquitoes constantly. There was a certain comfort and safety that accompanied staying inside a village, in a house—not so much his own security but that of his money. Four more lives were dependent on that money that had been scraped and put together out of everything they had. It included even the 100 that Peruma had put away bit by bit after spending on their household.

Without letting him see her welled-up eyes, she had removed her gold earrings and chain, bundled them in a piece of cloth and handed them to him. Only her thaali locket hung from her neck now. At the time of their wedding, Peruma had come wearing twenty sovereigns of gold. Of the four daughters-in-law, she was the one to have come with the most gold, making her the object of the others' jealousy. Peruma was prepared to wear a yellow thread in place of the gold thaali chain and give that to Muthu as well but Muthu refused to take any of her jewellery.

'If we settle down on a piece of land and start saving some money, can we not buy it back anytime we want? I don't need to wear all this every day to prance around at a chariot festival or a fête. Who knows when we will come back to this village for a wedding or a celebration? Let us put to use these pathetic things that lay untouched in some corner,' she insisted.

But Muthannan didn't want that. *This mouth will spew very different words later on. She will say, 'I gave you all that I had even if it meant that my ears and neck remained bare. If not for that, how would we have afforded this land or livelihood?' No matter where we end up living, we cannot avoid going to the village during a festival or for a function. The women will cover their mouths with the ends of their saris and murmur amongst themselves, 'Muthannan's wife doesn't have an iota of gold on her. That man, he must have sold off her jewellery and lost all the money.' I don't want to deal with all the trouble the relatives will cause.*

Little girl Vallamma will soon attain puberty. That ritual is coming up. In no more than five years, she needs to be married off. How can I find a piece of land, farm on it, see money from it and then buy her any jewellery by then? If we keep what we have, we can borrow some money from here and there to add more to it and settle her off in a good place. It will take another three or four years after that for the second one, Rosamma, to come of age and to be married off. We should be seeing some savings by then? As for the boy, if he is smart, he will find a way to survive. That was why he refused Peruma's jewellery. He wanted to buy only what his money could afford. Everything put together, he had about 2,500. At night, he kept all of it in a bag that he tied at his waist while he slept. He saw to it that it remained tucked in and didn't bulge out.

During the day, the money moved to his towel. He hid the towel under the hay spread on top of his cart. Every so often, he turned around to make sure it was still there and hadn't come undone with the bumpy movement of the cart. Kuppan offered to take care of it for him. 'Saami, don't worry about the money and focus on driving the cart. I will keep an eye on it all the time.' Muthu nodded in agreement but a little while later, turned to check on the money instinctively. 'You have an empty waist, Kuppanna. You can strip completely without a care. I, however, have a burden to bear,' Muthu reasoned with a smile.

6

It was only after he started making chartered trips that this fear intensified within Muthu—the feeling that there were thieves lurking in all directions. He couldn't see the good in anyone, couldn't strike a conversation with anyone freely. At the Rattoor market, he wanted to talk to the lady from whom he had bought the fodder mixture for the oxen. When she bent down to pick up the pot of water, he could not help but steal a glance at her cleavage that she had not covered properly. He could have exchanged a few flirtatious words with her, but he curbed himself out of the fear that she may be associated with scoundrels who were lurking around the market. That if he inadvertently slipped his intent to buy land while chatting with her she will send someone to follow them. He didn't have such fears during his life in the fields. But now, the sight of anyone fuelled the fear within him.

After Appa divided up his land among his sons and sent them away, Muthu spent some days feeling disoriented. The income from the portion of land he received was not nearly sufficient to run a family. In the state he found himself, he began to doubt if he could even afford a square meal for his wife and children. He did not have a job then. He spent his time curled up under the neem tree or in the shed during the day, and spread over a bald rock, staring vacantly into the sky by night, frustrated. He simply could not get a grasp on what to do. It was during that time when Vatthan, who delivered loads for a depot in Karattur, happened to come by the bald rock one night—a night brightly lit by the moon. Vatthan's breath reeked of arrack.

He lit a beedi and exhaled some smoke. 'Muthu, what are you doing lying here like this, da? Did Peruma sister not let you near her?'

'Mock away, da! You get to say anything because you can afford to belch on a full stomach. What can I possibly say when I belch because of an empty stomach?' replied Muthu angrily.

'Don't get angry, maaple. How will I know if you don't tell me what happened?'

When Muthu explained everything to him in a sad, tearful voice, Vatthan said, 'Is that why you are moping like this? Don't you know of people who survive with nothing but their hands and legs? First of all, stop saying "I don't have this, I don't have that". Look at what you have. You can make a living with the cart you have, da. Nobody looks after their oxen like the way you do. Let them feed you. The depot owners are struggling to find men with carts to deliver goods. Show up there in the morning.'

From then on, Muthu started making chartered trips. He drove to all the villages in the region. He drove for at least four days in a week. Even after all the expenses incurred, he saved a whole ten rupees a day.

The loading of the carts began late afternoon and the carts set out mostly past sunset. The carts always travelled together in groups of ten or twenty—never was a cart sent out alone. Lanterns would hang from each of them. The first and the last carts were driven by men who were seasoned in delivering loads. Even a small mongoose crossing the road couldn't escape the eyes of the first cart's driver. If he felt a little tired, he let the second cart driver go ahead of him. The last cart driver had to direct all his attention to the back of his cart only. If he heard the slightest noise that was out of the ordinary, he would sound out to the others. His hearing had to be sharp enough to be able to listen over the crackling of the wheels, and the singing and general chatter of the other drivers.

No one knew how or when a thief might appear. They had to be extra vigilant especially while driving through lonely hills, away from the bustle of the villages. This was when each would be focused on cheering his oxen to keep going as they drudged uphill bearing the heavy loads. If one ox grew tired and slowed down, all the carts behind it also had to slow down. Such times were ideal for thieves. If they came in a group of ten or twenty, the drivers could handle them, as none of them were puny or weak. All the carts carried *arivaal* or billhook machetes, knives and spears. If a driver did not appear strong, the depot owners refused their services, regardless of the kind of cart they had. It was the single thief who was the most dangerous. No one could predict his moves and the damage he planned to inflict.

Equally dangerous was a band of two or three thieves. While one of them distracted the cart driver, the others would finish the job with ease.

Even when travelling through active villages, a single thief could get on a cart. Usually, his target would be the last cart. As the one that traversed the road in fear, he would climb onto it stealthily, like a tiny cat. The sack at the very bottom of the last cart would usually be his focus. He would tear it open quietly and let the grains fall into his bag until it either got too heavy for him to carry or the driver spotted him. If the load was rice, the owner would suffer a huge loss. Somehow, the knives that the thieves carried cut through the sack without making any noise. The cart drivers, too, would employ many tricks to outwit the thieves. They would load the last cart with groundnuts or bran. When the thief cut open the sack, the bran would blow up on his face like smoke. When the thieves figured this trick out, they began to use a needle to first pierce the sack and find out what was in it before cutting it open with their knives.

On days that rice was transported, the owners arranged for a few guards to follow the last cart. They followed the cart on foot and carried weapons. The drivers felt sorry for the guards. It was bad enough that the animals were fated to walk the whole way—it was downright cruel that those men had to as well. When the oxen walked slowly, they could walk too. When they trotted at a faster pace, however, the men had to run to keep up. Whenever the guards accompanied them, the carts didn't face any trouble. Without them, however, a single thief could plunder entire carts in the middle of the caravan. If they walked under a cart, the driver behind that cart would not be able to see them that easily. The thief could make a gash in the sacks with a long needle and let rice flow freely through it. Before the driver can identify the sound of rice flowing out and stops his cart to check, the thief could have got away with large measures of rice.

Muthu made deliveries for three months. He wasn't home for four days in a week. For a man who until then had spent all his time only in fields, he came to learn about depots, its people, roads, cities and more. He was always in awe of how much more there was to know. Peruma tended to all of the work related to the field. It wasn't as if their land amounted to much—it was quite like a tossed piece of komanam that had been left behind for him. Even one woman was more than was needed to tend to that land. All of it appeared to be part of the scheme to drive him out of the village.

It must be Destiny that I now lay alone like this in an unknown place full of unknown faces. A troubled Muthu lay with his eyes closed under a neem tree, when he smelled smoke. What was Kuppan doing to cause smoke? Unable to control a sneeze, Muthu sat up. Kuppan looked at him with embarrassment. 'Did I wake you up, saami? The stove wasn't lighting properly, so I added some plant matter to the fire. That is what is causing all this smoke,' he explained, upset that he had disturbed Muthu.

'No, Kuppanna, feeling sleepy like this in the middle of the afternoon fills me with absurd thoughts when I lie down.'

The smoke soon engulfed the pot. His mind felt the same way. Kuppan's puckered his lips around one end of a tube to blow at the embers. Until the fire caught on, the pot would remain veiled in smoke. Muthu decided that after he finished eating the kali and the sun began to go down, he would go into the village to enquire about available plots of land. The houses were quite a distance away. There were no huts on the farms either. Even if these people who kept their fields and their houses separate didn't welcome with open arms a complete stranger like him from an unfamiliar land, he hoped they would not cause any problems in his dealings. But he felt certain that he would find land here. *From what I see, the soil looks very fertile. Some spots are clayey, but it is predominantly red earth. The colour of the red earth in this region is a little different, it looks like dried blood. The earth around Karattur is the colour of fresh blood. Still, that should pose no problem in using it for cultivation. It doesn't seem like much farming gets done here. The stumps of fox millets and of other little millets are left standing over a foot above the ground. Why would anyone leave them like this? Maybe this was done so they could be used as firewood? The soil is perfect for several types of cultivation. Hope the people are nice too. At any rate, they can't cause mental strife like the blood relatives. Any amount of external strife can be handled.*

The fire finally caught on well. Kuppan added the bean seeds to the pot. Muthu lay down again in the shade and closed his eyes. *Relationships that start at birth become so tangled over time that it becomes impossible to resolve even the most ordinary problems. And relationships with no past can turn into deep connections instantly. Never ever did I think that I will find a bond in Kuppan. Even though we have spent only a few days in each other's company, it feels as though we've known each other for several lifetimes. And the people who I've known since birth are now fading into a mere dot far away.*

Muthu was the youngest of all his siblings. During his childhood, his older siblings had showered him with endless love. They barely ever let him walk on the floor; they each wanted to carry him around all the time. He had three older brothers and two older sisters. After the sisters were married off, the brothers continued to pamper him. 'Our Muthannan,' they would say in every conversation. When they got married, problems began to creep in slowly. Still, they all got along together. All of a sudden, like a mean rooster chasing after the other chickens and plucking out their feathers, the topic of property division arose and obliterated all bonds they had until then. Kuppan had been no one to him until this trip. Muthu had only known him as the farm in-charge who took care of his father-in-law's lands. Yet, in addition to being his companion on this journey, Kuppan was also developing a deeper connection with Muthu. The joy from bonding is but meagre. The sorrow from severing a relationship aches deep within.

7

Appa had announced six months ago: 'I cannot keep the family together anymore. Each of you now have your own wives and children. You will naturally only focus on finding food for your own offspring. Just like how a koel throws out the young crows when the fledglings in its nest grow wings. It doesn't say, "Oh, I have protected them all this while, I should now feed them too". Once it knows they aren't its own kind, that's how it treats them.'

No one knew the reason behind Appa's decision. It was true that there had been issues amongst the women. But if that was, in fact, the reason, they should have been asked to part ways a long time ago. Everyone concluded that the decision must have been driven by the eldest brother and his wife. Even then, Muthannan could not come to terms with the situation fully. *The eldest brother is close to fifty. Why would he want to go separate ways at his age?* Muthu had never ever imagined that his family would split ways one day. That was why as always, he remained observing all that was going on around him quietly.

The farm was eleven acres in all. The division of the property was witnessed by a frontyard-full of people—a few important men of the village, some distant blood relatives of the same lineage, a few people from each in-law's family. Muthu hadn't informed his own father-in-law about the development. Peruma too hadn't insisted. Hushed conversations and calculated planning had begun right after Appa had announced his intention to divide the property. Muthannan had not involved himself in any such discussions either. This was the first time he regretted being the youngest son in the family. Going by the way such divisions worked, he held no claims to the property. The elders would suggest strategies for how to go about it. The eldest of the sons had the right to accept or reject it as it was presented to him. The youngest had to quietly accept whatever was given to him and had no right to demand anything.

Everyone was seated on the plinths and the cots arranged outside the house and spoke in support of their own plan. When the head of the village and a few others returned after a private discussion with Appa and the eldest brother by the cowshed, the others stopped talking and turned their attention to them. The women watched the goings-on sitting in the verandah of the house. They didn't yet have to attend to work in the kitchen—the assembled visitors wouldn't drink even a drop of water until the division was completed. Kaliannan and Pongiannan stood glued to a side of the plinth. Muthu stood with them too. The village head finally spoke.

'Rammannan's family has lived all these years together in unity without any fights or conflicts. The whole village looked up at them as an example of how brothers should be. But everyone knows that no matter how good things are, it is not possible for families to live together forever. They all have mutually agreed on the need for this division even before inviting us into the discussion. We propose a division that does not harm anyone and takes all factors into consideration. The eldest son is now over forty-five. The youngest is only twenty-eight. The ones in the middle are also over thirty. Bearing all this in mind, here is our decision. Please listen. You are all familiar with our custom—one that has been followed for generations—that the eldest would get the higher land and the younger, the lower, and the younger brother must gratefully accept whatever the eldest brother offers him. We take that also into account.'

After all these disclaimers, this was the plan they presented:

Four acres of the upper region by the well →	Eldest son Periannan
Two adjacent acres in the upper region →	Each of the two middle brothers, Kaliannan and Pongiannan
Two acres in the lower region →	Youngest son Muthannan
The leftover acre →	The father, Ramannan

Appa and Amma could farm the land that had been assigned to them until they were alive. Upon their deaths, half an acre each would go to the middle brothers.

The village head emphatically repeated the logic of the division many times over.

'The eldest son Periannan is forty-five years old. His son and daughter are ready to be married off. He has worked for this family ever since he was young. He is only going to slow down going forward and is not going to be able to add much to his property. Therefore, out of respect to all his hard work for this family, he shall receive four acres. As the two sons in the middle are thirty-five and thirty-three respectively, they shall receive half an acre more than the youngest son. The youngest son is only twenty-eight years old. He has time to work hard and save. Therefore, he gets only two acres.'

Periannan accepted the decision happily. It was his idea anyway, why would he have a problem accepting it? The two middle brothers got together and had a discussion. They went indoors to discuss it with their wives also. Kaliannan was the first one to speak.

'We too have children and large families. In a year or two, our children will also be ready to be married. We request this council that we are given here and now the half acre each that we would inherit after our parents died, itself.'

The crowd buzzed.

'Looks like you *maapillais* will abandon your father and mother on the streets. Well, if that were to happen, we will take them in. We are married to the daughters of this family. As if we can't take care of Mama and Athai until their dying day,' remarked Raakiannan, the elder akka's husband.

That akka had been married and sent off to Chinnur. Her husband had come there hoping that he too may inherit something. But after the first round of decisions, nothing had been said about giving anything to the daughters. His words betrayed his frustration when he spoke and the gathering realized he was present too. They chuckled at his words.

'That's right, Anna. You take one of them and we will keep the other with us. Or, we will keep them both in our homes, alternating every month. We have so many relatives living off us. Why would we deny our own *mamanaar* and *maamiyaar* anything?' The younger sister's husband Kandhaiyan added. The younger of the two sisters had been married off into a family in Kacchur, a village close by. He too spoke to register his presence.

'Whatever it may be, our situation is not so dire that we have to send our parents to our *maman* or *machaan*'s house, *maapile*,' said Chellannan, a paternal cousin.

'Here, they have four sons sound as a bell. Why would they even consider going to someone else's house? *Maapilais*, if there is something specific you want, please ask. If not, why say all this? Each of you take care of your own fathers and mothers. That is enough,' another cousin, Chinnannan, said piquantly. That angered Raakiannan.

'Have we sent our fathers and mothers to your house to be taken care of? How can you say such a thing?' He shook his towel forcefully and stood up.

'You can talk about our mothers and fathers, but we cannot talk about yours? How is that fair, mama? Only because my sister is married to you am I speaking this patiently,' Chinnannan snapped back. The situation was ripening for a fight to break out.

But before anything more could happen, the village head and a few others returned after their discussion.

'Our people do not know how to talk to each other politely and share a laugh together. Everything has to lead to a fight. Look, the most-affected family members are taking the division well and not fighting with each other. Why can't you all cooperate too? Show up for courtesy's sake, say something nice, drink some coffee or whatever they offer you, and take your leave, that's all there is to do,' The village head spoke in a raised voice to placate the arguing group and then moved on to talk about the division further.

'What Kaali and Pongi have asked for is reasonable. Even if they are refused, we know they are not going to go against it. But since they have made a request, we have to take their point into account too. Therefore, just like they asked, they will each get two and a half acres right away. But the mother and father cannot be left out of the equation. They too have functioning limbs and the strength to earn their livelihood and feed themselves for at least another ten years. The acre set aside for them will remain theirs. The youngest has yet to tap into his strength. Given his youth, he can earn much more. Therefore, his share will be limited to one acre for now. After the parents' death, their acre will go to the youngest. What do you all say, does it work for everyone? Speak up now.'

No one asked Muthannan for his opinion. He too didn't think of questioning anything. Wouldn't his mother, father and brothers who brought him up all these years know how much he deserved? He didn't have the right to claim a share or to ask for less or more than what was allocated either. To allocate land among brothers, the elders had cited the custom being followed for generations which was to allocate land on the higher region for the eldest son and so on. Since Appa's land was eventually going to go to the youngest, it was adjacent to Muthu's.

The only thing left to do now was to measure out the land. The house too was divided similarly. The house they lived in was eight *anganam*, with two large rooms and a verandah. It also had a courtyard lined with plinths on two sides, with backs for reclining. At the back of the house were two small rooms. Across from them was a large shed with a thatched roof. All these years, the four families and the elders had lived in this house together. But now, everyone felt that only two families could live here. The two eldest brothers got the house. One side of the verandah was for Appa and Amma. There was no place for the thirdborn Pongiannan and the last-born Muthannan.

The family's common fund had 2,000 rupees in it. From that fund, the youngest two were to receive 500 each towards setting up households of their own. From the rest, the two sisters were to get 200 each. Henceforth, they were not going to receive any more gifts or money unless the parents wished to give something to them out of their own earnings. The sisters were not to expect anything from the brothers. Out of the 600 that was left, 100 went towards the division-related expenses. The rest of the 500 went to the parents. When the parents got older, the brothers were to take them home for a month each and take care of them.

After everything was settled, Muthannan was left with an acre of land in the lower region and 500 rupees for a house. Kaliannan and Pongiannan murmured amongst themselves that there remained an additional 2,000 in the common fund that was never accounted for which the eldest brother had kept all for himself. Muthu couldn't argue, because he did not know anything of the fund. That was all Periannan's responsibility—whatever he said, Muthu had never questioned.

When they divided up the cattle and goats, the cart and the oxen went to Muthu. When Peruma was married to Muthu, she had brought along two calves as dowry from her parental home. So the oxen belonged to Muthu anyway. He also inherited four sheep and one milch cow. Each woman took back the utensils, cookware, pestles and mortars, and anything else they had brought with them when they had married into the family. The common utensils went to the parents. There was a ten-vessel set that they each took two of and left the remaining for the parents. In three months, they had to pack up their belongings and build their homes to move into.

The very next day after the division took place, Peruma left for her mother's house and took the children with her. Going away to her mother's was her way of showing that she was upset with the new developments. She packed up all her things and stacked the bags in a corner before leaving, saying that she would return only after he had set up a house for them to live in. And that if they all continued to live together after the division, some conflict or another would keep coming up.

8

Muthu had stopped talking to his brothers altogether. *Was it for this that they had celebrated me as their dearest?* They had carried him on their shoulders and heads. They have now flung him from atop. No one was around even to check on him, to find out if he was wounded or even alive. After Peruma too left for her mother's house, he didn't know what to do. He went to an uninhabited, open, rocky area, drank toddy until he could drink no more and lay down on the ground there, all by himself. Years of unshed tears gushed down his face all at once.

When Peruma had once said, 'None of your brothers are good people. One day, you will come to see this for yourself,' he had paid no heed to her. 'I don't have the intelligence that she has,' he lamented.

Two days later, he collected himself and began building a shack on his allocated acre. He identified a spot for a cowshed too. Knowing this was his lot, he now had to figure out a way to make a living. He began to plan how to make his land ready and fertile. His turn to use the water from the well came once in five days. The well was near Periannan's land and the water channel from there absorbed more than three quarters of the water by the time it reached his land. Yet, he revelled in the joy of working for himself.

A fortnight later, he went to his father-in-law's house to bring Peruma back. Before the family that sent their daughter to him with twenty sovereigns of gold and numerous aspirations, he stood with his head hanging low, unable to look them in the eye. Still, he couldn't bring himself to tell them anything about what had happened in his family. Apparently, nor could Peruma. Whatever they knew they had found out from talking to the children. There was bitterness and tears all around.

'Did they leave you to ruin because you are the youngest? This is what happens when you are too timid to speak up. Shouldn't you have said, "I too have a daughter who will grow over my shoulder in four years, I too have to arrange for functions and a wedding and need money for that" and asked for more? A lousy divide they made, and you accepted it all quietly! Why will your siblings think of your welfare? Everyone waits for that moment when they can take advantage of the situation. Why, even your own father and mother left you in the lurch. Everyone sang praises of your family, but that wretch has indulged three of her sons and shunned the fourth! How will she prosper? In her final days, she will be eaten by worms until she dies. Had I known this then, would I have given my daughter away to them? Seeing how everybody pampered you as the youngest one and treated you like their favourite, I thought they would keep her well too. How could they have done this? I've never seen such a thing happen anywhere else, good lord!' his mother-in-law complained on, incessantly.

His father-in-law didn't miss a chance either. 'Aren't we all still alive, maaple? The rest brought their relatives for support and to be there for them, why did you not? Okay, you didn't tell us about it. You thought your brothers would look out for you. When you came to know they hadn't, you should have said, "I will discuss this with my family and relatives and announce my decision tomorrow", and talked to us. Did that not occur to you at all? If you live like this, how is your family going to survive?'

Everyone unloaded their burdens onto Muthu. But where was he to unload his? He didn't utter a word. He continued to lie down quietly when his mother-in-law said insinuatingly, 'If the husband and wife keep mum, will everything become alright?' In the morning, they served him a fragrant and mouth-watering mixture of soaked pearl millet, water and curd. The fat from the curd made with buffalo's milk coated his palm. Normally, he would nibble on a piece of onion and drink that mixture with the fervour of drinking elixir. But that day, he didn't even notice the taste of the preparation. His tongue felt lifeless. He got ready to leave with Peruma and the children. He left them with a 'goodbye' barely escaping his lips.

'Even though I have four daughters, I was happy that I brought them all up well and got them all married off into good homes. I cannot sleep at night now, knowing one of their lives has turned out like this. Only our Goddess Baavaatha can show you the right way forward. After all, they have cheated you like the *pithaalakkaaran*, the brassware man. At least that man was a stranger. But to imagine that your own siblings did this to you . . .' his mother-in-law's words rang in Muthu's ears for a very long time afterwards.

At that time, everyone was fervently talking about the pithaalakkaaran not only in their village but in all the surrounding villages too. It was the only topic of discussion at markets and festival gatherings. The stories that people from the neighbouring villages narrated were all identical. Clearly, a big gang had split into smaller groups and spread in all directions to execute their plan the same way everywhere, over approximately one month's time. At first, two men who looked like they wanted to buy a goat kid arrived at the village, empty-handed and no load on their backs. Their *veshtis* and shirts were white and bright as the thumba flower. These men went to the village choultry and engaged with the oldies curled up there. They told them that if they gave them damaged or hole-ridden brassware, they could remould them into new utensils. All they wanted in return were the making charges, proportional to the size of the vessel. At first, no one believed them.

The men spent the night at the choultry, went into the fields and farms in the vicinity the next day, explaining in detail the same deal to each houseowner who lived there. No one could believe that by paying a mere twenty-five paisa, an old, heavy brass *sombu*, a small flask, could be remade into a new one. If they pawned the same sombu at the utensils store, they would probably only get twenty-five paisa for it. How were they to believe that remaking it into a new one would cost the same? For two days straight, the men roamed up and down the village. Though every house most likely had broken or damaged brass vessels, no one wanted to give them to the men. But the strangers hadn't relented. They stood steadfast in their 'principle' to do good for the people at all costs.

On a rocky piece of land somewhere, a broad round brass plate was being used to keep chicken feed. The plate had a hole big enough to look through if held close. One of the brassware men picked it up, wiped it clean with a rag that was lying around and said, 'Give this plate to me. I will bring you a brand-new plate, completely identical to this one, in a week's time, and you can see for yourself.' His companion continued, 'There is a new machine available now. All we have to do is crush this plate and put it into the machine and it will push out a shiny new plate.' The first finished with, 'It is just a plate to hold the chicken feed. If it doesn't come back, it doesn't matter, right? But if it did, it would be a new one.' The plate's owners considered their offer and allowed them to take it. Similarly, the men found a holed sombu in the front yard of another farm. It was being used from time to time to carry water to mix in with cattle feed and would otherwise be left on the floor of either the front yard or the cow shed. They took that with them too.

And so, from here and there, they collected a small sack-full of hole-ridden or damaged brass vessels. 'We will return with new ones in their place,' they said before they left. The ones who didn't give any vessel laughed at the ones who did. A laugh that meant, 'Do you really believe any of that is going to be returned?'

The ones who parted with the old wares weren't bothered by all that. 'All these damaged pieces were lying around useless anyway. If they come back, our gain; if they do not, nobody's loss.' To everyone's surprise, the same two men returned a week later carrying a big sack each on their shoulders. They unloaded them at the choultry and gathered everyone from whom they had taken the damaged vessels there. 'We are carrying a lot of vessels for the neighbouring village too. It is not possible for us to carry the heavy load to each individual person's farm and deliver their goods.' Sounded reasonable. The ones who had given their old vessels received the new ones excitedly. The plate came back feeling heavier and looking sparklier. The sombu dazzled like gold.

They opened the bags to display the wares they were carrying to the neighbouring villages. All manners of items came tumbling out of the sacks—oil containers, pots, wide-mouthed vessels, spatulas, lamps. For the brand new wares they brought back, their charges were but a trifle; just twenty or twenty-five paisa per utensil. 'Even the lead lining on the inside of these vessels costs more than that. How is it that these men are remaking them completely?' the villagers wondered. 'A new machine has come from abroad. There is only so much expense we incur while doing this. Even at this price, we make a profit of five paisa,' said one of the men. This time, many more people were willing to give their old vessels to them. One of the men said, 'We have to complete our delivery of new wares for every piece we took back with us last week. Our credibility is at stake.

We will return in two days after distributing the rest. Keep your brassware ready.'

As promised, they returned in two days with large sacks. When they left, their bags were full. As they received a vessel, they flattened it with a large stone right in front of the owner before putting it into the sack. Many could not watch their vessels being flattened like that, but what could they do? They wanted them remade too. The two men returned in a week the next time too. This time, only a few of the people received brand-new vessels in exchange for their old ones. They said the rest would take another week. Because they had received so many vessels from all the villages, the machine had a lot of work to do. Overworking the machine would make it excessively hot. Then, they would have to wait for it to cool down completely before they could run it again. That's why they were a little behind. But all old wares would be replaced with new ones.

'Let it come when it comes. These vessels just sit in the attic anyway,' said the villagers and this time, they gave them large containers, drums, platters and a whole lot more. 'What a machine the white man has invented and sent to our country!' they discussed amongst themselves. 'He was the one to have invented the railways. And the bus. How many machines he has invented! And now, a machine that changes old into new. It seems one end of the machine has a wide inlet, like an open mouth. Drop a vessel into that and by the time you snap your fingers, 'nng!' falls a brand new vessel out the other end.'

The men flattened all the vessels they received, packed them in their sacks and left the sacks in the choultry. As long as the one who gave the article remembered how it looked, he could identify the new one in its place. Since they had collected a lot of utensils from all the neighbouring villages as well, they brought a lorry to transport their sacks next time around. The lorry arrived in the middle of the night and was welcomed by barking dogs. It was the first time a lorry had ever come into the village. Many stood around it, staring at it. It left with all the utensils as swiftly as it had arrived. They continued to stare at the road every day therafter, waiting for it to return with new articles.

A week went by. Two weeks went by. And then a month. There was still no sight of the lorry. Or the things that had come as dowry from women's parental homes. Or the vessels that had been collected to be given away to daughters at their weddings. Or those that had been bought to be used for cooking on special occasions such the Pongal festival, weddings, funerals, etc. Attics everywhere were empty. No one knew the names of the men who had taken them, where they had come from or where they had gone off to. Once the ploy became apparent, the villagers calculated each other's losses. The ones who had lost only a little were pleased, while the ones who had lost a lot were too embarrassed to admit to it and reduced the numbers when they talked about it. In the end, all they were left with was the term 'pithaalakkaaran' that they used to refer to those men.

Muthu felt that his mother-in-law was right in a way for comparing his family's story with the pithaalakkaaran. All that love his family had showered on him since he was a child—the honey-coated words that had uplifted him and made him feel valued; feeding into his sense of lofty hopefulness, only to eventually snatch away whatever they wanted from under his nose. Fanning the flame of his desire, only to rob him of everything. His family had done just that. Just like the pithaalakkaaran. Except, he had wrapped up his crafty scheme within a month. His family had skilfully stretched their act over a span of years before leaving him dispossessed.

When Peruma saw the shack made of thatched palm, she did not say anything. Yet, she made her irritation known constantly through other ways. *But what more could be done in a mere ten days? Even those who build palaces for themselves, have to live in a shed like this while the palaces get built.* On the second day after her return, Peruma kept only a couple of vessels that she had got as part of the division, and sold off the rest to those who make arrack. She only made a rupee or two for each utensil. When the men came to collect the vessels, her mother-in-law asked her, 'It isn't as though you have no means to feed your family. Why do you need to sell these?'

'Sure, a *pucca* house of four anganams has been set aside for me, let me just take these with me and stack them there,' snapped Peruma exercising no control over her tongue.

The mother-in-law latched on to this. 'Like you brought loads and loads from your father's house for us to keep giving to you. Beyond begetting and bringing up four sons, what else am I going to be able to give you? I will see how you are going to fare too, won't I? Why four, you build a house of eight anganams and give that to your children.

Let me see how much you make and what you give . . .' she
went on.

There was no way for Peruma to win an argument
against her mother-in-law. She had everyone from her
husband to her children under her thumb. It was only after
the division that Muthu lost the attachment he had always
felt towards his mother. 'I used to breastfeed you till you
were six or seven, da, that is why my breasts have become
saggy like this,' she would laughingly show him her breasts.
Muthu would shy away. 'Stop, Mother.' A massive rift had
now torn through that bond. By giving him the land at
the very fringes, she had pushed their relationship to the
fringes as well.

For three months, Muthu could not figure out what
to do. He cultivated the land and sowed corn. When the
corn plants grew to a quarter of their height, there was a
severe downpour. His land became so wet that he could
not even set foot on it. When the brothers all shared the
land, they would sow seeds of crops that were dependent
on rains in this portion of land and return only when it was
ready for harvest. This part of the land was not amenable to
irrigation farming as it was prone to waterlogging. So prone
that water bubbled up to the surface when one stepped on
it. He planned to bring soil from the lake and elevate his
land after the rainy season. But they would have to bring a
lot of soil in, just to elevate the shed he had built there. His
son Ponnaiyan did not like being there at all. He would run
away to his grandmother's house all the time.

Even though their son wasn't on speaking terms with
them and the daughter-in-law wouldn't even look at them,

the grandmother and grandfather did not dislike their grandson. 'Ponnu, Ponnu,' they called him affectionately. Often, he stayed overnight with them too. 'They coddled one child, calling him "Muthu, Muthu" only to abandon him. And now, they are coddling you. Wonder what trouble they are going to create for you,' Peruma would whine constantly. She chased Ponnaiyan and lashed him with a long, tender branch of a tree to stop him from going there. When the lashes landed on his calves, leaving long welts from which blood squirted out, he would go and fall straight in to the lap of his grandmother again. It is a mystery how regardless of the ferocity of grandmothers, grandsons always found their laps warm.

Inside the one-room shed, Muthu was afraid to get close to Peruma. For one, she was so full of bitterness with everyone who had put her in that shed. She also kept an oil lamp, large enough to stay lit all night, to spot any creepy-crawlies that may enter the shed at night. He struggled to stroke her with the light on in the presence of his daughters and son. The son would go to sleep very quickly. But the girls were at an awkward age—there was no telling what might wake them up. He didn't want to risk tapping her and asking her to come out. What if she resentfully refused him? That would crush him completely. Fearing all this, he refrained from courting her.

9

The corn leaves I cut up made for one large bundle, a kutthari. This kutthari isn't enough to last even three months for the oxen and the milch cow. They have to be taken to other farms to graze. I have to find a farm owned by someone who isn't foul-mouthed, and gather grass from there to feed my livestock. But there isn't a single person who isn't foul-mouthed. Otherwise, I have to buy fodder. If I don't have enough to eat, I can spread a wet towel on my stomach and go to sleep. But if the goats and cattle don't have enough to eat, what can they do except wake up in the middle of the night and cry loudly—no other living being can sleep listening to that. No farmer can call himself a farmer if he starves his own innocent beasts.

Determined to raise the level of his low-lying land, he left immediately after daybreak one day, to bring soil from the lake. The silt had settled and the earth was higher by a forearm's measure. No one was around to gather the sediment. The village head had announced repeatedly that anyone who needed earth could take it as they would be helping them desilt the lake. But no other farm needed it. All the lands had already been raised above ground-level two or three generations ago. Some had even raised their lands above the rocks by a forearm's measure. For crops like groundnuts and corn, the roots barely needed to grow a foot deep into the soil. A run with a shallow plough was sufficient. When he turned the cart around after pouring out one load of soil to fetch the next, he found Peruma standing in front of him. Along with her were the girls and the boy, hugging her, drawn in like fledglings. Everything that she had held back for three months, she let loose all at once.

'Even if you slogged away for ten years, you cannot fill this pit. Are you looking to starve us to death? In one acre of land, what we can do is plant four neem trees, break their twigs and make toothbrushes to clean our tongues with. What else can we do? I have been watching you for the past three months, wondering what you are going to do. You used to bring up your older brothers proudly in every conversation we had. Where are they now? Has even one of those dogs checked on us to see if we are dead or alive in this pit that they have pushed us into? All these years you worked your fingers to the bone for those ingrate dogs. Is your plan now to throw away the rest of your life into this pit? Instead, why don't you go and see if you can get two or three acres elsewhere on lease? Or else, go and do some other job. Don't waste any more time on this rock of a land and kill me and my children,' she said, resolutely.

Not only that, she also started taking on any work that she got. Whether it was trimming branches, de-shelling groundnuts, harvesting ears of grains—she didn't shy away from anything. She also took their daughter Vallamaal along with her. That small child. He couldn't bear to see her working on someone else's land in the unbearable blazing heat. The next daughter, Rossamma, took care of household chores and the goats and cows. She was also responsible for taking care of their son. He didn't run away anymore, seeking his grandmother out like he did before. Somehow she had managed to make him stay put. News reached Peruma through the grapevine that the grandmother was going around saying, 'He used to come to me all the time calling me, "aayah, aayah", lovingly. What sin did he commit? She already has my son tied to her lap, now look how she has managed to use some spell to keep my grandson away from me as well.'

There was nothing he could say to assuage Peruma. She would only have driven the dagger deeper into his heart: 'Of course, since this place is filled with riches, I shall bathe my daughters in rose water, dress them in gold and keep them like dolls at home', she'd say. He too began to help out, taking on jobs like building plot dividers and installing bores. For one who grew up spending all his time in his own farm on his own land, it felt a bit strange at first, to work for wages. *But work anywhere was work*, he comforted himself. And work came with wages. Somehow, the household survived. That was when he came to know about chartered deliveries through Vatthan. Muthannan's income from it was adequate to run the household. Peruma going to work and managing the goats and cows made for additional income.

During that time, there was no communication between him and his older brothers. If he saw them heading directly towards him, he would hang his head and walk away. He avoided greeting them or getting into a conversation. Still, he helplessly hoped that they would enquire about his wellness, even if only out of courtesy. Maybe they were afraid that he might cling on to them if they did. Or maybe they thought that if he, the youngest of them all, had so much ego, then why shouldn't they? If they saw him on the street, they would recoil from him like he was a dog. At least to the dog, they'd still have said something to chase it away. How did the same people who couldn't tire saying his name so lovingly, suddenly get tongue-tied in front of him?

Meanwhile, the other brothers' farms were doing well. Since Muthu wasn't irrigating his land, they were receiving his share of the water too. But there was a twist in that as well. The first two days were for Periannan to use the water. The day after was Kaliannan's turn. The day after that was Pongiannan's turn. The fifth day was Muthannan's. Because Muthu wasn't using his share of the water, that day also went to Periannan. In all, Periannan got three days of irrigation. Muthu hadn't thought about all that. Knowing that there was no potential in his land, why would he waste his time irrigating it? It took half a day to wet a *seravu* of land. And for that, he needed to dig a very long channel and that too, only for the water that did not get absorbed along the way. Aside from all this, what was he even going to grow there? Gold? 'Go on, start irrigating the land. I will stand here with a *mammutty* to direct the water. If there's enough water, I will use it to wash my daughters' vaginas,' Peruma rebuked him about the setup one day. After that, he stopped thinking about irrigation altogether.

However, the two middle brothers could not accept this setup. They discussed a lot amongst themselves. 'Luck finds you only if you are born as the eldest, da. At least in our next birth, may we be the firstborns,' they said to each other. And that, 'If you are the youngest, you at least get talked to affectionately for some time in your life. It is a dog's life for the middle-born.' And that, 'If I am born again, I don't want to be a farmer. A dog, a fox, a crow or anything else would be better' and so on. Because they both had received equal shares in all aspects, the two of them remained united. They thought about paying Muthu for his day of water. But who was going to ask him? Nobody had the guts to face him.

On the days of Periannan's turn to irrigate his fields, his buffalos were locked onto the irritating apparatus right at the break of dawn. So eager was he to draw water from the well all day. At the end of his second day, the apparatus was at work even after darkness had set in. Only after hitting sludge at the bottom of the well did he turn it over to the next in line. His farms were verdant and bountiful. The cotton plants stood spread out and covered with pods. One portion was full of vegetable plants. Baskets of vegetables were ferried to the market in a hand-drawn cart every day. The lead farmhand Raman realized that Periannan's farm was the largest and so, stayed on with him. None of the others asked for him either. 'I never thought something like this would happen, saami. What will I do, I too have a stomach to worry about. I have to go where I can find food,' he rationalised. Of course.

The two middle brothers drew water only in the evenings on their days. Almost all of Periannan's four acres got irrigated. His wife and children were energetically involved in the farm labour. Aside from grumbling about how his family had never showed such interest in helping out when all the families had been working the fields together, what else could the middle two do? They were resolute in finding a way to talk to Muthu and give him money in exchange for his day of irrigation. But even if Muthu agreed, would Peruma? In case she did, they decided they would take turns every other week. The only issue was broaching the topic with Muthu.

Pongiannan's wife Seerayi had a good relationship with Peruma. She was the youngest daughter-in-law in the household until Peruma had come into the family. So she taught Peruma, the new youngest daughter-in-law, how she had to serve everyone. They had to follow everyone's instructions. When the two were alone together, they bitched about the others. Occasionally, Seerayi would order Peruma around as well, but after a little while, she herself would come around and pacify her. 'Everyone glorifies this family from the outside, I hope you now know what that is all about. From the outside, the cemetery looks deceivingly attractive with all the decorative trees and plants at the entrance. But how does it feel when you go in? It's the same with this big house too, Peruma,' Seerayi had mentioned several times to her.

Relying on that bond she had built, Seraayi came to Muthu's shed one evening. He was eating, seated on a cot outside. The children were on another cot across from him, giggling at something trivial. Peruma was sitting on the ground outside with the pot of kali in front of her. It must have been four or five days after the new moon. The low light from the thin crescent lit the front yard. 'Ponnu . . . can I get some food too?' came a voice from the dark. They did not expect visitors at that hour. Who could it be? Before they could identify her voice, Seerayi sat on top of the oil press that lay in a corner of the front yard.

It was an unexpected visit. She didn't know how to continue the conversation. Muthu broke the silence and said, 'Welcome, *nanga*! Give nanga a dish with kali in it, *pille*.' He referred to all his brothers' wives as 'nanga'. To distinguish between them, he called them eldest nanga, big nanga and small nanga. 'Welcome, akka, did you only just discover the way to here? Had I known ahead of time that a special guest was going to visit us, I would have made rice for dinner,' Peruma said scornfully. They could see Seerayi's shed from their front yard. Their family also didn't have a house; they had erected a shack on their land and were living in it.

Peruma used the word 'guest' to emphasize the fact that they had ignored them all these days.

'What can we do . . . we were all standing together. Now, even though we live next-door, we behave like guests with each other. This rotten land has blinded us from the world beyond,' Seerayi said, speaking broadly.

'Why blame the land for the actions of men?' Peruma responded.

'Yes, yes . . . this is all because of men's actions. Otherwise how could a drama like this have played out?'

Piling on more insinuations, Seerayi went on to describe in detail how Periannan's family was sucking away all the water that was Muthannan's to claim.

'They hook onto the irrigation apparatus when the sky is still dark. On the last day, they keep a lantern lit and work until the nine o' clock alarm sounds—till they've drawn out all the water. If one is ever born to a farmer, he should be only be born as the first son. Or they should stop with one son. Like you, we are also leading a meagre life. In a single-room shed, just like this. When we do receive water, it flows through two fields before reaching us. For now, we are able to irrigate only one portion of our land. If you can give us your day's turn of water, then . . . maybe we can get past the water shortage and irrigate two portions of our land,' she finished.

The darkness, only slightly disturbed by the moonlight, turned out to be favourable for the conversation. Peruma and Muthu looked at each other without responding. *Now that nangaiyaal has come looking for us, cared to open her mouth and ask for something explicitly, how can we refuse her? There is no opportunity to discuss this alone with Peruma. Looks like nanga won't leave without an answer. Should I say, 'We are planning on using the water. If not, we will let you have it, please wait'? What is Peruma thinking?* Muthu wondered. 'Ponnu, come here to me, ayya. You used to call me '*perima*' all the time. See how things are now . . . I see you from a distance every day and hold you in my eyes, ayya,' Seerayi said affectionately. She picked Ponnaiyan up and held him in her lap as if to give his parents some time to think while expressing her affection towards the child.

Perhaps he understood that the perima who had been looking past them all these days was now using him to get her work done, but he barely spoke to her. After squirming in her grip for some time, he eventually managed to free himself and affix himself to his mother. *What is going to change by taking so much time to think? The rest have taken away almost everything except my komanam. As long as no danger befell that, all is fine. Peruma can be managed. There is no use for that water anyway.* 'Okay, nanga, we can do that,' he said.

Peruma got up and rushed into the shed and spoke to him from there. Her voice alone came tearing through the darkness. 'If you give away everything, what are my children and I going to live on? Are we to carry a dish and go door to door begging for alms? Whoever wants to take over our turn for the water can do so in exchange for two modas of grain every year. If not, let things be the way they are. The dog that snatched away everything to feed himself can have this too. They can perform our final rites with our water.'

Muthu thought Peruma was right. Seerayi hadn't expected this. She had imagined that she would only have to deal with their bitterness from having ignored them all these days. And that she could talk her way into assuaging them and letting her have their share of the water. Peruma was smart. But two modas of grain a year was excessive. Each *vallam* yielded four *padis*. 160 padis of ragi or millet in exchange for the water would be too much. Perhaps she should check with her husband. But then they would come to know that she had come to them hoping to get their water for free. She performed some calculations in her head.

'Okay Peruma . . . we will buy the water on your terms. I don't have any qualms giving you anything but I am struggling too, just like you, to take care of my children. I will give you one moda a year. Even that requires cultivating four seravus of land. Please don't ask for more than that.'

Peruma didn't say anything. Instead of getting nothing for the water, at least now they would get one moda each year. As she left, Seerayi said, 'Don't change your mind if someone else comes offering more.' They sent her away with the assurance that they wouldn't. The moon had fully risen by then and the night enveloped them.

10

'Saami, saami . . .' Kuppan woke Muthu up after he finished cooking. Lost in a flurry of thoughts, Muthu had dozed off inadvertently. Perhaps he was overcome with sleep at the joy of finding a place where he could settle down. In the ten days that they had been on this journey, Kuppan had never seen Muthu sleep so well. Abandoning all care, that too in the middle of a deserted piece of land. The burden of the money he was carrying hadn't allowed him to sleep. In all the lands they had seen so far, his eyes had immediately spotted one flaw or another. Either he didn't like the type of soil, or the location. The quality of soil was excellent at one place they saw near Thinnur. Access to water was good too. But a valuvu of labourers was close to it. 'If these people are close to the land, we will spend our entire life protecting it from them,' he declared. Kuppan could not object to that statement. He rejected the lands that were close to the foothills as 'they will attract wolves and foxes, Kuppanna'. He dismissed all the villages by Rattoor.

'I am seeking places this far out only to evade all my relatives. If I move here, this close to them, some of them might find me, claiming to be my cousins. And others could claim to be my relatives by marriage. In our caste, isn't everyone a relative of some sort, no matter where we are? If not on the father's side, then on my in-laws'. I don't want anything to do with any of them,' he said firmly.

The more they travelled past Saethur, the more enthusiastic he became. They didn't find houses among the fields. 'This place belongs to a different community, anna,' he said. He was very pleased that the ox sank to the ground here and that too with a direct view of the mound with Mansaami's temple on top. That was the reason for his sound sleep. The bulge in his waistband was noticeable but he didn't seem too worried about it here. Kuppan too felt that all the omens were favourable. It was difficult for him to wake Muthannan up from his drooling slumber but his stomach looked empty and shrunken. All he had eaten since morning was kali mixed with water.

Even though Muthu had appreciated Kuppan's cooking throughout the journey, Kuppan knew he wasn't quite used to this food. Women were truly more skilled when it came to this—they always managed to add a vegetable or two to the saaru. Every fortnight or so, they'd cook meat. They could gauge their husbands' appetites and feed them well. All that was beyond him. He didn't eat to his fill either. He consoled himself saying there wasn't any work to do to warrant filling his stomach. Still, he couldn't instantly cut back on the amount of food he needed to eat. His stomach became empty as soon as he urinated a couple of times after drinking the diluted kali. Moreover, Muthu had grown up as his family's favourite. He must be used to eating a rich

variety of food. Watching him sleep made Kuppan feel
sorry for him. Maybe Muthu could have stayed in his own
village, eating whatever he could get. But nothing can deter
a stubborn mind. It was his grit that held him by his neck
and was pushing him onward.

Kuppan patted him hesitantly and called out softly.
'Saami, saami . . .' Muthu woke up with a start. His hand
checked his waist instinctively. 'If I get so sleepy by midday,
how am I going to survive being a farmer?' he chided
himself. 'It is the peace from knowing you will find your
land, nga,' replied Kuppan. 'Yes, yes,' laughed Muthu as
he sparingly splashed a little water from the pot to clean
his hands. They refilled the pot whenever they found clean
water so that they could stop anywhere to cook.

Kuppan served two ladles of kali and some saaru on a
tin plate and handed it to Muthu. If they found a banana
leaf or any large leaf where they halted for food, they didn't
use plates. Muthu took some of the hot kali, soaked it in
the stew and put it into his mouth. Even before his tongue
could fully take in the taste of the saaru, the food slid down
his throat in a flash. Piece after piece, it kept going down as
fast as a crow's wings flapped. When Kuppan tried to serve
him another ladleful, Muthu stopped him. Kuppan didn't
insist—could he have? Maybe he had decided not to eat to
his fill. It wasn't easy for Kuppan to comprehend all that
went on inside his mind, but he found it pitiful that Muthu
was experiencing so much grief at such a young age.

Muthu stayed reclined on the trunk of the neem tree for
a little longer. He took a piece of tobacco from Kuppan and
tucked it in his mouth. It wasn't a habit of his to chew betel

leaves and tobacco. Whenever he drove his cart for hire, he smoked a beedi to stay awake at night and keep warm in the winter. But that was not a habit either. Peruma could not tolerate the smell of beedi. She would push Muthu's face aside and move away from him. He drank toddy and arrack. But in these ten days, he didn't drink either. He only had sunnanbu theluvu palm sap with lime, that was usually collected in the cold dewiness of the month of *Maasi* in a few places. It was Kuppan who craved some arrack; even just a *kottai*, a swig, of kallu would suffice. He felt that that was the reason his body was not brisk. But he couldn't bring himself to drink any because Muthu wasn't drinking. Perhaps if Muthu wasn't carrying all that money, he would have had some.

Muthu walked up to the cart and took out a yellow bag from the cart's underside. There were already two veshtis stuffed in there. He carefully tucked his waistband with the money into the bag. A yellow bag in his hand. A bright white veshti over his komanam. A towel over his shoulder long enough to extend from his back to his chest. The towel couldn't cover all of his dark skin. The only thing he lacked was a little more height. He sprinkled some water on his hair and combed it clean with a wooden comb. The beard on his face looked like a hive abandoned by bees. He appeared to radiate a charm only unshaven, youthful beards had. He looked like a new groom arriving from out of town for a feast. Kuppan stared on, admiring the beauty of his neatening-up process.

For ten days, he has been wandering unsuccessfully without a word of complaint. Let today's efforts culminate

in something good, Kuppan thought to himself. The oxen
were grazing. The field was covered in a motley of colours
by grasses that had dried up and the new verdant sprouts,
drinking up the morning dew. If the oxen grazed for even
just a little while, they will have filled at least half their
stomachs. Unlike humans, they didn't have to fill their
stomachs in each and every meal. If they were full by
night, that was sufficient—they usually began grazing in
the morning and filled their stomachs a little at a time.
Muthu instructed Kuppan to take them grazing at a spot
close to a water source. It was something that Kuppan did
all the time. Still, Muthu reminded him to do it before he
departed. Kuppan hid a sharp knife in his waist. They had
sharp lances and machetes in the cart. He had also kept a
kodhalam, a crowbar, and an axe, all tied up in a large sack.
Should a large mob attack them, there would be no dearth
of weapons.

The sun hung low in the sky. It was not very hot. *How
can I get any work done if I worry about everything?*, Muthu
thought as he walked a short distance on the cart road and
took a narrow path, one-and-a-half feet wide, leading to a
field. He expected that the path that ran through the area
full of fields with no one around would lead to the heart of
the village. The soil was of a good variety. What he didn't
know anything about, was the people. But people's nature
was the same everywhere. Desire, jealousy, deception—
there were no differences among men when it came to
these aspects. It was really habits and customs that changed
region by region. The people who lived in this region had
to be farmers of some sort. It wouldn't be easy to get close

to them and be accepted as one of them. But if he was going to live alone on his farm, why did he need to be close to the rest? Especially when closely knit relationships could unravel overnight anyway?

His eldest brother, the one who had chased him this far away, used to be the fondest of him. Anywhere he went, he would carry Muthu along on his shoulders. 'My youngest' is how he introduced him to others. He bought him everything he asked for. His own children weren't treated that way. As adults, however, it would seem that affection disappears and rightful heirship trumps everything else. Muthu, who tolerated anything he did without ever saying a word against him, could not stomach the injustice that he had meted out to him in the end.

On that day, he had been out delivering a load of sacks containing groundnuts. His cart being empty on the way back, he was able to reach home at a reasonable hour. When the low-lying land was separated, the cart road had to be paved further out along the stream. Muthu had managed to pave it right at the corner of the field. Just as he turned off the cart road onto the corner of the low-lying acre where his farm was, his dog came running towards him, barking. It was the dog's way of welcoming him back home. Barely a year old, he was quite the barker. Muthu parked the cart next to the shed and untied the oxen from the cart.

Normally, Peruma would have come out carrying a hand lamp. She could hear the cart from quite a distance. 'You have exceptional hearing, pille,' Muthu once told her. 'I lie there unable to sleep. Won't I be able to hear you?' she had replied. Maybe she was fast asleep tonight.

Between taking care of the goats and going out to work on other farms, she had no respite. He pulled out the bundle of leaves from a pile and fed the oxen. 'Pille, pille,' he called out but got no response. He suddenly felt a bit scared. It was common to live on one's own field. Muthu had full faith in Peruma's courage. Even though he wasn't around, it had never been difficult for them to live with two daughters. Because it was a low-lying area, there were the dangers of snakes crawling in. But they had a dog for that reason. What was going on?

Maybe she had gone home because her father or mother became ill? Or maybe one of the children was bitten by a snake? He shuddered at the thought. The only house close enough to run to for help was Pongiannan's. After they gave up the rights to the water day, things were amicable between them. But Pongiannan and Kaliannan had stopped talking to each other. Pongiannan's wife did not tell anyone about soliciting Muthu's water. It was not until Muthu's turn came the following week and Pongiannan drew water that day and the cows came home, did everyone come to know. Kaliannan was furious—they hadn't even bothered to inform him about it despite having agreed to alternating the water day between them.

'Peruma has said that they will allow only us to use their share of the water. That too, for a payment of a moda of grains every year,' said Seerayi.

Their relationship never went back to how it was. Kaliannan slowly began to join forces with Periannan. Even though the parents received one acre, they had decided amongst themselves that they were not going to trouble themselves with irrigation at their old age and therefore, had not been allocated a water day. On hearing that they could get a moda of grains in exchange for their water day, they demanded a day of water for themselves too. That was when Periannan lured Kaliannan to his side. If they managed to get a day assigned to the parents, then the two would pay the parents the fee of a moda of grains together and use the water between them, he schemed. After that, Kaliannan stopped speaking with Pongiannan altogether.

But their plan did not work out. Since everything had been discussed already and sealed with thumbprints, no changes could be made without everyone agreeing to them first. There was a price for changing plans too. Every time a plan was declined, rifts grew wider.

If Peruma had to leave in haste, she would have informed someone at Pongiannan's house, Muthu thought. Just as he started walking over to find out, he saw someone asleep on a cot on the southern side, covered fully. Who could it be that had slept through the dog's barks, the cart's noises and Muthu's calls? 'Who are you?' he asked as he kicked the cot hard.

From under the sack being used as a blanket, emerged a son of one of the labourers that worked at Pongiannan's house. 'Saami . . . it was the landlady who asked me to sleep here. She asked that you go to her village after you got home. It was nothing urgent. She has gone there for no particular reason, she asked me to tell you.'

'Okay, but did you have to sleep on our cot?' shouted Muthu. Frightened, the boy got off the cot instantly and stood up.

'She was the one who laid the cot and asked me to sleep on it saying there may be insects or snakes on the ground,' he said.

'Okay, okay, sleep now. What sort of guard are you if you sleep oblivious to all the noises?' said Muthu and splashed water on his face from a pot in the front yard.

He had not slept in two days. He had planned to go to bed and stay asleep until the next afternoon. But if Peruma had gone home and taken the children with her, there had to be a reason for it. She would not have left the goat kids alone even for one night, nor the shed unguarded. She must have hidden the money in her waist and left. They had given the 500 they received during the division, to her father. It was still unspent for they hadn't decided yet whether to build a house or buy jewellery with it. She had left the message that it was nothing urgent as otherwise Muthu would be worried.

Sleep drained from his eyes. *I cannot stay here any longer.* He changed his veshti, took the staff that stood in a corner in his hand and set off on foot.

11

Even at a relaxed pace, I can reach mama's house by the time the light of dawn scatters across the sky. Until I know what all this is about, I won't be able to sleep. Maybe Vallama has come of age? But she is twelve, that can't be. Like her mother, her cheeks are sunken and her eyes are lost in dark circles. After the property was divided, access to healthy food became sparse. Even when there was any, the mind had to will the body to absorb it. *It will take at least another three or four years for her to come of age.* But, if that were the case, Peruma was too proud to go to her father's for the rituals—she would have performed all the rituals at the shack itself.

When they were all living together in one household too, she remained very proud. If anyone uttered anything unpleasant, she didn't eat for two days. Each and every one in the household had to appease her and convince her to eat. Her mother-in-law did not condone this. On seeing everyone sweetly asking her to eat, she would say, 'For a troublemaker, what good is the food going to do? Just ignore her. If a horse starves its arse dry, it will come to eat

91

on its own,' or some such thing. Peruma once let her tongue lash out at her like a whip, 'If it dries out from starvation, that is still okay, what is worse is when it happens because it won't stop galloping around petulantly.'

'Who are you calling petulant?' her mother-in-law had said. It then grew into another big fight and Peruma did not eat for two more days.

Not just with her mother-in-law, but also to avoid trouble with the brothers' wives, Peruma would go away to work in the fields. She didn't tire from it even when working late into the evenings. She took her two daughters along with her. They too worked, trying to keep up with her. Her son was the youngest child in the whole family. No one could control him. Peruma and her mother-in-law were always locking horns. All the other daughters-in-law were related to the mother-in-law in one way or another. Peruma was the only one who wasn't. 'If you bring an outsider into the family, how will she have affection for us? If we let our guard down a little, she will feed us a mix of arali seeds and rice to poison us,' the mother-in-law said, once. Since then, Peruma stopped cooking for the family. She swept the floors, washed vessels, fetched water for cooking, but that was the extent of her chores. She did not step into the room where food was being prepared. No matter how much everyone tried to convince her, she did not relent.

If someone said, 'Check the salt in the sambar and take it off the stove,' she would reply, 'I may accidentally mix in arali seeds instead of salt. You check the salt, spice and everything else yourself. Ever since I came to this house, my tongue has lost its sense of taste anyway.' She did not say much but when she did, her words pierced like papercuts.

Despite all that was going on in Muthu's head, the walk early in the morning was comforting in a way. If only his sleep hadn't been ruined, he would have enjoyed his walk even more. When the darkness had barely begun to scatter, he was close to his father-in-law's village. He saw someone climbing up a palm tree on a farm. Muthu asked him for two kottais of toddy and drank it. He paid him fifty paise, twenty-five for each kottai. They were tapping toddy before dawn for fear of the police. By the time the sun was up, he was climbing the steps to his father-in-law's home entrance. His mother-in-law was the first to see him.

She started lamenting immediately. 'We have pushed our daughter into a pit! If it was any other woman, she would have gone straight to the grave. She looked at the faces of her daughters and came here instead. From now on, I will not send my daughter back to that place, even if I have to pay for it with her life. I don't know what or how, but you must settle your family somewhere else. Or else, let her lie here, right by my feet. We took care of her for fifteen years. We can take care of her for another fifteen, twenty years.'

Muthu did not know what she was talking about. Peruma's face was swollen from crying. She hadn't slept all night. 'What happened, pille?' he asked her. Instantly, she started crying.

It was always this way. She would never answer the question. No matter how many times she was asked, she always only responded with sobs.

If he wiped her tears, caressed her cheeks and asked her, the answer would be tears. If he held her to his chest, stroked her back and asked her lovingly, the answer would still be tears. If he straightened her face and asked her, 'Tell me what it is', that would be of no use either. Sometimes, he lost his patience and slapped her in anger. But she did not yield to that or his threats either. It was always just the crying. By the time he got her to describe the issue, he would be on the brink of an existential crisis. When she did tell him after all that, he would usually think, 'That's it? Was all the crying for this?' But he couldn't tell her that. If he did, she would say, 'What counts as a big enough matter for you? If I die, will that seem like a big enough problem?'

'Only if you tell me can I know,' he said angrily, not knowing how else to ask her at his in-laws' house. Peruma opened up amidst her sobs.

In the evening, two days prior, Muthu had taken the cart and left to go to the depot. On his way out, he had seen Periannan. He too had seen Muthu. Just for a brief moment. He had then moved aside and let the cart pass by. This was the man who brought Muthu up like a father. Anything Muthu wanted, he had only to ask his eldest brother. They had named him something else when he was little, but used to call him 'periyapayya', or the eldest son. When Muthu began to call him 'Perianna', he became known by that name. They were about fifteen years apart. Even after he got married and had children, Periannan used to say, 'Muthu is my eldest son'. Muthu could not figure out when and how such a tight bond had come undone.

He found it difficult to believe that it was only due to the allure of the estate.

When Peruma came into the family after marrying Muthu, did she wrong Periannan in any way? Did the sister-in-law's control over him separate them? Muthu never spoke against or questioned Periannan. Even after the division of the property, Muthu did not ask him once why he did what he did. Despite that, it remained a mystery to him why Periannan harboured such a deep need to destroy him this way. It still hadn't dawned on him that the times when he rode on his eldest brother's shoulder to the fields and festivals, now belonged to the past. He often felt as though he were still sitting on Periannan's shoulders. Everything else that happened after he got off his shoulders, like getting married and having his own children, had felt like an illusion. And then this. Muthu had driven the cart, thinking about his brother the entire time.

When Sellan, his fellow cart driver, joined him a little further on the main road, their conversation suppressed his thoughts. They were discussing the details of where they were transporting goods to, how many carts, etc., when Sellan said, 'I feel like eating parotta today. I hope they have us going via Malaiyur. I hear that a new place has opened near the market in Moddur. And the kurma stew is so good that people lick their plates and fingers clean.' The talk about parottas made Muthu forget all about his eldest brother. Not once did it occur to Muthu that the brother that he had seen on the way would get such a twisted thought.

That same night, Peruma had tethered the goat kids to the stumps installed at the front yard and had fed the children as the sun went down. She always went to bed early. Especially after they had moved into the shed in the low-lying area. There were no passers-by, no one to chit chat with. The only noise came from the children when they played together. She permitted them to play outdoors only on nights when the moon lit the skies brightly. Other nights, she kept a lamp outside for a little while. The lamp placed over a flattened ball of cow dung on top of the lamp stand lit up the whole front yard. They sat around it to eat too. After all this, she would take the lamp indoors. It was her rule that when the lamp went in, the children followed suit. The boy was stubborn, but she never hesitated to land a few blows on his back and drag him indoors.

'In the shed that your father has built, there is a crystal hall for you to play in. You can run and jump around without fear,' she would reproach them. Sometimes she got poetic, 'This palace that we live in, with gardens all around—if you run about and play catch, you may get lost. How will I find you then? Please come indoors and sleep, my dears,' she would say. And at times, sarcastically, she would say, 'Beauties born to a king, please come. Lie down on this gem-studded sheet that your father has splurged his riches on and go to sleep.' Muthu never reacted to any of this. Occasionally, he was astonished at her choice of words.

Ever since the property was divided, the smile on Peruma's face had dried up completely. Initially, Muthu had found it hard to cope too, but he had consoled himself.

If he couldn't buy a lot of gold and marry his daughters into richer families, so be it. They could be married into poorer families like his own, and work for a living. He got to meet a lot of men, especially after he started running chartered deliveries—and of different kinds too, including ones who carried the sacks on their backs and those who ran behind the carts breathlessly like the oxen. He felt more reassured seeing all of them. *At least we have some property. We have food to eat.* But Peruma wasn't one to settle for that.

She worried a lot about the girls and their future. She even reduced the amount of food she made. To feed five people, she used only two onions to make kuzhambu. How tasty could that be? The daughters became skinnier than before. The boy's face lost its light. If he refused to eat, she would knock him hard on his cheek with her fist. 'Come, I'll fill up a pot from the river of milk and honey flowing next to the house and feed you.' Fearing her punch, he let her feed him anything before he could safely run away. When Muthu returned from his trips, he usually brought back something for them: boiled cassava, pears, mangoes, whatever was in season. She mocked him indirectly for it. 'Your appan has saved enough to put a howdah on an elephant for sending you off. Eat, eat,' she would mumble. Or she would say, 'You lot finish off the money your father makes by buying things to eat. And then your appan will marry you off with a neck full of necklaces made with avaram flowers and a long chain made of karuvela bark, complete with earrings made of stone.'

He had tried to calm her down several times but to no avail. She simply would not smile. She didn't talk to anyone properly. At the field where she worked, she did not have a cheerful conversation with anyone. She considered everyone her enemy. She felt there was no point in talking to anyone—she did not like them. She thought everyone wanted to harm her. She read between the lines all the time and the intent behind people's words and actions always felt wrong to her. All she worried about was how she could get the daughters settled owning just the one piece of bad land they had.

The door to their shack was made of palmyra leaves. There was a rope on the inside and a rope on the outside to tie across. Once she tied the rope and lay down, she got up only in the morning. If she woke up early, she did not step out. 'If they come to know that the male in this house is away, a thousand mosquitoes may show up,' she said. 'Let any of those dogs try to come here. I will break his leg and throw him into the pit.' Even though no one came by their land, she worried as though many did. In the middle of the night, she would sit up and listen intently to the chirping of the crickets. Suddenly, she would shout loudly, 'Who is that?' No one could sleep properly because of her. On the days that Muthu didn't go to the depot, he put his cot in front of the house and slept on it. Those days, she would come out bravely. And allow herself to sleep peacefully too.

That night, however, after the children had gone off to sleep, she nodded off too. Suddenly, the dog's barking filled the air. Usually, if it saw a snake or an insect, the dog would start barking nonstop. But this was a different sort of bark. It usually stood itself in front of the snake and produced an 'urrrr' sound, softly at first, as if to give it a warning before barking loudly. It alternated between the growl and the bark. The dog didn't let a snake go unless it changed its course and escaped. If it was an ordinary snake, it would tear it into pieces. Even a cobra couldn't escape it.

One night, the dog was making a strange, low, wheezing sound. She didn't know what it meant. There was a nasal 'mmm' sound followed by the sound of a bark. This went on for a while. Peruma slowly looked through the palm barrier. The sight she saw in front of her right across their threshold, froze her heart. In the light of the moon, she could clearly see a cobra seething to strike. Across from the snake, the dog stood beyond strikable distance, its tail standing erect. She could see the hair on its back standing erect. If the cobra struck forward, the dog could grab it by its teeth. If the dog went any closer, the snake could bite it. The two were locked in a staring match with each other. The snake also moved slightly whenever the dog snarled. Peruma had never seen a sight like this. She stood there arrested, her body withdrawn and shivering.

There was no movement on either side. As Peruma wondered what was going to happen, a fear overtook her— the thought that if the dog lost, the snake may enter the house. She looked across to see if the spear was in its corner. Even though she wanted to grab it and hold it in her hand, she thought she might distract the dog's attention and stood still instead. Just when she was wondering how long this was going to go on, the dog grabbed the snake by the middle completely unexpectedly, and flung it into the air. The snake, half the length of a full-grown palmyra tree, went flying across like a twisted rope and fell on the ground with a thud. Because its mid-region was wounded, it could not move at all. It lay writhing where it had fallen. The rest of the night, she and the dog stayed outside on guard. By dawn, it had stopped writhing—its tail alone moved a little. From then on, with the dog standing guard, she did not fear the snakes at all.

But the bark on that night sounded like the dog had spotted a person. Because she was alone in the shed, Peruma had given her thaali chain to her mother. She wore a thread around her neck and a pair of earrings, that was all. The earrings together could add up to half a sovereign of gold. She wore them so she wouldn't look like a widow. She had heard stories of ears being chopped off for stealing gold. She had made a note to herself to buy a pair made of lead at the next chariot festival market. In their lone shack, there were no brass vessels either. She had taken them all to her mother's. Only the mud vessels that she regularly used for cooking remained in the shed.

As she lay wondering if she should get up or not, she heard a voice call out 'Muthu . . . Muthanna . . .' She couldn't identify who the voice belonged to over the dog's barking. But it sounded very familiar. She held the spear in her hand for protection, stood behind the palmyra screen door and asked sternly, 'Who is it?'

'Hmm . . . it is me, Periannan,' replied the voice. Perplexed by what that devil was doing outside her house at this hour, she asked, 'Yes?'

'A matter . . .' said the voice. Because it was disrespectful to talk to a family elder from inside, regardless of the situation, she opened the screen.

She had never stood in front of him or engaged in a conversation with him. Kaliannan's wife and Pongiannan's wife used to call him '*machaan*' coyly. Peruma referred to him as the eldest machaan only when she talked about him to someone else. At that moment, she was tongue-tied. When she knew it was him, she kept the spear against the wall and brought a hand lamp with her. She stood close to the screen, looked into the darkness and stuttered, 'He has gone out for a delivery'. Seeing Peruma talk normally to the visitor, the dog realized he was not a stranger. It stopped barking and went away to lie down near the goat kids. Periannan sat on the cot in the front yard.

Whether Muthu was around or not, the cot remained outside. She arranged a broomstick on it in such a way that it appeared as though someone was asleep. Over time, that became a spot for the dog to sleep on. 'He will return only tomorrow night,' she murmured, barely letting the words out of her mouth. She thought he had come over personally to ask for their consent to assign a water day to the parents, since sending messages through the others had not worked out. As it is, everything had been taken away in the name of the love that Muthu was surrounded by growing up. Maybe they were planning to strip him of the komanam he wore. 'He will return only at dawn, the day after tomorrow.' Peruma stood vigilantly but even she couldn't hear her own voice. Her tongue had gone dry and remained drawn in.

He suddenly stood up from the cot, rushed over to her, and grabbed her breasts. 'I came only to see you.' The part of her sari that covered her chest couldn't stop his hands.

Peruma, who had not at all expected this, pulled back instantly, falling against the palmyra barrier in front of the shed. Still, he didn't let go of his hold on one of them. 'I've been watching you since the day you got married. You keep running away and hiding. Do you know how much I desire you?' he said, seizing her. 'Muthu won't mind. He's never going to deny me anything I want. Come to me . . . a younger brother's wife is like one's own wife,' he whispered into her ears. It was so late in the night that even a fart would have sounded like an explosion. 'Chee, you dog!' she cried and pushed the man off her.

The mouth stinking of toddy brushed against her body. The hand that held her breast still wouldn't let go. Her sari had slipped completely off her chest. She grabbed the spear that was within her reach and struck his foot with all her might. The moment his grasp loosened, she pulled herself away from him and ran into the fields, screaming, 'Aiyooo, aiyoo!' It was only when Pongiannan's dog started barking that she remembered that there was someone close enough to call out to for help, and went running in that direction. By then, they had all woken up hearing Peruma's screams and the dog's barks and came outside. 'Akka, akka!' she cried, holding Seerayi. After calming herself down, drinking some water and straightening her appearance, she narrated all that happened. She suddenly remembered her children were still asleep in the shed. This man who did this could do anything. He may even decide to set the shed on fire. 'Akka, come with me akka, the children are still sleeping there,' said Peruma.

12

Peruma returned to the shed with Pongi, Seerayi and their eldest son Rangannan accompanying her. She hugged her arms tightly to hide her shivering. All these days, she had feared the dark. But it was the darkness that had been protecting her all along. Periannan had grabbed her in the light of the lamp. Darkness gave her the spear and safeguarded her. It was helping her hide her shivering too. If it remained dark everywhere, all the time, there would be no need to look at anyone's face. Darkness won't reveal them either. In the embrace of darkness, she leaned against the leg of the cot and cried. Quietly. The dog was barking in the direction of the low-lying area. The man wasn't there; he had left. Darkness would have dragged him away.

The children had not woken up; in spite of everything that had happened—they remained asleep. It showed that they had no fear in their minds. Darkness was keeping them safe and, in that darkness, they were asleep, abandoning all care. At the light of dawn, fear will consume them too. Instantly, she had an awakening. The sun will rise and the light will spread everywhere. How would they survive

without fear? 'I will drive home the point to the girls in the
morning,' she resolved. The boy was young. A child. He
could sleep deeply after tiring himself out. But how could
the two donkeys who were grown enough to be at the verge
of coming of age sleep like this? At just the slightest sound
of a snake hissing, they should wake up as if their own hair
were was on fire. How could one get any sleep at night if
one was born to a farmer?

'Today it was you. What is the guarantee that it won't
happen to me tomorrow? Come, let's go and ask that akka
and those oldies,' said Seerayi. Seerayi's continuous chatter
felt soothing to the worn-out Peruma. Most of what she
said simply rang hollow in her ears. Still, she wanted her to
continue talking. Pongi also insisted that they went right
away. Rangannan was asked to sleep on the cot outside and
the three left. 'I'll be here. You go, akka,' he said. He did
not address her as 'chitti' or 'chinnamma'. When she had
been married into the family, he was still tottering about,
barely able to walk. Now, in the middle of all that, she
found it astounding that he was reassuring her like a grown-
up, sporting a beard and moustache. If her first child had
been a boy, would he have reassured her that way too? Her
son had been born last, after two daughters. How much
more was going to happen by the time he was old enough
to reassure her like this? In a farmer's household, the first
child must be a boy. She stood up staring at Rangan, who
appeared like a shadow in the dark.

Ever since they had moved out with their belongings
after the property division, they had not gone back to that
house. She had spent ten or twelve years of her life there,

yet she did not have any happy memories from living there. She didn't even like being with Muthannan in that house. On occasions that they went to her village, he found that the affection she showed him was very different. 'Only if you like the people can you like the place,' she would say.

When everyone called him 'Muthu . . . Muthannan' and coddled him, it burned her like dried ginger powder on an open wound. 'They will rip everything off him with this sweet talk,' she muttered. Muthu suffered, feeling caught in the middle. The women coined the name 'Raangi' for Peruma—the insolent. 'Has Raangi come?' 'Has Raangi gone?' or 'What did Raangi say?' they would refer to her when they talked amongst themselves. Usually Peruma was already in the fields by the time the rest of the women drank the water and rice soaked overnight, in the mornings. Assuming that she had left as usual, her mother-in-law once went into the house asking someone, 'What did Raangi do today? Did she drink some soaked rice or was she pulling a long face?' Peruma, who was inside, combing Rosa's hair, realized that she was referring to her. 'Being insolent is much better than being a dick sucker,' she had snapped back, loudly. After that, she did not hear that name being used around her at all.

Fearing her anger, they preferred giving in to her whims over saying anything to her face. 'Muthannan is so timid. He never says anything to her. How did he end up with this demon of a woman?' they would say. It was their mother-in-law who grumbled aloud once in a while. Peruma usually remained silent when she did. But whenever an opportunity presented itself, she finished her off with a fittingly cutting retort. Every bit of that eight-anganam house was teeming with bitterness. She could not speak affectionately to anyone there as she held strong prejudices against each one of them for one reason or another. It was there that she had slept with Muthannan and borne her three children. She had always felt that she could have brought them up better if they lived elsewhere.

Pongi and Seerayi conversed about a lot of things as they walked. Peruma followed them like a wooden doll. 'If one's own sibling behaves like this, wouldn't an outsider think of you as an easy target that lives alone in that shed?' Seerayi's words caught her ears sporadically. The house was still awake. Even after the village died down at night, the house was always lively. The four brothers together had ten children. They used to run around the houses clamorously like a flock of mynah birds and played late into the night. On moonlit nights, children from the neighbouring fields joined them too. They played kho-kho, freeze-melt and hide-and-seek, until someone shouted 'Go to sleep, all of you' and shooed them away.

On dark nights, the cots were spread across the front of the house and it was tales and riddles galore. Paati always told the same story about a girl from Kodamaala. If the kids asked to be told a different story, she said, 'This is the only one I know'. Kaliannan's wife Poovayi was a good storyteller. There was no end to the number of stories she knew. Just when they thought they had heard the last of her stories, she'd spring a new one from nowhere. When they all asked her, 'Where was this story all these days?' she would casually reply, 'My grandmother told me this one. I remembered it only now.' Even after two families moved out and the children living in that house had grown past their parents' shoulders, the front of the house was still buzzing with life.

Periannan's wife took on the riled-up visitors all by herself. 'Look at the three that have arrived here with their half-covered heads. Who knows what calamity has befallen whom and where.' Periannan wasn't home. Perhaps he was lying somewhere and would find his way home only after the inebriation subsided. At that point, Peruma lost all her strength and started sobbing. She was lost and had no words. For a second, she thought she felt the warmth of comfort get the better of the bitterness in her heart. Regardless of all that had transpired, they were still her relatives. Whether they called her insolent or obstinate, they were family. If a thorn poked a foot, wouldn't the hand—a part of the same body—pull it out? She expected that they would offer her solace.

It was Pongi who narrated all that happened. 'You sent us away to some corner. If you come after the women too, what do you expect us to do? Do you want us to take our piddly possessions and wander from village to village to find a place to live?' he asked forcefully. 'What happened to her could happen to me tomorrow. How can we live peacefully in our land and in our home?' Seerayi added. Hearing the rumble and the barking of the dogs, the mother-in-law, father-in-law and Kaliannan's family came out too. Periannan's two sons came out too but stood silently without uttering a word. These were the same children who used to call Peruma 'chinnaaya' fondly. Peruma

stood leaning against the wall with her sari end over her
mouth and continued to cry uncontrollably. Kannayya spat
a mouthful of betel leaves with a loud 'thoo' outside the
house. Peruma inadvertently wiped her face as though she
had spat on her.

'And you all thought this was worth talking about at
this hour and marched over here? That my husband went
alone to her house. And grabbed her. And she shook
with fear? That man is barely different from a dog with
everything shrivelled up. His children have grown over his
shoulder and are old enough to be married. Would he lug
his junk over there at this hour? And even if he did, she
must have slept with him when they lived here. Maybe he
remembered that and went over for some more. Let him
come back. I will be sure to thrash him for ignoring this
house where food is available in plenty and craving instead
to feed on scraps at the bottom of the vessel.'

The mother-in-law, too, was unfazed. 'Why have you
come in the middle of the night as though something
dire has happened? How is it a crime if an older brother
grabbed the wife of a younger brother? In our times,
the sacred wedding thread was tied by one man but his
brothers were all husbands in practice. You think all of the
six children I had were sired by your father? Who knows for
sure? Whoever got on top, got in. If he did come seeking
you, instead of inviting him discreetly and serving him a
feast, you have come here to create a scene. Must be the
changing times in the name of civilization. Listen, aaya,
from now on, I denounce your husband as my son; he is not
a brother to Periannan anymore. Why will anyone come by

your place from now on? Build yourself a fort and rule it all by yourself too. Let my eldest come home. I assure you I will ask him why he went seeking this bitter bitch when he could have gone anywhere else. Go back now and take great care of those precious parts of yours,' she spat out words without control.

Hatred fully took over Peruma as she stood there. A fear crept into her mind that if she stayed any longer, they may drag her by her hair and beat her up. In Muthu's absence, it was wrong of her to place her trust in Pongi. These people were not the relatives she knew from before who fight over something one minute and share a laugh together the next minute. That story had ended. These were strangers. This house, these people and memories of living with them were all a thing of the past. Not one word of reassurance was available here. Only a knife to the neck. Everything was clear now. She took a step back and continued to walk into the darkness.

'You shouldn't have spoken to her like that, amma. Muthu was born to you, not to some rival wife. You treat one eye with butter and another eye with lime . . . How will you live well in your old age?' asked Pongi. That's all he could do.

'Butter and lime indeed! Just because I am not physically as able as I used to be, you think you can talk to me anyway you wish. You come here defending her, that repulsive wretch. She hates the very scent of a man. Like an *aalanthaapatchi,* a fire bird, she never let anyone close to her even when she lived here. She flies in quest of human flesh, picking up the trace of a man or woman. If you are not careful, she will use her words to pierce your skin and feed on your flesh. You listened to her and showed up at this hour. Since you live close to her, did she manage to lure you to her side?'

Unable to listen to the words that were pouring out of his mother's mouth, Pongi too returned. No one said anything. It was clear from the silence that no one had expected that outcome. Seerayi and her son slept in the shack to be close to Peruma. At least Pongi's family was there for her. If not, what could she have done as a lone woman? If she got beat up, no one was around to support her. That must be why Periannan came over. The wound from the spear she had stuck into his foot would take a while to heal. Let him be reminded of her wrath every time he looked at it. Let it be seared in his heart that such lowly acts will not be tolerated by Peruma.

The next morning, no work got done. She had waited restlessly for the sun to come up and then took it out on the two girls. 'The grown-ups are behaving like dogs. What will these two saplings do? Don't hit them,' Seerayi stopped her.

'Won't you wake up even if they come to kill the mother who gave birth to you? You sleep like corpses. Don't you have any fear in you that we live alone in this shack? You think you can shield your vagina and sleep through everything after being born to a farmer, di?'

The children accepted her blows and cried. They did not have any inkling of what had transpired. Not telling them seemed to be the right option. Peruma remained lying in the front yard, doing no work. The girls did not know what to do. They sat in the same spot and cried every now and then. The boy alone played with the dog and the chicken. Seerayi went to her house, finished her work, came back, made kali and fed the children. She was the one who told Peruma about the plan.

'The men from my house went around and found out all the details. They don't want to have this land divided up into four farms. Everyone has children and responsibilities. So they have decided amongst themselves to consolidate this into two farms. First you. Then us. We may not agree to the plan if they told us directly. That's why all this. Once your husband returns, tell him to find a farm far away and leave this place. We will relocate to where you are in a few days. Let them keep this land for themselves.'

Was chasing them away from the village the motive behind all this? That seemed to explain everything that had occurred. When they lived together for ten, twelve years, not once had Periannan behaved this way. He looked at her with a wandering gaze occasionally, but Peruma had quickly moved away at those times. Since this had occurred after the division, the explanation Seerayi gave made sense. Whatever it may be, she could not continue to live here with her children anymore. Seeing their mother frozen in one place, the girls got up and did what they could. The boy didn't go anywhere beyond the front yard and played within the boundaries. When Peruma felt the scorching heat on her body, she got up as though she just regained her senses. She had made a decision. She informed Seerayi, instructed a labourer boy to guard the shack, arranged for him to sleep there until Muthu returned, and set off in the middle of the day. She did not even turn to catch the last glimpse of the land or the shack as she left.

If their portion of land was not sufficient for farming, is this how they planned to deal with it? Will the eldest of a family come in the middle of the night and grope a woman? Her breasts still ached in the morning. She removed her sari and examined them. Her left breast was withered. The way he had seized her, his grip did not seem to match their intent of chasing them away from the village. It was more a manifestation of several years of lust steeping in his heart. From then on, she was going to remember his hand every time she saw that breast. She wanted to chop that breast off of her body. If she hadn't got hold of the spear, he may even have torn it off her that night. She could sense his passion. The more she thought about it, the heavier her breasts felt, until they felt like massive rocks atop her chest. She could not live there bearing that weight. From then on, come what may, even if it meant living away from Muthu forever and in the corner of her mother's house as a burden, she resolved never to return to that land.

*

After Peruma managed to narrate everything between tears and whimpers, she leaned on his chest and let out an unassuageable loud bawl. Muthu didn't notice anybody else around them. He held her in a tight hug, patting and stroking her back. No words were going to mean anything. He too felt like crying. With a lot of effort, he controlled himself.

'A faraway place with no relatives close by will do just fine. Even if it is so remote a land that even lizards don't live there. If we have to live on one meal of porridge a day, my children and I will live contented. Don't ever think that I will come back to that place in my lifetime. If you insist on it, you will only see my corpse,' she cried.

Muthu did not expect his eldest brother to stoop so low. He had imagined that a tiny bit of the love from his childhood had remained, hidden somewhere deep in that heart of stone. He had hoped that the brothers would get back together. He didn't care that he couldn't live in that village anymore. He wanted to smash his elder brother's head and demand answers from his parents.

'I cannot ignore this. I will go back and settle this once for all,' he said and got up. Peruma rushed towards him and blocked him.

'Everything is over. From now on, there will be no bond and relation between us and them—ever. They will say the same thing to you too. Your mother called me aalanthaapatchi. So be it. From now on, none of them will come anywhere near us. They said many more things. Being a woman, I stayed quiet. If you lose your temper and your actions lead to something unpleasant, what will happen to my children and me? Don't pick a fight. Focus on finding a buyer for what we have and sell everything. We will go somewhere and start over. Once they have decided to chase us out, they will do anything to achieve that. He has nothing to lose, his children are grown. He has snatched the bulk of the lands. What leverage do we have, tell me?' she said. Muthu stopped, bound by her words.

They sent Peruma's father and brother to the village. With Pongiannan's help, they would get as many things done as possible. Peruma may find the village and its land bitter. She was, after all, transplanted there. But it was not the same for him. He had germinated on that soil and was rooted there. Thirty years of memories lay buried in him. He lay down on the cement floor of his father-in-law's house and remained that way for a long time. He did not know when sleep descended upon him—two days' worth of sleep. Moreover, his mind must have sought an escape in sleep, tired from bearing all that burden. Peruma did not disturb him. Long after the lamps were lit, she woke him up gently.

It took him a while to fully regain his consciousness. They had cooked rice from paddy. She served it on a plate and placed it in front of him along with a lamp. As she bent down to serve him the saaru, his fingers tried to move her sari from her chest. She instantly clutched her sari tightly. 'Don't see it!' she said and cried. Barely audible whimpers. With a large sigh, he directed his hand to his plate instead, when he heard the cart pull in. It was his cart. He knew it just by the sound of the turning wheels.

13

The footpath led to another cart road. From there, the village seemed within reach. It was full of houses made of palm thatches. Thatches that hadn't been replaced for many years. There were a lot of small huts. Interspersed among them were a few houses with roofs made of U-shaped terracotta tiles. They too invoked the feeling of being in the shadow of sadness. By the way the houses were organized, he could tell that the roads were not planned. He wondered why there were so many farms that lay wide open but not with proportionately enough cattle or goats—the bunds were full of grass. *They have left the grass untouched even in summer. They must be people who did not farm for a living. How are we going to spend our lifetime with them?*

At the entry into the village, he was invited by a lone little temple and a peepal tree adjacent to it. The platforms built around the tree were very wide. An intense game of *thaayam* was taking place on one side of the platform. The other sides were filled with people napping. Should he enquire about available land from the people here or walk further into the village and enquire at one of the houses? No one seemed to have noticed his arrival. Yet, if he went past them, he may need to give them answers. The sound of the dice rolling caused a commotion among the spectators—all sorts of people stood around watching. Two people rolled the dice. Whoever got the higher number, won the game. The game was played for money; bets from one to five paise were placed. Getting their attention was not going to be easy.

In the same loud voice that he used to push the oxen to go faster, he asked, 'Say . . . where is the house of this village's *naattamai*, nga?' The entire crowd turned around. 'What did you ask?' said a young man from amidst the crowd. Muthu's face shrank at the lack of respect in that question. 'The naattamai's house' he said politely. Everyone sized him up as though a strange creature had arrived at their village. 'Where are you from?' asked another man. 'I come from the west, nga.' By then some of the men who were napping woke up too. One of them looked at Muthu and said, 'Come here'. He approached the platform. The man pointed to a corner and said, 'Climb over and sit there.' The man looked like the responsible sort. 'Where have you come from? What do you want?' And the enquiry began. There was no hint of respect in their words.

Muthu had noticed that already. Beyond Rattoor, any sense of politeness gradually vanished, to the point that no heed was paid even to the differences in age.

When he told them that he would like to buy land in that area if there was any available, they mocked him,

'Look da, the agriculture minister has come!' commented one sarcastically. Everyone laughed at that. Another said, 'Each kuzhi, or 144 s.f., will cost you a thousand rupees. Will you buy it?' Muthu took a look at the man's head. His hair was matted and full of knots. *Must be months since he has bathed*, he thought. 'If the land supports farming with good water access to grow paddy and other crops, a thousand can be reasonable,' Muthu replied. When he said that, they all turned their attention to him, finally acknowledging his seriousness.

Muthu understood that the man who had invited him to sit down at first, was the village's naattamai. He spoke very clearly. 'There isn't any good setup in place for water access in these areas. There may be a well somewhere. Sweet potatoes and maize are grown around here. Other than that, we also sow kodo millet and little millet. The selling price ranges anywhere from 100 per ten kuzhis, all the way to 200. There is just no one to sell or buy.' He then looked at the men standing around and asked a question. 'Does anyone here want to give their land?' There was no favourable response.

One man who was intoxicated and had stumbled past the crowd to stand in front of Muthu, asked him, 'What do you do?'

'I am a farmer,' replied Muthu.

'What rubbish. I'm a farmer too. Can you afford to buy land here? Do you have that much money? Dei, admit it . . . you've come to steal chicken, haven't you? Did that Subbukodukkan send you here to spy?' he asked, grabbed Muthu's towel and pulled it.

'Leave him alone, Mooka. Look at how respectfully this visitor speaks. Stop troubling him.' Mookan did not at all pay heed to the naattamai's reproach.

'What is in the bag? It is definitely a knife. This man is certainly a chicken thief,' he tried to snatch his bag. Muthu held the bag tightly under his arms. *This is a new place; these men are different. Stay patient.*

'Ayyy . . . just because you come wearing a new *vetti*, you think we will believe you?' continued Mookan. He walked around Muthu clapping mockingly. Everyone around them found this amusing. 'Move away,' the naattamai brushed Mookan aside and took Muthu with him, saying 'Please come'. Muthu took a good, hard look at Mookan. When travelling to other unknown places, being deemed a robber was common. Muthu had mentioned that he had come in his cart and that he needed a place to stay for the night. The naattamai told him that he could ask around if anyone wanted to sell their land and that they could talk more about it that night. He invited him to stay the night at his place.

There was room in the village choultry, he could leave Kuppan there. He found his way back and turned away from the village road when voices of laughter drifted towards him from the choultry behind. They must be talking about him, he thought.

He mentioned 'kuzhi' but I left without asking them how much land that was. I suppose we can discuss that at night. The very first interaction with the locals began with a conflict. How are we going to live with these people? He perched on a large rock he found on the way.

Where has Periannan pushed me into?! What sort of language has he made me listen to? Is it a good idea to buy land here? Even their language wasn't pleasant, how will the people be alright? Should I look elsewhere? But it was this location that Mansaami had pointed to. He closed his eyes, held his head in his hands and leaned back all the way on the rock to lie down.

Why be pessimistic about everything? Why don't I think of the benefits of buying land here? Muthu slowly sat up. *This is a region of people different from mine. Their way of speaking sounds strange. They refer to everyone, from little children to older people, using the same uncourteous 'nee'. That is their habit. There must have been more than twenty people in the choultry. Only one person wanted to pick a fight. He was heavily intoxicated. Every village has a drunkard, especially one who got drunk and picked fights. Finding a village without a drunkard is not possible.* It is only the past ten days that Muthu has refrained from drinking, otherwise he too is in the habit of drinking every day.

Whether or not one continued to climb trees, the skill of climbing remains with him. That shouldn't be a concern. *The soil is good. There is water too. Can't spot any deep wells but water will come with digging. There is plenty of space to graze the goats and cattle. Even for a whole pen full of goats. If help is needed, seems like there are labourers available. What do those people napping in the choultry do for a living? They will probably accept lower wages. There is so much work that can be done in summer. A new place. New people. Everything feels new. All the experiences will be new. As long as the curiosity to explore remains, anything will be interesting. You will be the first man to get out of that place which has been paralyzing people for several generations. How long can you live in a pond full of stinking stagnant water and moss? Let's give the overflowing spring of fresh water a chance. And if you set everything the right way, maybe more will follow your way. If you turn this land green, Pongi will move here soon too. When he does, you will have company and support. Together, you can create everything anew. If the land lends itself, work hard and develop it.*

First, a farmland. But not by paying a lot for land with nothing in it. We will buy some land right here. In a land that has everything, there won't be much to do. Much work will be required in a land that has nothing. This is a land with nothing. None of the fields looked like they had been worked on. The bunds are missing. The circular tracks of the ploughshares haven't made their way to the borders yet. There are palm trees here and there but their fronds are dry. Not a single coconut tree can be seen around. Somewhere at a distance, there is a cow or a goat or two. But it doesn't seem like there are many more of them, unless they are bred in a pen setup. These people don't even know that if they only used thatches made of kodo millet or pearl millet in their roofs, they would last for several more years.

The more he thought about it, the more it seemed that the decision to purchase land there had a lot of benefits.

There were no signs of labour-class families in the area. Saethur was about ten kal away. He should find out if there was a market closer by. Even if Saethur was the closest, it wasn't very far. He got up and started walking. There was still some daylight left. When Mookan had tried to snatch his bag, his heart had skipped a beat. He had placed one vetti at the bottom of the bag with an indent in its middle into which he had placed his waist pouch with the money, and covered it with another vetti. If Mookan had grabbed the bag and spilled the contents, the waist bag would have fallen out. What could he have possibly done if they had declared the money stolen and taken away all of it? Seeing their state of affairs, he imagined they would have taken the money and divided it among themselves. Until he bought a farm and everything was settled, the money had to be kept safe.

Peruma had said to him before he set out, 'I hear they knife people for mere earrings. Everyone talks about how a woman's chain was snatched when she was walking alone. The stories that we hear at the market don't stop at one or two. Our entire property down to the very last bit of it is now in that waist pocket. It is in this pocket that the futures of my three children lie. If something were to happen to it, I will make a paste with arali seeds, feed it to the three, consume it along with them and die. After that, if you are smart enough, you will be able to marry someone else and live well.'

The warning continually rang in his ears. If a single robber attacked him, he could manage it. Even if they came in a group, he could somehow manage that too. But if a whole village gathered together to rob him of his money, how could he handle that? *Surely, there must be a few good people in any place?* As long as he remained connected to them, he could handle any trouble. The naattamai seemed to be a good man. It would be good to hold onto him. But even if they were able to settle on a piece of land, he should not breathe a word about the money. He needed to remind Kuppan about that too. It was money from returning a pittance of a land that was given to them like alms. Thanks, but no thanks.

It was money from severing ancestral bonds.

14

Ever since he had left his village, early that morning, Muthu had not gone back. Peruma didn't let him. If he had, a mere conversation could end in blows. There was no predicting what might happen with the frenzy everyone was in. They couldn't afford for him to lose a limb or two. 'Your eldest nanga spat right on my face. After that, why would we ever cross that house's threshold?' she said. His father-in-law and his brother-in-law Veerannan had gone in his place. They met and talked to Pongi. Muthu's land was adjacent to his. So, if he bought it, he could farm on both. If some outsider bought Muthu's land, what would he do with just one acre? Pongi was very happy to buy that land.

Seerayi had said to them, 'We are buying the land only for the rights to the water. Other than that, of what use is that land? If we sow corn, the forage will be over a quarter of the crop's height. And if that happens during the rainy season, we cannot even weed it out. The soil is full of gravel. Larger stones aren't a concern but this land is full of small stones. It has been left alone only because nothing can be done with it. They gave them that piece of land and forced them out of the village. Don't know what they are going to do to us.'

After the deliberations, Pongi had agreed to pay 500 rupees for the land.

The land was a mere four kals away from the road that connected Karattur to Ottur. It was practically within stone's throw from the road. If one had to go to the market, one could easily walk the distance. The land could be used just to feed cattle. One could rear cattle on that land for milk. Enough people from Karattur would buy milk if it was delivered early in the morning and it can be delivered by foot. The land may not be conducive for agriculture but the cows could find sustenance. But who had the money to pay for all that? They were churning the land and barely feeding the family. Maybe if more people were interested in buying that land, they would have received a better price. But there were no other buyers—that too, at such short notice. Someone may have come forward if they were able to negotiate the price, register a deed, allow for one or two years for the buyer to save the amount and then pay the money. But in a rush, there was no other option available other than to go to Pongi.

Now, they could irrigate all the lands from Periannan's to Pongi's, and grow anything they wanted. If they grew one portion each of vegetables like green chilies, tomatoes or snake gourd, they would all sell out at the weekly market. That income would be enough for meeting basic expenses, even for a large family. As for the grains and cotton seed plants, those roots needed watering merely once a week for

a significant yield. Because Karattur was so close by, the
land value, in general, was not bad. But Muthu's land was
a useless pit. What would they do with it? Maybe in the
month of Kaarthigai, it could serve as the gathering spot
for all the wild dogs to create a ruckus. Yet, the father-in-
law asked for a thousand for that land. A greedy move.

'They gave me 500 just like they did Muthu when the
lands were divided, to build ourselves a house. I have only
that money. I have not been able to save a single additional
paisa since. For now, we live in this thatched shed. If
Muthu finds a place that works out, we will follow that way
too. We can build a proper house and all that. I will give
you the 500. Please ask him to make the transfer. I cannot
do better than this,' Pongi had declared decisively.

They had no choice but to accept the deal. Veerannan
who knew Peruma's stubbornness, immediately agreed. He
went around the land that was given to Muthu a few times
too. 'Even if they laboured on this land their entire lives,
they couldn't fill a quarter of their stomachs with it. Do
they even have a conscience, those people who allocated
this as their share?' he said to his father. He wanted to tell
Muthu, who was a seasoned farmer, 'Sell this at any price,
you can get and find a job as the farm in-charge. You will
be able to settle your girls down,' but how could he? The
land could fetch another fifty or 100. But finding a person
who could afford to buy was going to be very difficult,
especially in a rush. With Pongi, the work got done easily.

Next was his parents' piece of land that was to go to
Muthu after they passed on. The two of them were still
as fresh as recently harvested tubers. Who knew how long

before they passed on and the land went to Muthu? His father-in-law thought it would be best to speak directly with them. He would tell them, 'Muthu does not want this land. He is not going to come back here, what can you offer us?' and get a verdict on that as well. The best option would be if one of the brothers took the land and gave money for it, although they may have to wait five or ten years to get possession of the land. It would not be surprising if those oldies lived to touch 100 either. But who would trust that arrangement and pay for it now?

They could not approach an unrelated person or a distant relative to sell this land to, either. 'Let's try anyway and see what happens,' thought the father-in-law. It was ancestral property after all, so if nothing worked out, it could remain as it was. Sometime in the future, it would come to Muthu. He wondered if they had clearly stated that in the documents. They could easily cause any amount of trouble to the last-born son at any time they wanted. Especially if he was as timid as Muthu. When the father-in-law brought this land up with Pongi, he too wasn't clear about the setup. But Pongi did not have the heart to send Muthu's father-in-law over to talk to his parents either. The relationship was already suffering. He didn't want more rifts between the in-laws to worsen the situation. His mother's tongue wouldn't stay quiet. 'That foul-smelling wretch has gone home and sent her father, has she? Look how they demand the land when the owners are still alive. Go, tell her to drop a rock on us while we are asleep and then take the land,' she would spurt. Wanting to avoid this, Pongiannan offered to approach them instead of Muthu's father-in-law.

'Your father's wife is hardly going to seat you on her lap and shower you with love and kisses if you go! How long do you think it will take her to throw you out just as she did her last-born? Remember you are the last-born from now on,' shouted Seerayi.

'Ada, leave that alone, won't you? The last one was everyone's favourite. He is leaving the village altogether now. My heart is pounding with worry over where he is going to go and how he is going to manage. Those fellows are his brothers too. Won't they have concerns too? My mother has breastfed him, won't she think about it for a moment? People don't remain the same. Will we have the same mentality tomorrow as today? Let me try talking to them. At worst, I will bear a few blows for Muthu's sake.' Pongi made his big speech and headed out.

It was evening time. Pongi sat down on a cot set outside Amma's and Appa's place. Amma was inside and thought it was her husband who was sitting outside. 'It took you this long to pluck a couple of green chilies and a handful of curry leaves? Yet, as soon as you sit down, you will demand that you be served food. Like I can simply cast a spell and have the rice and stew cook on their own instantly. All these days, you ate whatever and however your daughters-in-law cooked. Now, at the tail end of time, your tongue wants tasty food,' she snapped. Appa never responded to anything. He held onto that habit like a vow. Before she said anything more, Pongi said, 'Amma, this is Pongi.'

She came out in a flash. 'Have you come to see if your father and mother are still alive or lying dead? Just what have we done to you that hasn't happened anywhere else?

We divided up everything in the presence of others and with everyone's consent. Yet, you hold secret deliberations here and there. You say your father and mother cheated you. What sort of talk is that? Are all five fingers created equal? Even though they are uneven, the hand has to adjust to all that,' she sputtered.

Pongi let her talk for some time and quieten on her own. While she was talking, Appa returned too. 'What has the sire come seeking?' he asked. The residents of Periannan and Kaliannan's houses peeped through the windows. The brothers hadn't returned from the farms yet. Periannan's wife thought that he had returned to discuss what happened the previous night and was ready to use her voice any moment.

'I don't want anything. Our stomachs are already brimming with whatever you have given us. I have not come here to grab the gold you have kept heaped on your verandah. Muthannan is leaving the village for good. I have told them I will buy his land for 500. We are registering it tomorrow. That's why he wanted to see if he could settle the portion that is with you as well. "I don't want anything to do with you, I don't want even the wind of this land to touch me again," he has said. What is your offer?' Pongi poured it all out in one breath. If he paused even a little, they would cut in and say something to create confusion.

'That sire will not come by this village at all, is that so? That luckless wretch will not let him. She will drag him to her father's house and keep him there with her. That wretch with no affection for the family. Until he turned six, he drank the milk from my breasts and found it sweet. Now it is her breasts he finds sweet. Let him be well wherever he is. Not one day did I imagine that I would cut off and discard my last-born. I brought him up with so much love. When I thought my womb was barren forever, he took root within me as if to give me life. He received support that no one else did. Now he doesn't even want to see my face. Let it be. We are not dependent on anyone. As long as our hands and legs are functioning, we will work and feed ourselves. If not, we will find ourselves a four mozham rope from somewhere. Alright. I will give my land to whoever takes care of us in our final days. Be it a man or a woman. If no one takes care of us when we are old and invalid, we will sell the land off to some stranger and live off that money. I don't want his curse. Did you give him 500 for one acre? Here, let him keep this 500 too. When you register your land tomorrow, get mine written in my name too.' She brought the money wrapped in a cloth, dropped it on Pongi's lap and went back in.

No one had expected such a reaction from the old lady. '*Le* . . . what are you doing, le!' exclaimed the old man. The wives watching all this rushed to inform their husbands. Pongi knew that if his mother had made a decision, nothing could change it. He took the money and left immediately. They could try to change the old lady's mind and then chase him down to take the money back. He would not put that past Periannan. He rushed back home, gave the money to Muthu's father-in-law and asked them to leave immediately. 'We can talk in detail later. The work is done. There is another 500 in here. Please take this and leave. We will take care of the documents tomorrow.'

The bullock cart was ready to leave. The labourers had loaded it with all the utensils and other possessions, and tied the goats to the back of the cart. He sent them away in a hurry. He watched the cart until it got on the road and disappeared. It was beginning to get dark. No one had come after him so far. It had to be Periannan who was angry with Pongi because he had bought that one acre of land from Muthu. Kaali had always been fond of Pongi. Even though they didn't speak with one another, they enjoyed a closeness that could unite them again any time. Pongi had the old lady's support too now. He felt he didn't need to worry about what had happened.

As he was thinking about the arrangements to register the transactions, he realized that they hadn't discussed Muthu's shed. He could ask for it to be left behind for him. Muthu could give him at least that in return for taking care of the daunting work of obtaining money from the old lady. He needed a work area like that. He could use the space to feed the cows and the goats, to store firewood and tools, like his *manvetti* and plough.

Everyone was quite a bit surprised to see the old lady just hand over money like that. Pongi had assumed that the one acre of land was a lost cause. The old lady acted as though she had already thought it through and planned for such a scenario. Perhaps she had seen Muthu's father-in-law and Veerannan arrive in the afternoon. Maybe she foresaw that this was how things were going to turn out. Muthu was unable to comprehend all that had happened.

Her characteristic way of speaking with spite had transformed into action filled with compassion. They took out the money wrapped in a cloth and started counting it all together. Pongi had handed the money wrapped in the cloth and dropped in his lap to Muthu's father-in-law in a hurry, who, in turn, handed it over to Muthu without opening it. In the bundle were 684 rupees; on top of the 500 that she had received when they had divided the property—she had added up her entire savings until then and handed all of it to Pongi, even though she had mentioned only the 500. When they finished counting the money, Muthu burst into tears. 'Why are you trying me like this, Amma? Just when I thought you have flung me away, you lift me up!' he cried, beating his chest.

All this while, he had thought that the old lady had had a hand in the scheme to chase him away. By sending extra money, she had adequately expressed her heartfelt well wishes for him. Even though he had wanted to sever all ties with them, a small unintentional knot now refused to come undone. The extra 184 rupees were no small knot. Peruma didn't say anything. To her, the money that had been sent was akin to being handed a glass of water after being beaten with slippers.

The old lady was no ordinary woman. She made sure to maintain a small knot in each of her relationships. Even though she didn't like Peruma, when the other daughters-in-law were not around, she would tell her, 'Why subject yourself to all that smoke from cooking? Go, work in the fields, out in the open. That would be better.' So much so that Peruma wondered if her mother-in-law actually wanted to help her. It infuriated her when she spoke that way. It is true what they say, a tongue lacking nerves speaks from all sides of the mouth. A crafty one, she was. The one who had called Peruma an aalanthaapatchi. But it was really she who cast a spell on everyone and made them come back to her. The spell she had cast on Muthu was this money. She planned these gestures time and again, foreseeing opportunities to have her sons come back to her. Peruma did not trust the old lady's intentions. However, the money that had reached them at such a difficult time in their life gave her joy. Whose money was it anyway? It was money that they had earned over the span of all those years of toil.

But it was different for Muthu. That money came steeped in his mother's love. Every time he thought about how she promptly handed that money over, his eyes welled up.

15

When Muthu returned to the field where the cart was parked, Kuppan's face lit up with excitement. To have Kuppan's encouragement to buy land in the area was a good thing. The man's life had remained centred around the earth from the time of his birth. He could read the secret dynamic between the soil and the seasons—it nonchalantly revealed to him the nitty gritty and nuances hidden from the layman's eye. More so than humans, he had fostered a deep connection with plant life.

'When I tell people that plants and foliage talk, they laugh at me, saami. This *panguni* season, go to the fields right after you wake up in the morning and see for yourself. With their bodies dripping clean in the morning mist they will look at you and laugh at you, calling you a dirty little fellow. I get quite embarrassed, you see. Don't think of them like humans. Even a single blade of grass does not truly die. When there is no rain, it simply hides inside the earth. You should see how it peeps out of the soil with just a few drops of rain. Like little children peeking out of their hiding spots.'

When he spoke, Muthu marvelled at Kuppan's passion. With him by his side, he felt confident that he could accomplish whatever he wanted. He narrated to Kuppan the story of his trip to the village.

'The naattamai has invited me to his house. There are always a few good people in every place. The way they speak is very different. Not one of our people lives here. If we thrive, we may inspire a few to move here and then we may acquire some company. Until then, we have to comply with the people of this village as much as we can. Let's see if we can't find someone or the other with land to sell, as soon as the day breaks. If we give five or ten rupees more, we should be able to get a farm. These people are slackers, they will give in,' he opened, sounding hopeful.

'My only fear is about the money, Kuppanna. There is a drunkard dog called Mookan or Naakan or something like that. He tried to seize my bag. He was flat as a plate but what a commotion he created! If this had happened in our village, I would have slapped him right then. I bore it all quietly as this isn't our village. The way he pulled the bag—if I had kept the money at my waist, it would have shown through. And they would have taken all of it. These people must never even have seen a thousand or 2,000 together. Even if we agree on a land and conclude all negotiations, we should we give them the money only after the land deed has been registered. Someone I know lives there, in Saethur. We will tell these people that we gave all the money to that person for safekeeping. Or we will tell them that if we inform the bus driver, someone one will bring the money from our village. Don't indulge in any loose talk, Kuppana,' he cautioned him.

As if waiting the whole time for Muthu to finish, Kuppan jumped up. He said cogently, 'I already found the field and met a person who is going to sell it to us, saami.'

'Really! My brother! Come, show me,' Muthu said hastily. He did not know what had happened while he was at the village. *Even though Kuppan has spent most of life playing with the earth and being indifferent to the rest of the world, he is quite sharp*, he thought. Muthu never left the oxen unguarded. To him, everything would be lost if someone passing by untied them and took them away. But at that moment, he didn't even stop to think about them. Kuppan also said, 'Let the oxen remain grazing here. The field is within view,' and started walking.

Once Muthu had set out for the village, Kuppan had placed the utensils and the plates back on the cart. Muthu had set up a basket with a pot and a wide-mouthed vessel with a rope around it. When it was irrigation time at any well, they would ask someone there to draw some water for them. If there were labourers already drawing water from the well, Muthu would send Kuppan alone with the basket and its contents. Kuppan would then request them to draw some water for him. He would take help in placing the water-filled vessel back inside the basket too. The oxen drank water from the wide-mouthed vessel. Their setup came in handy whenever Muthu left Kuppan behind to go about his enquiries.

Because they needed water for the oxen, Kuppan had balanced the basket on his head, held the oxen rope in his hand and walked aimlessly. Once he climbed over a mound, he spotted two or three coconut trees. Wherever there were coconut trees, there was sure to be a well. What he didn't know was whether there were any labourers nearby. Halfway to the coconut trees, Kuppan spotted a man standing clad in long trousers—he seemed quite young. Must be less than thirty, Kuppan estimated. His body was in excellent form and he looked good. He could tell just by the way he moved that he was not the kind to see a task through diligently. When Kuppan told him what he was looking for, he took him to the well. He had come there to take back two cows that he'd left in the fields to graze with two long ropes around their necks. 'What people are you?' he asked. When Kuppan answered his question, he asked, 'Oh, are your people around this region too?'

'I don't know. There are people who speak Telugu too. We speak only Tamil,' Kuppan elaborated. When the man heard that Muthu had gone into the village, he asked, 'What sort is he? Is he from the west?'

'Yes,' said Kuppan, 'We come from the Karattur region, west of here.'

Everything Kuppan said was new to the man. Kuppan mentioned that when the family property was divided between the brothers, Muthu's wasn't given enough land for farming. That was why they had come here.

The water source in the field hardly fit the description of a well. It was more like a pit, about five-men deep. The man referred to it as a '*kaeni*'. There was barely any water in it and there was no irrigation apparatus either. Perhaps they used a tub to irrigate their lands. The man told him that he had four or five brothers and that they didn't get along well and constantly fought with each other. Because of that, their farming had suffered.

'That man's name is Vellaiyan, saami. His body seemed like it was sculpted out of iron. He alone could plough through this entire field by himself. But as good as this man looked, his work is sure to be bad, you see . . .' Kuppan told Muthu and continued.

It appeared that one of the brothers was vehement about moving to his father-in-law's house. Another one wanted to move to Irumpaalai and find work there. Two of the others did not have any money to invest in farming. Under the circumstances, they were considering selling a portion of their lands. Kuppan couldn't control his excitement when he heard that bit of news. But without letting his feelings be seen, he said, 'If we like the soil, we will consider.' The man showed him the land. 'That man kept drawing more and more water as the oxen drank, you see. That itself made me like him. He saw our oxen and said that we were taking good care of them. He is the sort that can tell just by looking at the oxen if they were the small but fattened type.' Kuppan couldn't stop praising the man. As easily as he had been able to judge oxen just by looking at them, Kuppan could also guess if someone was suited for farmwork or not. The man had left saying that if Muthu liked the land, they could discuss the matter further, the next day. Hence, Kuppan decided to take Muthu along to show him the land.

Two broad cart roads flanked the farm on the north and the east sides. The same road where they had stopped the cart continued until here and turned to the east. To the west was a slope that ended in a dense, thorny pit. To the south were farmlands for a very long stretch. 'How much of this, Kuppa?' asked Muthu. The man had said ten kuzhis or 100 kuzhis, however much they wanted. One kuzhi equalled eight cents. Twelve and a half made an acre. Starting at the road, about 300 kuzhi seemed to belong to them. The land that was available for sale bore no traces of prior farming. It was very uneven, with rocks and stones. On the side that ended in the pit were huge trees, mostly of the seemai karuvela or black thorn variety. How good was the soil, though?

Muthu broke off a twig lying on the ground and prodded the soil with it. It was indeed red earth. He dug into the earth a little—the red earth was mixed with a bit of black soil. That was not a problem. Not much farming had been done on the land. Wherever the land was flat, he could see the occasional circular tracks of the plough. They hadn't ploughed it much—just a little, using only a single plough. A few vellaivela trees stood here and there. He spotted one or two neem trees as well. And ten or fifteen palm trees. Their dried fronds hadn't been removed in two or three years and clung to them like matted hair. A stork was perched on a palm tree with its mouth wide open. That was a sign that water was available in abundance close by.

Would Peruma accept this land? To get to a tar road, they had to walk two kals. It must be about seven or eight kals to Saethur. The land wasn't repaired either, there was a lot of work yet to be done on it. In about four or five years, they would be able to cultivate properly. Ten years and they would have a glorious farm here. A well had to be dug. They could graze cattle and goats. Will they be able to manage? Will Peruma blame him for dumping her on untilled land? But they would certainly have a lot of land. Assuming it would cost them twenty rupees a kuzhi, he could buy 100 kuzhis. That amounted to over nine acres. That was a lot. Even if he reared only one pen-full of goats, he could get his elder daughter married off in four or five years.

This was the land that Mansaami had shown him. The name of the place was Karunkaradu. The one who stood in this *karadu*, this rugged land, would be known as Karattuchaami. It would be nice if they could acquire this land. Because there were roads on two sides, there was almost no possibility of encountering any problems with the owner of the neighbouring farm. On another end was the lowland, bordering a brook. That had to be poramboke land. So there was no problem on that side either. Only one side was adjacent to another farm. Once they had measured the land, he could install stone dividers close to each other and erect a fence there. Since this was a new land where he knew no one, there was no one to support him through any sort of problems. Indeed, even in a place filled with one's family and relatives, fights over dividing ridges could go as far as to draw blood. In a place where he had no connections, he would have to be cautious about such things. This was a land best suitable for that.

They went around the farm once. There were rocks scattered all around. In one particular spot there was a large, rounded rock. There were tall rocks in a couple

of spots. Small, rounded rocks were spread around
everywhere. Should they want to build a house, there was
no dearth of rocks. They could use the rounded rocks for
drying grains. The matura shrubs were full of blossoms.
In one spot, a matura shrub had grown into a tree. Muthu
affectionately touched the tree which looked like a thin, tall
man standing with his arms bent over his head. When they
clear all the undergrowth, they will leave this one alone.
It was a wonder. Every farm should have one. Whenever
anyone visits them, they will want to know about the tree.
When he realized he was planning out things as though he
already owned the land, he chuckled.

All the neighbouring farms in this region were like this
too. None of the farms were ready for farming immediately
upon purchase. Not one farm seemed to have a house in it.
How could they farm without living on the land? That's
why they had only sown millets and ragi. He conjured up
an imaginary map of the land as best as he could estimate,
and imagined growing finger millet, corn, pearl millet and
cotton crops. If he managed to dig a well, he could even try
growing paddy. The lush, healthy paddy plants swayed in
the breeze in his mind, and the breeze gently blew against
his face. He closed his eyes, looked up and took it in.
*Adadaa, is there anything more comforting than this! Will it all
come true?* His blossomed face was radiant.

Muthu got some experience of growing paddy when
they had leased some land by Padalur for a few years. It
was only Muthu and Pongi who spent all their time on
that farmland. Kaali shuttled between the farm and home.
Periannan paid a visit once in a while. During those years,

the entire family enjoyed rice from paddy and puttu at least once a week. The cattle got hay too. The two of them spent six months in a small shack to work there. Due to the distance and the inconvenient living arrangements there, they did not continue farming that land. But the smell of that paddy rice was still fresh in his mind. Muthu used to balance himself carefully on the border bunds which were shaped like the haircuts given to children, and take in the air every morning and evening. 'Dei, you are the only one who gets high on air,' Pongi used to tease him.

If water was available, growing paddy was no big task. Kolunji plants had sprouted in abundance around here. Even in this heat, they stood bearing delicate red flowers. For paddy, there was no better fertilizer than that. He was speechless. So many images flashed in front of him. He didn't need any food that night. His mind and his stomach felt content and cool. They had to squint as the sky was barely lit. The two returned to the road. Kuppan looked at Muthu's face closely. He appeared to be deep in thought. He should be. This is not a decision he can make so easily. It was about the place where they were going live for years to come.

'Saami?' Kuppan interrupted Muthu's thoughts.

'Mm . . . Kuppanna, what do you say? Do you like it?' asked Muthu.

'I like it, saami. The soil is good. We will surely get water. If we work on it for a year or two, we can rectify it to be suitable for farming. The landlady will also like it, saami. Looks like the cost may be reasonable too. For the money you have, you can get much more than what you thought you could,' replied Kuppan. Just then, a bird squawked in its baritone voice and caught Muthu's attention. It was an Indian Roller bird. Comfortably perched on a tall palm tree, it appeared to be staring right at them. A good omen.

16

Kuppan had expressed in words exactly what Muthu had been thinking. In their ten-day journey, Muthu had come to appreciate Kuppan's experience and his agility to be able to accomplish anything. Since Muthu did not drink, Kuppan did not touch it either. It did not even occur to him to drink without Muthu's knowledge.

Muthu knew Kuppan, but he did not know anything about his work. All he knew was that Kuppan had started working at Muthu's father-in-law's house at a very young age. From being a labourer boy, he eventually became the person to take care of the family's farm, and practically lived in the house. Whenever Muthu visited his father-in-law, he saw him around but hadn't paid much attention to him. Kuppan would refer to Muthu as 'saami', bowing to him while holding his towel under his arm. It was a mark of respect extended to him for being the son-in-law of the family. Back then, Muthu's mind hadn't even registered his face fully.

They gave him his share of the annual bounty as part of his annual wages. Kuppan went back to his home only if he felt like it. He ate his three meals at the landlord's house. He was seldom seen in the labourers' quarters, where his family lived. The younger generation that grew up entirely in the quarters would look at him as they would at a stranger. On the occasions when he was spotted at the quarters, everyone assumed that his family was hosting a guest. He took on all types of work at the landlord's house. He continued to do so even after he got married and had a couple of children. His wife, Thangaa, was easily scared. She helped out at the field when there was work. Otherwise, she stayed at home and looked after the children. Kuppan had mandated that she not work in anyone else's fields. Because he spent day and night working in the fields, he could take home anything that grew on the farm. He had the right.

Muthu's father-in-law had said about him, 'For a month after he got married, Kuppan wasn't seen at the farm at all. I thought that was the end of him. That he found something he'd ever experienced before and that had possessed him completely. And that he was going to seek work in some other obscure place now. But he didn't. A month later, he came to the field tightening his komanam. And we found out that Thangaa was pregnant. A few days after their first child was born, Kuppan wasn't to be seen for a month again. He had gone to make the next one. If that man wasn't seen for a month, then poor Thangaa was bearing another child is what it meant. Just like cows and goats, Kuppan too had a season.'

'True, saami. It is only man who wanders around all-year around holding it up anytime, with no regard for time or tide. Sparrows, crows, goats, cattle—all their actions are reflective of the seasons. That's how it should be. If man follows that principle, he can focus on other things properly, saami. If not, it is only this that runs through his mind all the time, you see,' came Kuppan's response. When he was young, everyone made him repeat this over and over again and laughed. If anyone asked him where he learnt it despite having spent all his time in the fields, the unflinching response would be, 'In the fields, saami. That is where sparrows and crows keep their families.' He explained, 'I know more about a sparrow's family than a man's. Followed by the families of goats and cows. I like the way they live. I believe that's how it must have been for man too. Somewhere along the way, things changed for us. We lost any sense of order or reason. But like crows and sparrows, I will go through this life waking up in the morning and feeding my family.'

When Muthu was preparing to leave for his journey into unfamiliar lands after getting the money ready, Peruma was afraid to send him alone by himself. Her father and her brother had a lot of work to attend to on their land—land that remained undivided because her brother was the only male heir. The fields had to be irrigated every day. Peruma was seated on the plinth worrying about her husband having to travel alone—tears came rolling down her face, inadvertently. Kuppan took a long look at her as he walked by to take care of some work. He had brought her up sitting on his shoulders, ever since she was a little child. He thought of her as his own daughter. 'Everything's coming together, *thaayi*. Why the tears?' he asked her affectionately. 'Things are coming together, Kuppa. Only,

there is no one to go with him,' and her voice gave way to a
sob before she could complete the sentence.

Kuppan said sympathetically, 'I will go along, thaayi.
I have nothing binding me. The boys are married. They
take care of themselves. Thangaa only needs to be fed.
Whichever son's place she goes to, they feed her platefuls.
The daughters are like that too. Even if they don't have
enough for themselves, they never say no to their mother
or father. Setting all of that aside for a minute, if she comes
to this house, will Amma send her away without feeding
her a mouthful? I will go with saami, thaayi. All these days
I have remained here like a frog croaking inside a well.
Let me see some lakes and rivers too.' Peruma felt the life
return to her as Kuppan presented his offer.

When the cart was all set to leave with everything
loaded and tied up, Peruma told Kuppanna, 'Please
look after him well, Kuppa.' Muthu had found that
amusing. Maybe Peruma had said that to make him feel
less unhappy as they left, he had reasoned. Kuppan was
a man with grandchildren. Muthu was just beginning to
itch for a life of his own. Who was going to take care of
whom? Muthu had travelled to many places and seen a
lot of things. Kuppa had not stepped outside his village.
But now he knew that if Kuppan had not come with him,
Muthu would have struggled a lot, as Peruma had implied.
Starting with cooking meals, Muthu had found Kuppan to
be of immense support for everything. A man who had not
been anywhere—his landlord's house was his sole refuge
since he was a child. But because of that, his experience of
working with the earth, agriculture and rearing livestock,

was unparallelled. It was exhilarating to hear him say that the soil could be readied in a year or two.

If he had a lot of money on hand, he could hire labour to get it done. However, once the land is paid for, he would be left empty-handed. With those very hands and his entire family working together, he could make sure they didn't have any dearth of food within a year's time. Beyond that, with a little more growth every year, they could reap the full benefit of the entire land in ten years. Patience is the name of the game. He could rear cattle, goats, chicken to manage in the interim. *This land is going to open its mouth wide and swallow anything it is given and not let anything out for the first few days. It is like conception. One has to wait ten months. For this land, it is ten years.*

17

They parked the cart by the village choultry. They untied the oxen and retied one of them to the yoke at the front of the cart and the other to the spokes at the back of the cart. They placed two large rocks on either side of the wheels. They gave the oxen water and the half bundle of grass that Kuppan had gathered. For the night feed, they still had some corn greens left in the cart. Kuppan slept on the cart itself. Muthu reminded Kuppan to be careful before he left for the naattamai's house. A few people were sleeping in the choultry even at that hour. *Don't they say that misery befalls those who sleep as the sun leaves the sky?*

He decided he would inform the naattamai about what had happened, come back to have kali for dinner and then go back to his place again since the arrangement was that he would sleep there. The street was filled with children jumping about and playing. Just seeing that made him happy. The houses were small, most of them with thatched roofs. It was surprising to see so many children together. That must be the joy of living in a village. He felt as though the whole world was filled with children.

Muthu's children liked to play too. When the family was living as one, they, along with his brothers' children, made for a sizeable crowd. But they weren't this animated or excited. Because the children were born to brothers of different ages, there were few children of the same age. Periannan's oldest son was twenty years old. Muthu's youngest child, Ponnaiyan, was six. Only when children of the same age get together do their games evolve. When children of different ages play together, their games fizzle out rather quickly. But Muthu hadn't had even that opportunity either. When he was born, there were no other children in the family. He grew up only with older people, the ones who coddled him and carried him around. The only company he had for play were the boys who herded goats in the lands over the hills. He was amazed to see the children playing together here, their din akin to birds returning to their nests at the end of the day. Ostensibly, a loss meant a gain too.

It wasn't easy for him to cross that street filled with merry voices. The children barely noticed that he was new. They bumped into him and then continued to run unperturbed, colliding into him time and again. He wanted to grab hold of the children running around, their dark skin mostly bare, and coddle them. Aattur village had a few houses too, but only for the sake of it, with only old and invalid people living there. Only the few houses whose lands were closer to the heart of the village showed any life. The rest of the homes in the village were just people's property and usually were used as storehouses for a year's worth of grain supplies or harvested bounty. They were cleaned only on festival days. Otherwise they mostly remained locked and unused.

He found Karunkunnu to be a bit different. The people seemed happy here. They didn't seem to pay much attention to agriculture or working hard. Even if they did toil, it did not appear as if they did so purposefully enough. But then, the streets were filled with joy. The neighbours spoke with each other easily, without raising their voices. There was enough space in the backyards to tether a cow or two and a few goats. Everyone chit-chatted at leisure. Not a mouth here that didn't chew betel leaves. Even lads and girls just about as high as an adult's shoulder roamed around with their mouths reddened and stained with betel leaves. He could tell that these people remarried liberally—there was not a single woman in a white sari. Paying utmost attention to the bag that hung from his hand, he continued walking down the street and observing the village.

The naattamai's house was small. It did not seem that his family lived in much luxury. He was sitting on the cot outside, on the street. Even the cot looked different—the supports were only a foot tall and the braiding had been done with two cords. There were only one or two cots per house. Muthu recalled his parental home, where each adult had their own cot. When the girls grew up, they got their own cots too. During summer, all the cots were brought out into the front yard. More than twenty cots would be lined up next to each other. The children would fight amongst themselves over who got to sleep next to whom. On one such night, a visiting relative saw the cots and asked in surprise, 'Have you started a business of selling

cots?' When everyone chuckled, he said, 'It makes me so
happy to see these many cots lined up like this. If anyone
else sees this, they may get jealous and give you the evil
eye. Who knows, even I may have cast one inadvertently.
Devakka . . . You should rid the family of any evil eye, aaya,'
he said to Muthu's mother before leaving. Who knew who
had cast an eye on them? The yard remains, but the cots
no longer do.

The naattamai was old enough to be considered
elderly. It could be that his sons were taking care of the
farms with him cursorily overseeing everything. In a place
where so many people lived, there must be no dearth for
disputes that need settling. Even if he heard a case a day,
it must take up all his time in discussing and resolving it.
Maybe they had a practice of paying him a token for his
involvement. The mud wall in his house was cracked in a
few spots. It wasn't polished with cowdung, nor had it been
stained with slaked lime. If the house was maintained well,
the walls and floors would be in order. Any cracks can be
attended to from time to time. Apparently, all such habits
were wholly absent in this region.

A cot was brought from somewhere and placed across
the naattamai for Muthu to sit on. When he told him
about the land that Kuppan showed him, he understood
whose it was. He called one of the boys playing on the
street and said, 'Bring Vellaiayyan'. Muthu had all his
questions answered by the naattamai. The price of a kuzhi
of land was somewhere between ten and twenty rupees.
He would be able to gauge their expectation once he spoke
to them. If they finalized the transaction, he could give

them a small advance of a ten or a twenty, and then, in a day or two, pay them the entire amount. If he informed the bus driver who drove by his village, someone from there will come in person with the entire amount, he told the naattamai.

It did seem that the naattamai's words carried some weight in that village. He requested him to negotiate as much as possible because the lands were only suitable for grazing and not at all fit for agriculture yet. The naattamai laughed. Muthu said he was ready to pay him a small amount too.

'I have no connection with you. I come from a place far away. Even though I met you only this afternoon, you spoke to me affably and even invited me to stay at your house. I recognized the kindness of your heart right then. Wherever one goes, the only necessity is to associate with good people. You have to speak on my behalf and see this deal through. I am bound by your words. I consider you to be an avatar of the great Karattusaami Himself, and I will pay you with a token proportionate to my means. You must not refuse it,' he said.

The naattamai declined his offer. 'You do not have to give me anything, I will do what I can.'

'No sir, if I do not gift you something for helping me—a complete stranger from a distant land—my mind will not let me be at peace. The same way we feel content only after we drop a few coins into the collection box when we go to the temple, for my satisfaction, I will give you a five or a ten. You don't have to take my side. Please just help me negotiate a fair deal.' Muthu looked at his face.

By then, a blinding darkness had enveloped them; Muthu could not see his facial features clearly, but he felt confident that he could close the deal through him. Ten rupees must be a big amount for him. It was worth a kuzhi of land, after all. He thought it was going to work out well for him. The boy returned with Vellaiyan. He seemed to be about the same age as Muthu. As soon as he saw him, he stood up from the cot, put his palms together and said politely, 'My name is Muthu, nga. I come from the west.' Vellaiyan raised a hand slightly. His hand didn't move beyond that. 'Mm.' The habit of putting one's palms together to greeting one another seemed completely absent in this region. Muthu wondered what else was different.

The naattamai brought Vellaiyan up to speed and added, 'If you bring your brothers now, we can discuss the deal right away'. The man said he would bring them all and left. The naattamai called Muthu to the plinth outside the house. A small lamp was placed on it, that looked like the lamp used by an auctioneer who had visited their village in the months of Thai or Maasi, spread a blanket and auctioned the things wrapped in it. Muthu removed the bag from his lap, placed it by the wall and leaned over it. If he kept the bag in his lap all the time, it may raise suspicion. The naattamai enquired about the members of his family. Muthu talked about them in detail.

He did not reveal any of the problems within his family. All they needed to know was that there wasn't enough land for him to farm. That much was true. Even if he somehow survived on his portion of the eleven acres, it was going to be impossible to get by when their sons took over. Periannan

had two sons and two daughters. Kaliannan had three girls
and one boy. All three children of Pongi's were boys. The
daughters could be given away in marriage. That would
still leave them with seven sons. How would eleven acres
suffice then? They were ready to buy any land available but
no one within the village was willing to sell.

18

In the midst of the conversation, a group of people plodded over. One of them sat on the naattamai's cot. Some sat on the floor, some others remained standing. Muthu estimated that there were five of them. It was too dark to see their faces. 'Each kuzhi costs a thousand. Not free,' came a voice. The voice of the one who had caused trouble that afternoon. Mookan. Evidently, he was one of the brothers. Muthu was going to have to navigate futile arguments. If there were five of them, why would they have left the lands untended like that? A family could easily grow grains on a ten-acre land. They must be a lazy bunch. He didn't have a good impression of them.

This was the family of Mookan who had threatened Muthu as soon as he had entered the village. As long as the land was good, it didn't matter how the people were— Muthu didn't say anything. The naattamai commenced the conversation. 'How much are you asking for a kuzhi? How many kuzhis are you giving away? Which part is it? Give all the details clearly, Vellaiya.'

'Each kuzhi costs a thousand rupees,' said Mookan.

'Mooka, won't you stay silent?' the naattamai chided.
'You have been troubling him ever since he got here. If
you continue to speak this way, he is going to say no to the
land.'

'Doesn't matter how big a fucker he is, it is still a
thousand for a kuzhi,' insisted Mookan.

'Just ignore him. You state the price,' said Vellaiyan.

'How can I? You should decide the price,' said the
naattamai.

He said that a kuzhi was worth twenty-five rupees.
They were ready to sell up to a hundred kuzhis. The location
was the same as had been shown to Kuppan. They could
measure the land starting at the two roads that flanked the
land on two sides. Muthu said the area of land he could
buy depended on the cost per kuzhi. He mentioned that
his plan was to buy at least fifty kuzhis. He also said that
twenty-five rupees for a kuzhi was too high; that the land
was not conducive for farming; that he was buying the land
to create sustenance by raising cattle and goats. He added
that only if they quoted a price less than twenty-rupees for a
kuzhi did it make sense to continue the discussion. Muthu
himself was surprised to hear himself speak that way.

He had held no responsibilities in his parental family.
His brothers took care of everything from keeping accounts
to transportation—all things good and bad. His only
exposure to it had been witnessing conversations or dispute
settlements. Today, he was in a position of authority. He
had learned everything he knew about what to say and how
to say by observing Periannan—he spoke clearly and in
a way that didn't offend either side. All of that was fine.

Only, the way he had behaved with Peruma had been utterly despicable. When Muthu did see her chest after quite a bit of insistence, he was reduced to tears. The rage in Periannan's mind had manifested in the violence of his hands. It was only after seeing her bruised breasts did he agree unequivocally that he wanted nothing to do with his village anymore.

Peruma always said his hands were rough. She liked it when he caressed her breasts tenderly with love. If he ever grabbed them or squeezed them in a moment of passion, she pushed him away immediately. 'Do you think this is a ball from the chariot fete? Will it not hurt me?' she'd cry. He had been roaming about like a dog all these days, obsessed with her. He simply hadn't found an opportunity. In some way, what Periannan had done had worked out well. Instead of being bound to just an acre of land, he had now stepped out and was about to become the owner of a lot more land. Vellaiyan's brothers discussed amongst themselves. After that, the naattamai took them to the street and spoke to them in whispers.

Muthu thought that the naattamai must have told them something along the lines of 'There is no one to buy land in this village even at the rate of ten rupees per kuzhi. That too, who will buy land that has nothing on it? This outsider is offering to buy it not knowing all that. If you bring your price down, it would be better for you. If not, he will look elsewhere. If he offers twenty, plenty here will want to sell him their land. I would give my ten kuzhis at that price too. But only you have so much land. Only you can offer a hundred kuzhis. That's how I see it.'

For the ten rupees that Muthu had promised, why shouldn't the naattamai negotiate at least this much? Would he accept a ten from the other side too, like the cattle brokers at the market? *He can't extract a single rupee out of that group*, Muthu thought. After wrapping up the discussion with the brothers, the naattamai returned and said to Muthu, 'They are refusing to accept less than twenty a kuzhi. "Make it an even twenty," they say.' Muthu decided to test his negotiation skills again.

'I can give twenty, nothing wrong with that. But the land is not suitable for farming. It is full of rocks. There is no water facility. Even though I come from the west, this money has come to me only through hard work. How can I just throw it all away on rocks, you tell me? Thirteen or maybe fourteen is all I can give. You think about it.'

'Are you asking to buy the land for thirteen? Dei . . . it is a thousand, a thousand for a kuzhi!' shouted Mookan. Another one slapped him hard on his cheek and told him to remain quiet. He sat down on the ground, softened his voice and whimpered softly, 'A thousand a kuzhi'. They regrouped a few times on the street and lowered the price little by little, every time they came back. Muthu continued bargaining. They quoted nineteen and Muthu countered with fifteen. When they quoted eighteen, he said sixteen. Both parties remained adamant at eighteen and sixteen. If they came down to seventeen but Muthu stood firm at sixteen, what would they do? And if Muthu went up to seventeen and they stood firm at eighteen, what would he do? Both sides were thinking the same way.

This was the time for the naattamai to step in. 'I'm not saying this to anyone in particular. I am simply stating this in general. Let's close this at seventeen. Having come this far, it shouldn't fizzle out over one rupee.' After a few murmurs here and there, and just before they could agree on seventeen and start getting into the details, a few women came running down the street, screaming. 'Aiyo, aiyo!' their voices tore through the darkness. Along with them were toddlers and tiny children. 'I won't let the land be sold'; 'They will drink and squander everything'; 'We will die along with the little ones', they wailed on and on loudly. In response, the men yelled back, hit them, ran after them and caused a big commotion. To Muthu, it as like watching a murder of crows cawing and fighting amongst each other.

He wondered if he could live with this group. Just as everything was coming together, it stopped abruptly with the inauspicious 'aiyo'. *Should he declare that it would not work out and leave?* Mookan's wife was crying bitterly lying on the street with her hair completely dishevelled. He continued to circle around her and hit her. All the villagers came out to the street to gawk at the scene with lamps in their hands. Voices both in favour of the women and against them could be heard from the crowd. Muthu was utterly embarrassed. The naattamai and a few others had to shout over the noise to control the situation. It took more than an hour for everything to settle down.

'If it doesn't sit well with the family, then I don't want it,' Muthu said slowly. 'These fellows are drunkards. They will drink away all the money. That is why I told the women that I will hand the money over to them,' said the naattamai and continued. 'There are over 200 kuzhis of land in all. They can survive on the remaining land.' Perhaps he was afraid that he may lose his share of ten rupees.

The negotiations resumed. It was decided that arrangements would be made to meet the registrar the very next day and explain the deal to him, measure the land and register the new ownership. Only ten rupees needed to be paid in advance the next morning. Since they had agreed to seventeen per kuzhi, Muthu committed to buying 100 kuzhis. He repeatedly stressed that they all come back to put their thumbprints on the papers the next day and acknowledge the transfer. He was still suspicious of Mookan. 'Give that dog a quarter paisa and he will show up wagging his tail,' assured the naattamai.

19

Muthu ate his meal at the naattamai's place after everything was settled. The naattamai had insisted a lot, even though he had told him he had food in his cart. There was millet rice and thumbai broth for dinner. He didn't know that thumbai could be used to make broth until then. He wanted to learn how to make it. The naattamai's daughter-in-law explained with a laugh. 'The same way one cooks amaranth. But don't eat too much of it,' she warned him, 'it generates a lot of body heat.' The millet rice got its taste from the broth. When the broth was mixed with the fluffy and flaky millet, its taste transformed completely. After eating cold kali all these days, he found that food delicious. He knew Kuppan must be waiting for him to eat. Muthu told them he would return after telling Kuppan about all that had happened. The naattamai offered to go with him but Muthu declined, saying it was too dark outside. The naattamai sent him off with a small lantern.

The bag was in his hand. Fearing that the naattamai may ask him to leave the bag behind, he hid it in the dark. The street was awash with darkness. It was a few days after the full moon—the moon was now waning. It would rise in some time. The waning moon, the 'aiyo!' right as they were about to agree on the deal—these signs made him feel uneasy. What did the future hold? But then, the waxing period was still twelve or thirteen days away. Could he have afforded to wait that long? As of this day, eleven days have gone by since his journey had begun. Peruma must worry about him more and more with every passing day.

Muthu usually fell asleep as soon as he lay down since he was perpetually fatigued from the travelling. Peruma laid awake staring at the perimeter of the house. As it is, she wasn't one to deal even with small problems and lately, one after the other, a lot of big events had occurred. If Muthu was not around, she always blew everything out of proportion in her mind. She ran scenarios in her mind until she had thoroughly confused herself. However, life is never without its problems. Even though the negotiations were over, it would be a full week before they completed all the legal formalities and returned home. Until then, it was going to be difficult for her, waiting for him restlessly. He couldn't leave things hanging in the middle. With people around who were trying to cause problems while the negotiations were still ongoing, he couldn't risk taking a break to go home. He had to sort out everything related to the purchase promptly within a day or two and move onto the land. It is true that he was shaken by the women crying 'aiyo'. But there was no time to check for auspices prior to closing the deal. Often, it is the work that gets done out of necessity amidst many constraints which completes quickly and brings one more satisfaction, than the work that is executed only after days of planning and deliberation. Moreover, only a person who has everything going for him could afford to check for omens. For someone standing alone with nothing, the only way to advance was to keep an open mind and seize any opportunity.

He walked on, filled with thoughts, sighing. The road bumped into a pause here and there, before meandering on. Most of the houses were dark and quiet. Only small lanterns and *gada* lamps were glowing. Understandably so. How much kerosene could one afford to buy to constantly refill oil lamps? Muthu struggled to afford kerosene for the hurricane lamps he hung from his cart when he did chartered deliveries. Out of the pittance he received as his daily wage, fifty paisa went just into buying kerosene for the lamps. All the cart drivers who rented out their carts got together and asked the depot owner for a kerosene allowance. On days when rice was being transported, it was the depot owner's responsibility to arrange for men to safeguard the caravan from the front and the rear. In the same way, they argued, the depot should bear the kerosene expenses for their lamps too. The owner said he would look into it, but never did anything about it.

Using castor oil for the terracotta lamp at home had helped alleviate that burden to an extent, but castor seeds didn't seem to be cultivated in this region. How did they get through a whole year of crops with just little millet and kodo millet? The cart was parked a little distance away from the choultry. He could see a few figures moving under a tree in the choultry and hear voices in conversation. One of them asked, 'Who's that?' upon seeing Muthu walk towards them with a lamp.

The voice sounded like it belonged to a middle-aged person. 'It's me, nga,' he replied. 'Who's "me"? Don't you have a name?' *The people here sure like to sound important*, Muthu thought and answered, 'It's me, the man from the west, nga. I'm coming from the naattamai's house,' Muthu responded.

'Have you completed your negotiations with Vellaiyan over his land?'

'Yes, nga.'

'How much for a kuzhi?'

Muthu wondered whether or not he should respond to that question. There are five people in Vellaiyan's house. Internal disputes over selling the land were ongoing. On the other hand, the news would have spread by now. There was no point in trying to hide it. Back in Muthu's village, even after a land was registered to a new owner, people outside the deal did not know the exact price. The price that was declared publicly was different from the actual negotiated price. The buyer claimed that the price was lower than what he actually paid; and the seller claimed the opposite. One deduced that the price was somewhere in between the two numbers. This was set up to prevent unconcerned third parties from providing unsolicited advice and affecting the minds of the persons involved. But it did not appear that such strategies were practised here.

He thought for a little bit and said, 'An acre comes to over 200, nga.'

A momentarily befuddled man asked immediately, 'How much for a kuzhi?'

'Seventeen per kuzhi, nga.'

'*Adengappa!* Seventeen for a kuzhi? Looks like I could sell ten kuzhis of my land for that price too,' came a voice from the dark.

'The people from the western region are loaded with money,' said another.

'Someone must have said that the land has a treasure buried under it.'

'If their location fetches such a price, I wonder how much a land irrigated by the water channels through it would fetch?'

Muthu's ears rang from the constant onslaught of voices as he struggled to stay calm.

'How many kuzhis have you negotiated in total?' asked a voice that sounded as though it had got up and was approaching him. When he responded with '100 kuzhi', they all got busy trying to calculate how much that cost. Listening to them discuss things made Muthu wonder if he had offered to pay more than what he should have. But the tongues of spectators always wagged. The same people would go to Vellaiyan's family and ask them why they had parted with their land for anything less than twenty. It would be no surprise if Mookan listened to that and decided to interfere with the decision. Until the transfer was completed, his heart was going to thump loudly. It was only because he had gone up to seventeen that everything had worked out so swiftly. In the rush that he was in, there was no time to deliberate further. When one's head is on fire, should he be wasting time choosing between a lake or a river to put it out? It only makes sense that he grasps the closest pot of water to douse it.

They remained discussing things amongst themselves as Muthu walked to the cart. Night or day, the choultry always seemed to be filled with people. He thought of his fellow villagers who found excuses to leave even if they were asked to gather to discuss temple festivities. 'I need to guard the pen' or 'I have to feed the dog', they said. Here, the people gathered together all the time. Should he need it, would any of them be willing to do any work, lend him a hand in the field?

'Saami . . . have you spoken to them?' Kuppan asked eagerly. The discussion at the choultry would have reached Kuppan's ears too. Muthu narrated all the details to Kuppan. Even though Muthu's voice couldn't be heard over the loud, animated conversations at the choultry, he spoke in muffled tones. He informed Kuppan that he had eaten, warned him to stay alert and hurried back to the naattamai's house.

20

As darkness began to leave the sky, Muthu awoke Kuppan. The oxen were lying down, chewing cud. When he made them stand up, they each expelled a stream of dung that piled up into what looked like little stone baskets. There were already seven or eight such mounds of dung piled at the front and back of the cart. Muthu couldn't leave them there. He looked around. He realized that the human forms lying fast asleep with their veshtis covering them from head to toe were not going to stir anytime soon. He took out a basket from under the cart and started piling the dung into it. The warmth of the fresh dung sent a soft shudder through him. Understanding Muthu's intent, Kuppan came forward to help him too. But Muthu asked to him to get the cart ready instead.

The cowdung filled up half the basket. When he loaded the basket on the cart, he felt a sense of satisfaction similar to the one after cleaning the cowshed every morning. He asked Kuppan to drive the cart. What a surprise! Not wanting to disturb him who appeared to be deep in thought, Kuppan took the reins without any questions. Muthu

asked him to stop the cart when they arrived at the land
he had negotiated for. He emptied the dung basket into a
pit-like spot, broke a few branches off an Avaaram tree and
covered the pit with them. The cowdung could be spotted
only if someone went near it and stared into it deliberately.
But who was going to come by here? He felt satisfied that
the first task he had done after negotiating the deal was to
take cowdung to the land. If anyone saw him do this, they
would say, 'Look how impatient he is, the land has not
even been measured yet.' But how could he waste all that
cow dung? He had lost ten days' worth already. Must have
been around ten full baskets. For those ten days, he didn't
have a choice but to leave it wherever they had stopped.
When they halted at choultries, they collected the dung
excreted overnight and flung it into nearby fields to avoid
being called out for leaving the place dirty. Ten baskets of
dung would have made for sufficient manure for a whole
seravu of land!

In the shadows of the still-dark sky, he took an intent
look at the land. 'One more week and I will be back,' he
told the land in his mind, boarded the cart, and relaxed.
He told Kuppan to drive to the road. 'Let us go to the
hilltop first to offer our prayers before we begin any work.
He is the one who showed us this land. It is now in His
hands to ensure everything goes off well.' 'Everything
will be fine, nga. One of these days, we can also make
offerings to satisfy Him,' Kuppan replied enthusiastically.
The damp air in the morning when the dawn was yet to
break touched Muthu's face and cooled it. *It will be good
if it rained in a week or ten days. Then, the whole land can*

be tilled at once. It needs to be tilled four or five times before the seeds are sown. The land lays dark and marshy for now. They seemed to have simply scarred the lands to sow seeds previously.

The hill was close by, merely a stone's throw away. It was not difficult to climb atop it, they could come and go at will. The hill at Karattur was about five *kal* from Muthu's land. Still, someone from their household went there every new moon day to offer their salutations to the God, unfailingly. More often than not, it was Muthu who went. When there wasn't much work to do, Pongi joined him too. The two of them competed against each other to see who would reach the hilltop first. Pongi typically conceded, unable to beat Muthu, and rested in one of the *mandapams* on the way. When would that ever happen again? Although Pongi was with Kaali for a while, it was because of him that Muthu got 500 rupees from the old lady.

Deep down, Pongi still had affection for him. After he got the lands ready for farming, he could convince Pongi to move here too. How else would he divide up that tiny piece of land between his three sons? He turned to Kuppan suddenly and asked him, 'Would they have given us ten or fifteen more kuzhis if we had asked?' Kuppan wanted to laugh at Muthu's stream of thought. *No amount of land is enough for the people who are landowners by lineage*, he thought to himself. 'We can keep adding little by little as time goes, saami . . . where is the land going to go? There is so much available in this region,' he replied.

Along the path was a vast stretch of grazing land, so big that they couldn't even tell where it ended. The dawn's light continued spreading across the entire field. Even in this heat, greenery prevailed. A few large trees stood here and there. A lot of vellaivela trees—one couldn't find these at all around Aatur, there were mostly only black babool trees there. A few neem trees could be seen too. He could identify them by the way they stood tall with their branches spread wide. They always reminded him of tall and lean people. This must be poramboke land abutting the hill, serving as grazing lands for the neighbouring villages. A whole pen of goats could graze here without wandering much. And it was not far from the field either. He made a mental note to arrange for goats once he moved here with his family. *Sheep will be well suited for this place. And they will need a pen.* As an image of a large pen filled with sheep appeared in his mind, they reached the cart track. The same cart track that had caught them by surprise yesterday, seemed familiar today. Once this spot was settled on, everything near it seemed agreeable.

He left Kuppan at the cart and bathed at a well on the foothill. The water was warm with no trace of the early morning chill. When he washed his mouth with it, it tasted sweet like jaggery. He filled the pot that Kuppan brought over. Kuppan could bathe with it. The oxen could graze until they returned from the hilltop—they gave them some water too. Even as they climbed up the hill, Muthu's mind was filled with thoughts about the land. 100 kuzhis was about eight acres. He could have bought twenty or twenty-five more kuzhis to have around ten acres. 100 kuzhis had cost him 1,700. He still had 800 left.

But was everything simply going to appear without effort as soon as the land came into his hands? He needed some capital to purchase goats and cattle, to build pens for them, a plough to till the land, tools to dig a well, to cut palm fronds, to erect a shack—there were so many expenses. No matter how hard he worked, could he avoid spending money? He was yet to pay for the land purchase. If he had borrowed a little from here and there, he could have bought ten acres. But he had had to work so hard to save even this amount. He had to scrape together every bit of what they had. Maybe he could have asked his father-in-law. But the man himself hardly had anything left after getting his four daughters married off. He was already doing a lot by being supportive and providing words of comfort. 100 kuzhis were enough. Just as Kuppan said, if he survives for long enough, he would be able to purchase another 100 kuzhis.

He had to give ten rupees to the naattamai. It would be another fifty to pay the men who measured the land and the official who collected land revenue. There was the expense of purchasing and installing perimeter stones. He had to bring his family over, he would have to build at least a small shack for them to live in. Until the land started yielding produce and income, he had to feed five hungry mouths. If he kept Kuppan for help, he would have to feed him too. Moreover, it would be best if Kuppan brought Thangaa along as well. They would need a little place to live in. All this would use up the 800 he had. The land may not generate any income for at least two years. He would then need to invest some money. It wasn't enough just to buy land. There were so many expenses around it. It was only after he did the calculations could he sufficiently convince himself that stopping at 100 kuzhis had been the right decision, and he was able to climb the knoll happily.

The knoll was very small and appeared to be made of dirt. A scant rock or two stuck out, but it was mostly dirt. That's why it was fully covered with trees. A few were neem trees but the majority were oonja trees. The leaves had begun to turn yellow. In a month's time, they would stick out like poles after shedding all their leaves. The whole knoll would appear to be covered with sticks. So what? Tender, new leaves would then sprout from the same trees. The shed leaves would get washed downhill by the rains into the grazing lands. They make for good fertilizer. That's why the grazing land was so verdant. There were no steps, only a person-wide mud path that broadened and narrowed at various along the way.

The Karattur knoll had steps that were almost vertical. They were quite frightening to climb for those who came from the low plains. The knoll was taller too. This one wasn't even a quarter of it in height. It took him about ten minutes to reach the top. He didn't need to stop to catch his breath. From the top, he could see all the farms in the region. They were all shrub lands. Even palm trees were sparse. To his surprise, he spotted one or two coconut trees too. There were five or six settlements around. He even noticed that there were two settlements in the village. Apparently, the labourers did not live on the side of the village that he had been to. *If the state of ones living on the east itself was pitiable, that of the ones dependent on them must surely be worse,* he thought to himself. Anyway, he should face no problem hiring a helping hand. But he shouldn't get anyone to help him just yet. If he did so before generating a steady income, he would be left with nothing. For now, it should suffice if the people of the household helped out. Moreover, Kuppan was with him too. Thus far, they hadn't discussed his wages. He could check with his father-in-law and pay him annually.

Aattur was full of palm trees. One could see rows upon rows of palms in abundance. But water was scarce. If they dug very deep, there would be enough water to irrigate just four seravus in a day. That is why they cultivated low shrubs there that barely covered the land. Fitting for the terrain, the knoll in that region too was full of rocks. The heat that the rocks radiated reached far. On the other hand, this region had water. Wherever he drank from, there wasn't a hint of salt in it. The wells were all shallow, created by invisible hands that had scooped away the soil. They were ditches, rather. If they dug a little deeper, water was bound to gush out. There would be no dearth of water to farm. But these people have let their lands dry up. They now needed to be corrected before anything could be planted. He looked to see if he could spot his land from there. He then chuckled at his impatience, already referring to it as 'his' land. He could see it well.

It was right where the cart road flowing with white sand paused and meandered. The thorn trees that filled the lower plains appeared dense. To imagine that entire region green with fertile farmlands brought him joy. Karunkarattu Mansaami sat on top of it with a big head, a broad face, wide open eyes, flaring nostrils, thick lips, a delicate smile, plump cheeks, deep ears, a small neck, bolster-like arms, a broad chest, a slightly discernible stomach, vast legs and spread out toes. God in a form which seemed to be enfolding the land in a heartfelt embrace. The lips split by a smile the width of a thin line. He held a spear straight and stood tall. It was a small temple. It was more like a hall in which to light lamps. He couldn't find a priest. He went in, touched the feet of the god in salutation. He dropped three coins on a plate set in front of the god. A five paise, a three paise and a two paise. Ten paise in all. 'Don't wonder why I'm offering only a few coins, saami. Make everything come together smoothly. I will bring you offerings to your heart's content,' he prayed.

The morning sun shone bright outside. He smeared the holy ash on his forehead and took one of the paper packets containing holy ash from the plate. If the priest was around, he would have asked him for a prediction. Maybe because everything was moving favourably, God was preventing him from seeking a prediction. He made a note of all the roads that went by the hill and the villages they connected. Though there were stretches of farmlands, they weren't isolated. They were surrounded by villages on all sides. A call for help could be answered from all directions. He must make some acquaintances in the neighbouring villages too. He climbed down the hill faster than he climbed up.

After a bath, Kuppan sat watching the oxen that were grazing. Muthu sprinkled some holy ash on his palm.

Kuppan smeared it across his forehead. 'Oh God of the Hill, protect us from any trouble,' he prayed. There were a few thatch-roofed shops at the base of the hill. One of them was open. It was a tea stall. The two of them walked to it. About two or three people were already at the stall, sitting and watching them closely. The owner seemed like a smart businessman. 'Two teas, please,' said Muthu and seated himself on one of the two benches placed on either side. The stall owner looked him up and down and asked him, 'Who are you?'

'A farmer from the west, nga,' replied Muthu. By now, he was used to giving that answer. Kuppan, who was standing by the road outside the stall said, 'I am one of his men, nga.'

'You will find *kottaangkuchi* tucked between the bamboo over there. Wash one and bring it here,' said the stall owner, looking at Kuppan—he went looking for them. When he found them, he realized that the stall owner was referring to the hard coconut shell halves; they were known as *thengai thotti* where he came from.

It was only afterwards that the men seated on the bench spoke up. Muthu gave them non-committal answers to all their questions. He gathered that Sikkur, Vallur, Mottur were all villages that were located along that main road. The tea stall served all those villages. When the hot tea made its way to his stomach, he experienced a newfound clarity. They gave the oxen some water to drink, put harnesses around them and set off. 'What is this, saami . . . this tastes like the starchy water we feed the oxen. How can they charge fifteen paisa for this?' complained Kuppan.

Muthu laughed. Kuppan had never liked tea. He only drank it because he couldn't refuse Muthu. 'Once you get used to it, you will trade even liquor for this. You should see those cart drivers, Kuppanna. Some of them will go on without food but they just cannot survive without tea. Even I have now come to grow very fond of it,' said Muthu.

When they got back, a large crowd of people had assembled at the village choultry. One of them spotted the cart and announced. 'There they are!'

21

The naattamai came forward hastily. 'Where did you go? There are a lot of rumours going around that you decided to sneak out in the middle of the night without informing anyone because a couple of useless fellows told you that you were overpaying for the field,' he gushed and held Muthu's hands.

'No one from my family has ever gone back on their word, nga. So what if one or two people say things like that. I have to use my brains too. It is for the faith we have on the lord of this land who sits atop the hill, that I am buying this land. I had to see him and inform him of this transaction, didn't I? That's why we left while it was still dark. Ask the men to get going. We need to get the deed of purchase and have the land measured. The sooner we get it sorted, the better it would be for me. Today, it has been twelve days and twelve nights since we left home. But at home, they must feel like it has been twenty-four. Only when I go back and see them will I find peace,' said Muthu, smiling.

All of Vellaiyan's brothers, old and young, were there. They appeared to have fought with the men in the choultry who said that the price was higher than it should be. There were telling marks on the faces of the men. Muthu also gathered that they were keen on not letting him or the deal slip by. Mookan was sober now. He didn't utter a word. They must have discussed late into the night about how they were going to divide up the 1,700 they would receive after completing the sale. At dawn, when the cart was no longer in the choultry and Muthu was not to be seen on the plinth outside the naattamai's house where he had been sleeping, they must have concluded that he had run away and all their plans had gone to waste; they must have cursed him for that. No one was awake when Muthu and Kuppan had left the choultry. The naattamai would have been upset too at the loss of the ten rupees he was slated to receive from the transaction. At his age, earning ten rupees was a lot. Seeing Muthu now had put everyone at ease again.

That day, Kuppan did not make kali. Both of them were served food from the naattamai's house. Since Kuppan had to keep an eye on the things by the choultry, Muthu had brought the food to him. It was rice from paddy and meat stew. They had cooked chicken. The stew tasted unusual, like eating a lump of horse gram mixed with rice. If only they had ground some paste to add to it and made it a little runnier, how tasty it would have been! In any case, it was only because of the good impression they had of Muthu that they were treating them well like this. Muthu complimented their cooking, asked them how they had made the dish and helped himself to many servings of the stew. 'On the days we have kari kuzhambu, we always make paddy rice,' said the naattamai. Muthu continued to find their language peculiar. 'Kuppanna, this is not kari saaru, it is kari kuzhambu, remember,' he said and laughed. 'Even though the kuzhambu is ordinary, the chicken is quite tasty, saami,' Kuppan laughed too.

'From now on, everything is going to be like this, Kuppanna.'

'Agreed, saami! I say that in a land that eats snakes, simply choose an agreeable portion of the snake and start eating.'

They were told that the land surveyor lived four or five villages away, on the way to Saethur. He was apparently a good man and was known to be punctual with his work. Even though he belonged to a different community, he was favourable to the people from the east and of other castes. Muthu unloaded the kodhaanam, a long container that attached to the underside of the cart, and kept it at the naattamai's place. There were so many things in it. The manvetti, kothu and kadapaarai were for agriculture. A machete, sickle and spear for protection. A few things for cooking, a rope for climbing palm trees, a box, a few baskets that were in a sack. They had tied it to the underside of the cart and filled it with many things. Some had been put in by Muthu, some others by Peruma. They had loaded the top of the cart with bundles of corn husks.

When he left his things in the backyard, he repeatedly requested the naattamai to keep an eye on them. 'Theft is rampant in these parts. But no dog would dare to touch a thing in this naattamai's house,' he assured him before summoning his daughter-in-law and instructing her to take special care of Muthu's things. Muthu covered the kodhaanam completely with gunny bags. Everyone left on Muthu's cart. Things were moving faster than he had expected. Yet, until everything was done, he decided not to count on it or discuss it with anyone. Nothing was more embarrassing than bragging about a deal that then doesn't going through. There was plenty of time after the deal was done, to talk about it. But until then, his focus and energy were always devoted to the task at hand. Even Periannan used to say, 'Give Muthu a task and he will not sleep until it is done.'

Within just three days, the surveyor had measured the land, checked for encumbrance on the property and drafted the deed. Right before signing the deed, the naattamai asked Muthu, 'Has the money arrived yet?'

'I'll be right back,' said Muthu and drove off in his cart towards Saethur. There, he wandered around for some time before returning to the village. He told them that he had sent a message through the bus driver to his relatives, and that a relative had left the money with a shopkeeper. He pulled out the money from his bag and counted 1,700 rupees. Muthu's eyes welled up when he handed the money but he managed to compose himself. Everyone involved placed their thumbprints on the deed documents only after that. The five brothers placed their thumbs, one after another. His name was written as 'Muthannan, the son of Ramakkan who lives in Aattur Mandrakaadu of Karattur Taluk in Malaiyur Jilla'. *No matter how much I try, I cannot seem to shake off the bondage of my umbilical cord*, Muthu thought to himself. He gave five rupees to each of the witnesses. The naattamai was one of the witnesses too.

When they finished everything and walked out, they found the wives standing there. There was a lot of shouting and yelling. The money was divided amongst them right there. The grasping hands of the wives and the brothers created more pandemonium. The naattamai could not do anything to control them now.

Outside the registration office premises, a restless group of people, all relatives of the sellers, stood waiting. It seemed that the entire village was gathered there. If they were all to be taken out for a meal, that could set him back by at least 100 rupees, he thought in complete befuddlement. *How could people be like this? Could they not have brought only a handful of their closest relatives? Is selling land a happy event?* It seemed liked a gathering for a feast. They invited Muthu and Kuppan to join them. Muthu mumbled as he walked over. How would his body digest the food bought with the money made from selling land? He only went on the naattamai's insistence. It was the first time Kuppan had ever entered a place like that to eat. Only Muthu seemed distressed about the situation, however, everyone else, including Vellaiyan's family, did not seem to mind at all. Muthu sat in one corner with the naattamai beside him. When Kuppan was asked to sit with him, he did not think it appropriate to be treated as his master's equal. He made up an excuse and sat by himself elsewhere. The food and the stew were quite tasty. They served meat on tiny dishes. *If we eat like this, how will our bodies digest this food?* He looked around. Everyone was eating with great relish and in high spirits. Not a single person's face expressed dismay. Muthu felt that when all their money was spent, their anger was going to be directed towards him. They were going to behave as though he had beaten them up and taken their lands away for nothing. Their rage was bound to develop. They could bring harm to him in so many ways. What would he do should such a situation occur? Muthu felt confident enough to relish the food only after thinking through these thoughts. That was when it occurred to him that one just has to have the right mindset and feel blessed even to enjoy the food served to him.

22

Muthu scarcely noticed that they had reached the village, owing to the meal. Kuppan, who drove the cart back, reached the choultry and called out to him. Muthu snapped out of his drowsiness. Even though he had fallen asleep sitting up, it was the sort of deep sleep that had eluded him for several days. He felt a peace from not having to carry the money on him anymore and from completing the task of purchasing the land. He left Kuppan there and took the cart to the naattamai's house. When the naattamai and the rest of the people alighted from the cart, he took the help of some labourers who were around and tied the kodhaanam back onto his cart. 'Are you going back today itself?' asked the naattamai.

'I'm planning to leave tomorrow morning,' replied Muthu.

'There are no big houses in the village, only a couple of small ones. You can bring your family to live in one of them for now, until you find a more comfortable one later. It should not cost much. You are now one of us. We will see each other every day,' the naattamai spoke cheerfully.

Muthu took him to the backyard and placed ten rupees in his hand. When the naattamai's hands hesitated, he held them and pressed the money into them firmly. The naattamai's face lit up.

'You have helped an outsider so much. I owe you a lot but this all I can afford. Please accept this,' Muthu said and smiled.

'I don't think we will need to rent a place here. I'm not used to living in the middle of a village amidst the bustle. I will erect a shed on the land and live there, nga.'

The naattamai looked at Muthu intently. 'Alone, in your land? How will you, with your wife and children?'

'We are used to all that, nga.'

'No, what you are doing is not right. Robbery and theft are rampant here. They may even kill people, those heartless fools.'

'What do I have to spare, nga? I have given away all I had to buy this land. From now on, my earning is dependent on it. Whenever I reach a time when I actually start saving some money, I will worry about robbery.'

The naattamai sprung up and instantly brought his son and daughter-in-law out. 'Listen to what he is saying,' he said and went on to explain Muthu's plan. They too tried to convince him not to do so. 'Are you concerned about living in a community different from yours? We are farmers too. We will make sure you don't run into any problems,' they said.

Soon, a group gathered on the street. They tried to scare him with stories of snakes and ghouls. But Muthu did not budge from his stance. His attention was on the sun, which was headed towards the horizon in the west. He had planned to get some work started on the land before the end of the day. He felt a little annoyed that he couldn't seem to find a way out of this conversation. He slowly started moving towards his cart, smiling all the while.

'Are you headed to your village already?' asked the naattamai.

'I'm going to the land now, nga. I will go to Saethur tomorrow and take a bus to my village from there. Kuppan will be here only. Please take care of him. I will be back in two or three days,' he replied.

'With your family?'

'Not really. They all must be waiting for me, wondering what became of me. I will inform them of all that has happened and then return. Once I erect a shed and set up the place, I will go back and bring them over.'

'You can sleep here tonight.'

'It will be on the land that I will sleep tonight. Tomorrow, Kuppan will leave the cart by the choultry and spend the night there. Please look after him,' Muthu replied as he drove away.

If he stayed for longer, the questions would not cease. He found it astonishing that it was not the practice here to return to the village and their homes from the fields only after the sun had gone down. He wondered how many more surprises awaited him. Eventually, he would get used to them. He shared this observation with Kuppan and chuckled as they rode the cart. Even though Kuppan had a home in the valavu, it was the fields in which he lived. He too did not find it odd that they should live on their land.

There was still much of the day left. Once they reached the field, he untied the oxen from the cart, tethered them in the field and took a good look around. The stone erected to demarcate the property was beyond the farthest point his eyes could see. He felt a sense of pride that he owned all this land. He let the oxen graze. He pulled out the manvetti and the digging bar from the carrier under the cart. 'Get the basket, Kuppanna,' he said. Kuppan figured that Muthu was about to commence work. but he didn't know what he had in mind. Many a times, it was only after Muthu had already embarked upon something that Kuppan could understand what he was thinking. He planned everything in his mind. When the land was being measured, they had chopped off some thorny branches that were in their way. There was quite a distance between the end of the property line and the stream.

'Kuppanna, I spoke to the surveyor in private. There are three acres and sixty-four cents of land between this property and the low grounds that don't belong to anyone. I have requested him to create a deed for that land as well. He said, "Come back after the registered deed is in place. But in the meantime, you can plough the lands and farm on those lands as if they are yours and pay taxes for a couple of years. The settlement record can be created only after that." I will take care of that when I come back from home. I will pay the tax on the bit of land that is sixty-four cents in your name, and when the settlement record is ready, I will pay for it and have that registered under your name. That way, you will also have some land to call your own. You can bring Thangaa here. If any of your sons is willing to move, they can come too,' Muthu said, unveiling his plan.

The idea had struck Muthu when they were measuring the land densely covered with thorns. Yet he had brought it up with Kuppan only now.

'What else is left in my life . . . saami . . . I will stay here at your feet until I die. What am I going to do owning property, saami . . . You think we are people that can survive owning a piece of land . . .'

'Kuppanna . . . your own people may ask you, "He took you that far away in return for nothing?" Why leave room for such talk? It doesn't seem like there are people from your community around here. If we thrive here and need help some time, we can bring any of your sons who is willing to come. Having some land for yourself will help. I am going to arrange for the land to be yours. End of the matter,' finished Muthu.

'Will I ever go against your decisions, saami? Do as you please,' Kuppan finally agreed.

As they talked, they walked through the thorny shrubs and reached the middle of the stream. They could see the dried bed. During rainy season, the water level must reach the height of one's chest. At one spot, they saw a wide pit that displayed signs of holding water. He pierced the centre of that pit with the digging bar. 'God of the Mountain . . . I consider this land a treasure that you have given me. For this parched mouth, it is water that we need first. Even if it is only enough to wet the tongue, you must show me some water, my sire,' Muthu prayed loudly and venerated the land. Kuppan's eyes sparkled with tears. He too prostrated on the land in reverence. Muthu aimed at the centre of the pit and sunk the digging bar in. About half the length of the bar went in with ease. His eyes flickered with satisfaction. Kuppan too smiled in happiness. The two of them did not exchange a word after that. As Muthu drove the digging bar in, Kuppan heaped the soil into the basket with the manvetti. Together, they carried the basket and emptied it close by.

Water must have stagnated there for a long time but the soil was of the gravel variety. It looked dry on the top but there were traces of moisture below. The digging bar loosened the soil and piled it up. Clumps of soil tumbled down. Kuppan remained bent over the entire time, digging further and shovelling the loosened soil into the basket. He straightened up when the basket was full, to lend a hand to carry and empty it. As they dug deeper, there were plenty more signs of water. Once they had dug a three foot square and stood about knee-deep, they were convinced. Muthu drove in the bar with renewed vigour. If only there was more of the day left. He had spent too much time at the naattamai's. If not, they could have drawn the water out by now. Since Muthu hadn't worked for the last twelve days or so, he gasped for breath. But he couldn't stop because of that. Everything would be okay. His body was covered with sweat, yet he didn't stop digging.

Kuppan straightened his back and asked to drive the bar. Muthu now shovelled the soil and filled the basket. It was easier to shovel the soil than to dig. It was only a small pit. By the time they dug to the level of their waists, they felt slight dampness. If they had left it there, water would have seeped into it at least to the level of the ankles by the morning. Daylight was diminishing. The yellow evening sun glittered on the horizon. The thorn bushes appeared to be covered by a yellow umbrella. Muthu grabbed the digging bar and struck it into the soil. It went in so deep that he couldn't pull it out easily. He wiggled it around and drew it out. Instantly, Kuppan got into the pit, filled up the manvetti with soil and handed it to Muthu. Muthu tossed the soil into the basket and handed the manvetti back to Kuppan. From then on, they didn't need the digging bar; the hand shovel was sufficient. Had the pit been wider, they could have taken the basket into the pit to fill it. This one barely had space for a man and a manvetti. If they had had an *ottukoodai*, a shallow wicker basket, perhaps he could have kept it between his legs. For now, though, one of them had to dig the soil and hand the manvetti to the other to empty it into the basket. Together, they went through five or six basketsful this way.

Since Kuppan was inside the pit, it was difficult for Muthu to carry the basket by himself. He dragged the basket just a little bit away from the pit and emptied it there. He could have brought an ottukoodai along. But how could he have known that he would need it? On a journey that he commenced without knowing his destination, this is all he could have gathered and brought in anticipation of needing them. Only when the time comes does the need become clearer. After emptying another five or six basketsful, he could only see Kuppan's head. 'Saami!' Kuppan called out eagerly. Muthu peeped into the pit but could not see anything. The pit was completely dark. The sun's rays had gone down and darkness had engulfed everything like shadow. Muthu gave Kuppan a hand to help him get out of the pit.

Muthu then got into the pit himself and bent down to check. It was tough to bend inside but his feet felt the tingle of the water trickling in. At least ten pots full of water were sure to get collected from here every day. There would be no need to go looking for water elsewhere. He reached down and scooped up a handful of water. It was muddy. He poured it into his mouth. The water was sweet. There was no way he could have found water this tasty anywhere close to his own village. 'If we dig a larger well, we can even sow paddy, Kuppanna!' he cried out with joy as he took Kuppan's hand to climb out of the pit carefully without letting the piled-up soil slide back into the pit. He turned eastward and said in earnest, 'Karattu saami, you found me this land. Now, you have given me water. Please protect me, who has complete faith in you.'

As a person who came from an arid region where they had to dig eight or ten *muttus* to begin to see traces of water, this was great fortune, finding water at a mere four feet. A spot in a stream bed. A pit where water had stagnated in the past. Moreover, they wouldn't need to carry their pots around looking for water to meet their immediate needs. If they dug at this very spot a little more, they would be able to get enough water to irrigate a seravu of land. The oxen could drink it. If they waited about half an hour, the mud would settle and the water would be crystal clear. But the daylight would not last that long. *Let me light the lantern*, Muthu thought. For feet that have roamed mountains and forests, walking amidst these thorn bushes in twilight was hardly challenging. When he crossed the thorn bushes with his basket, digging bar and manvetti, there was still a trace of daylight left. The oxen were grazing in the shallow grass. They had lost a lot of weight in these twelve days.

When they were pulling chartered loads, the oxen were well taken care of. No matter what time they returned home at night, there was always water mixed with oilseed and punnakku waiting for them in the trough. At least one bundle of green grass lay waiting in a corner of the shed. All Peruma's arrangements. She took care of the animals better than she did her own children. Once they set out on this journey, all he could give them was plain water for every meal. The only time they had thavidu and oilseeds was at the Raattoor market. After that, they had to go searching for a pond or a well, even for water to drink. Even though he had corn sheath bundles in the cart, he had to be sparing with them lest they should run out of it and be left with nothing to feed them.

Whatever the oxen grazed on when they halted to rest and whatever grass Kuppan and Muthu gathered for them was all their stomachs got. The taste of water too varied from region to region. For a tongue that is used to a certain taste, it takes a few days to adjust to another. But for these cattle, it was a different taste every day. Sometimes, it was two or even three variations in the same day. They did not like drinking water. They took a few sips only to quench their thirst. Once he returned from home, he would nourish their bodies, he thought.

At that moment, the sky appeared to have shrunk to an umbrella propped up against his land. He ran as fast as he could, eastward. Kuppan watched him break into a run, with his komanam tossing about, and thought to himself, 'Has this man gone crazy?' Muthu felt as if he could run to the sky and touch it. Only after he reached the mud road did he realize the umbrella sky was now sat beyond the knoll. He looked around. The umbrella seemed to be receding into the distance rapidly. It was, after all, an illusion that the sky had appeared to shrink to sit propped up against his farm. To touch it, he would have to run so much farther.

23

He sighed and returned to the oxen. The oxen that had frozen in panic upon seeing him jump and dash towards the horizon, were now at ease. He untied them and told Kuppan, 'Get the brass *thookuposi* and join me.' By the time they retrieved the large vessel, the thookuposi, a small bucket-like vessel, and the ropes, and walked back to the field, there was no daylight left. It was pitch dark amidst the thorn bushes. Muthu tied the oxen at the outer edge. They lit the lantern. Even though they had brought it with them, they hadn't used it until then. Muthu usually stopped for the night while there was still daylight. Even when they could drive just a little more and reach the next village, he never rushed.

To look into the pit that they had dug with the lantern, he had to lie flat on the ground. His body was covered in sludge. But that didn't deter him at all. He could see the water clearly in the light of the lantern. It could be almost ankle-deep. Finding water was momentuous. He tied the rope to the handle of the thookuposi and scooped some water that had collected in the pit. The water was sweet.

He waited for Kuppan to bring the pot over. He then gave him the bucket-like thookuposi to try the water. 'Pour some into my hands, saami . . .' Kuppan said cupping his hands to receive the water. 'This water trickled around your feet, Kuppanna . . . just drink from this.' Kuppan took the bucket hesitantly, held it high and poured the water into his mouth. Muthu neither kept him away nor held him close. He never uttered an insulting word at him. Peruma's father and brother have shouted at him and hurled abuses on many occasions. But they also spoke kindly to him soon after. Whenever they shouted at him, Kuppan took it as them having some other problem which was manifesting as anger at him and never uttered a word in his own defence. Later, when they would come back to him regretting what they had said in anger, Kuppan would chuckle to himself. When a bull wants to scratch an itch in its horns, it attacks the base of a tree until the itch is gone. Even if the tree gets scratched, it doesn't do anything to stop the bull. Kuppan thought of himself as that tree.

Every time Kuppan thought about how Muthu treated him, his heart filled with tenderness. Not one demeaning word was ever uttered. While Muthu readily blamed himself for any mistakes, he never pointed a finger at Kuppan. 'Saami . . . you gave this to me, calling it water. This is not water but *paanagam*, the sweet beverage that we make on our village festival using fresh palm jaggery.' Muthu rejoiced at hearing those words, as though he was floating in the air. They scooped out bucket after bucket of water and poured it out for the oxen. The oxen seemed to drink the water more fondly than before. 'From now on, it

will only be this water. Hold on tight to the taste,' Muthu
whispered to them, gently patting their backs.

Muthu and Kuppan bathed next to the pit. Kuppan
poured water on Muthu as he cleaned himself. The
fatigue and dreariness from the past twelve days dissolved
away. A thought dawned upon him. How would it
be if they had a large well full of this water? He could
hop, jump and play in the water. Will such a time ever
come? A sigh followed. 'Why do you do that, saami, do
you sigh like this often?' Kuppan asked. 'It has become
a habit now, Kuppanna,' Muthu who had turned away
from him, replied. He removed his komanam, squeezed it
dry, wore it properly again and walked over to draw water
for Kuppan to clean himself. Peruma too asked about his
sighs often.

'You keep thinking about things, as though you are
planning to capture a fort, and keep all that bottled within.
Then you simply let out a big sigh . . . this is what you do,'
she said. On several occasions, she could even discern what
he was thinking about. 'Isn't this what you were thinking
about?' she would ask. He would simply smile and not
give her an answer. When he let out a sigh, he felt lighter
in his mind. He continued to scoop and pour water for
Kuppan. 'Bathe at ease, Kuppanna. This is our water. I will
keep drawing water for you even if you want to bathe until
dawn.' Kuppan's body cooled down. His mind felt peaceful.
He could now stay in one place. He also felt a little joyful
knowing that he too would get some land for himself.

The two of them finished bathing and walked back to
the place where the cart was parked, along with the oxen

and the lantern. Nearby was a small rock. Kuppan got busy
setting up the stove to make dinner. It was not going to
be possible to cut grass for the beasts tonight. Muthu took
out some corn stalks from the bundle in the cart and gave
that to the oxen to eat. Had there been a little daylight, he
could have bathed the animals too. He should tell Kuppan
to take care of that first thing tomorrow morning. He
caressed their backs. The right-side ox folded its tail and
did a little jump. Did it know the good news that he had
bought the land? This ox had been the one to point out
this village to him. Surely, it knew all that had happened.
He walked to the front, lifted its face from amidst the corn
stalks and hugged it, placing his cheek against it. The ox
stuck its tongue out and licked his cheek. The left-side ox
watched them. He lifted its face too and planted a small
kiss there too.

The man who had sat in the driver's seat of the cart
felt that a sip of toddy or arrack would be a good idea that
night. When he worked in the fields, he had at least a
thimble of toddy every night. When not in season, he had
a steady supply all year around from the palm trees that
bloomed out of season. When he drove for hire, there was
no access to toddy. He bought arrack and kept the bottle
hidden in the backyard. Whenever he reached home, he
drank a lid-full before going to bed. Peruma knew all about
where he hid the bottle and of his drinking habit, but
she acted as though she didn't know anything. The man
worked so hard, he was allowed to have a little. If he ever
got drunk, he couldn't remember anything. He lost control
of his tongue.

Pongi was the one who made fun of him. 'Just stop after taking a good whiff of the bottle, da. If you drink, you are barely human.' That was a big fear of his. If he didn't touch it, there was no concern. If he got started, he could not stop when he should. Peruma herself had got scared once. She had tried to stop him but he had gripped her and tried to force her to take a sip as well. 'It is bad enough for a family if the man drinks. If the woman starts drinking too, that would be the end of them. The whole family will be packed off to the heavens,' she said. But he didn't stop. She finally had to forcefully push him down to free herself. The next day, she did not speak to him at all. He didn't remember what he had done. He couldn't recall the sequence of events, no matter how hard he tried. With no other option left, he surrendered to her demands. From that day on, she watched him drink to make sure he didn't overdo it. If he tried to, she snatched the bottle away from him.

If he had thought of it earlier in the evening, he could have arranged for it through the naattamai. Maybe it wasn't too late just yet. If he sent Kuppan, maybe he could find some. He lay down on the front of the cart and thought for a little while. He had tucked the leftover money, 500 rupees, secretly in the underside of the cart where no one could ever find it. Even Kuppan didn't know about it. It was again only the cart and the oxen. No one could take them away easily. If a stranger were to grab the ropes, the oxen would shake their heads and chase after them with their horns pointed. Muthu had sharpened their horns as well. Even if they touched the intruder lightly, the damage would be severe. If he had a little bit of toddy, he could wake up at any time. Nothing could pacify the mind once it starts demanding it. He went up to Kuppan and discussed the matter. He could see well in the light of the stove how Kuppan's face brightened at the idea. He felt bad that he had kept this man who seemingly loved his drink, away from it for so many days. He told him to buy only a glassful for each of them. If there was no more available, how could they drink more?

'Once I return, we can start tapping from our own trees within a week,' he chuckled. 'There are at least four or five trees that look ready to be tapped. I think they would produce good, thick theluvu. They look like they can be climbed. I can spot the tracks of the leg covers climbers wear. Looks like they have been left alone for a couple of years. Alright, we will do it. We can keep tapping and tapping and drinking away, Kuppanna!' he exclaimed while examining the trees.

'The older landlord has spoken very highly of your talent. But so far, I have not had the pleasure of seeing it for myself, saami . . .' Kuppan said and left.

Was finding an arrack shop really that difficult a task? It was easy to find the spot that usually had the most bustle. 'Kuppanna . . . if anyone asks, you must say you are buying it for yourself and that I don't drink. The entire village knows we are staying in the open fields. Some fellow may follow you back here thinking the two of us are going to get drunk and pass out,' Muthu warned him before he set out.

Kuppan had made a stove using three stones. The three stones were perfect for holding the pot. In a field full of stones, it was not surprising that he could find even ones. They were so many stones on this land. As though someone had brought cartloads of them and deliberately strewn them all around. How could he do any farming with all the stones in the way? After a long time, Muthu was going to cook. In those years when they went to the fields to till and ended up staying there, the responsibility to cook invariably landed on Pongi and himself. But Pongi used to trick him. He used to distract him by talking about something or the other, and eventually get him to prepare the meal. That's when Muthu learned to cook well. After he got married, there was never a need for him to utilize his skills. If he did walk into the kitchen for any reason, Peruma chased him out. 'You work like a slave to all in this house. Do you really need to do menial work too? Your mother declared that I will mix arali paste into the food. Now, if they have any stomach disorder, even if it is just acidity, they will suspect that I asked you mix something in.'

No matter who cooked, he could instantly tell what was missing or if there had been any mistakes in the preparation. Peruma had sent with him a few padis of flat bean seeds in a bag. For any kali, the flat bean seeds were the perfect companion. He put the seeds into the pot, added onions, green chilies with care, poured a drop of castor oil into the mixture and closed the pot with a plate. There was nothing easier than smashing cooked beans. He had forgotten to bring a churner but he used the spatula and smashed the beans as much as he could. He also didn't use oil to temper the food. After it was well-cooked, a drop of oil was all he added. To chase the arrack down, the tongue would want some heat in the food. So, he added a little more chillies into the dish. How good would the arrack from this area be?, he wondered. He hadn't seen many toddy tappers around here.

24

Most of the palm trees had two or three years' worth of
dried sheaths, and were dense and overgrown like a boy's
full head of uncut hair offered to a deity. He should trim
the dried palm sheaths and tap the trees for sap after he
gets back. Even though Muthu was wronged a lot—for
being the youngest meant being the fool—his father had
also done many good things for him when he was a young
boy. It was because of him that he had learned to climb
trees and tap for sap like a toddy tapper. He remembered
loathing his father for making him do that. When others
made fun of him, Appa said, 'Let them say what they want.
The skill you've learned will help you for life.' Only now he
understood what he had meant. As a boy, he once spent six
months climbing trees in a field in a village where he did
not know a single person and was perpetually covered with
palm sap from the climbing.

There were palm trees everywhere along their
farmland. It seemed there were even more of them during
his grandfather's time. The dense palms were cut down
as they blocked the sunlight that fell on the arable lands,

making them difficult to cultivate. When all four sons
began to work on the lands, the trees in the middle of the
farm were also cut down. Even the fifty that were left were
too much. Of them, forty were climbable. It was Kandan's
family that had climbed them for generations. The deal
was to provide four padi of toddy every day, four padi of
theluvu, two *manuvu* of palm jaggery every year and one
manuvu of palm jaggery with dried ginger. During the
Tamil months of Margazhi, Thai and Maasi, when the sap
gushed out plentifully, collecting the four padi every day
was easy. After that, the quantity varied with each tree. The
years of good rainfall meant an abundance of sap. If the
skies dried up, so did the poor palms. Even during verdant
years, if the northeasterly winds blew a little strong, the
palms tightened their supply. It was understood that all the
quantities promised were dependent on the season.

Once, when Kandan's grandson Chinnaan was
climbing on behalf of the family, a new tree climber arrived
in the village from Vittoor. On Muthu's family land lay a
rock, large and open like a threshing ground. It provided an
ideal spot for selling toddy after the harvest season. It was
easy to access and provided seating suitable for long hours
of drinking. The new climber approached Muthu's father
with a deal of five padi of toddy a day and one additional
manuvu of palm jaggery. It sure took mettle for a complete
stranger to approach a land that was being serviced by a
family for generations. But was the lure of only one extra
padi of toddy and a manuvu more of palm jaggery going
to make them hand charge of all the palms over to him?
Muthu's father was livid. He sent him away after giving

him an earful. 'You think if you promise an extra padi, my mind will go to eat shit? If you really want to make a living by climbing trees, first go to that tree climbers' valavu and request them to find you a farm. Instead of that, you thought you could lure me into giving you mine? Even if the toddy and theluvu you promised me flowed like a river in my land, I wouldn't let you have my trees, da,' Appa sizzled. The new climber listened to him with his head hung, realized that he was at a dead end, and left.

It must have been two or three days after that incident that Chinnaan was atop a palm tree. His wife Koyini was seated below with balls of palm jaggery. Muthu's father, who happened to be passing by, stopped and brought up the subject of the new climber. 'Look at how he walked over and asked me directly for my trees just like that. What guts! I'm sure someone must have instigated him,' he said. Koyini couldn't keep her mouth shut. In her youthful overzealousness, she replied, 'Is there anyone who can give more than us from climbing these trees? If someone like that comes by, go ahead and give him your trees.' Appa did not like that one bit.

Here he was, explaining how he would not give his trees to anyone else. And she carelessly said he could give them away to someone else if they asked. It must be their temerity that led them to think that no one else could climb those trees but them—that no one else would dare enter the farms without their approval. 'Remove your harness right now, Chinnaan, and climb down. I was being mindful of the fact that your family has been climbing palms for us since your grandfather's time. But see how callous your

wife's words are. And you didn't even open your mouth or
say anything to stop her? Clearly, she sets the rules here. It
does not matter if the palms remain untapped, or the dry
sheaths keep piling up like unkempt hair. I don't want you
to set foot on my property again,' declared Muthu's father.
Even though Chinnaan tried to send his apologies through
others to try to convince him to take them back, Muthu's
father stayed firm on his decision. 'She's a woman . . . she
challenged me to give the palms to someone else? How can
I keep them on my land after that? My self-respect is at
stake,' Appa maintained.

He expected that someone from the tree-climbing
community would ask for the job, but no one did. He sent
word to the new tree climber. That man had found work in
Semmur and had even collected a couple of rounds of palm
sap already. Appa seemed perturbed. The entire family
enjoyed toddy and theluvu. They made for one square meal
every day. The sunnambu theluvu was for the women and
children. Whatever was left over in the morning could be
heated slightly over the stove and made to last until the
evening. The kids drank some with relish every time they
passed by. And in the household with five grown men,
there was never any toddy left over. Appa himself drank
a kottai. Periannan never touched toddy during the day;
his favourite was evening toddy. Pongi and Kaali always
ended up fighting over how much they each got. One padi
wasn't enough for either of them; they drank as and when it
was being tapped. Sometimes, the quantity of theluvu was
reduced to meet the toddy demand. While the two brothers
were fighting, Muthannan usually took whatever he wanted.

Appa knew then that the job abandoned by a woman was not going to be picked up by anyone else locally. 'How could he ask him to take off the rope and climb down right in the middle collecting? Such conduct is bound to continue with anyone else who takes on the work. In the face of such a problem, what he should have done to handle it was to say "Finish up with this year and don't come back next year." How could he throw him out all of a sudden? How will the climber find another farm in a flash? He is now stuck without a job in the peak season. What he has done to him is akin to slicing his throat. He should allow Chinnaan back into his farm. No one else should step into that farm,' was the common opinion and verdict of the community. When all the climbers united against him, Appa became even more stubborn. 'If these climbers that only need half a brain to climb up a tree and back down have so much audacity, how much should I have as the one on whose land the palms stand? Just watch if I don't make them come crawling back to me,' he went around saying to everyone.

Early one winter morning, when Muthu was about twelve years old, he woke him up. It was about the time he had started wearing a veshti over his komanam. He was dark-skinned and had shot up like a palm sapling. He looked like a seventeen- or eighteen-year-old. His father didn't offer him any explanations. He simply asked him to get ready, and so he did, with a few komanam strips and a veshti. He took him up to Karattur on foot, and then they boarded a bus. Once they got off the bus, he took him far into some farmlands. By the time they reached their destination, the sun was high up in the sky. Luckily, he had bought him some puttu in Karattur itself. Only when they were walking through the farmlands did he explain to him what was going on.

Muthu didn't speak much to his father. Just a word or two here and there. It was Periannan who was more like a father to him. Muthu listened to whatever his father said and acknowledged with an 'okay' or 'hmm'. He was also afraid of him—sometimes he hit him suddenly, mid-sentence. They arrived at Pattur—with the Gandhi Ashram—next to Mollur. His father had a friend there who was a palm tree climber. He told him that he was going to leave Muthu with him for six months and that he was to learn the art of climbing trees from him during that time. 'I didn't tell him that you are my son. I told him you are the son of a tree climber from our village. Don't let me down. Learn everything there is to know about the skill and when you return, you will take care of all the palms on our land. If you create trouble instead, I will hang you and strip the skin off your back,' he added.

Appa's friend Adhakkan was of an advanced age. He and his wife, Aarayi, had built a small hut for themselves in the middle of a farm. He continued to climb a dozen trees or so within his capacity. As the Gandhi Ashram was close by, he did not want to tap toddy and get into trouble. He only collected theluvu. Aarayi stayed busy until afternoon making palm jaggery. They tapped toddy only from one tree for their own consumption. Appa had made up a grand story about how Muthu had lost both his father and mother and was loitering around uselessly and so he thought he could learn something from Adhakkan. 'Even though we only got to meet at markets here and there, we've known each other for what, twenty years now? I have come this far with this tree-climber's son so you can teach him something and set him straight. Treat him like your own son.'

Adhakkan told Appa that he could get veshtis and blankets from Gandhi Ashram for free. Appa said he would do that when he came back to pick up the boy, and left. Muthu spent nearly six months with that old couple. Not one person came to see him during that time. It was only after he came back home that he found out that Appa had not told anyone where he had been all those months. 'He'll come back,' was the only answer he had offered. Appa did not come to see him either.

Muthu had found the first week with them very difficult. Coming from a large family and a house full of people, he couldn't settle in with the oldies in their mousehole-like hut on an empty farm. Then he figured it out—there was no one to yell at him or scold him. No one was after him trying to make him work. He began to enjoy the bliss of a sacrificial goat that gets to roam free as it wants. He slept until the sun was full in his face. 'This is the age to sleep till late,' the old man would tell the old woman, 'Don't disturb him.' By the time he woke up, the two would be under one of the palm trees. He would feel ashamed and rush to join them with the drool on his face barely washed off.

With a laugh, the old lady filtered some toddy into a palm shell and handed it to him. The toddy, chilled by the cold of the night cooled his body. That was breakfast. He had a few more shells-full, pausing between each. His body felt like it was gliding like that of a cuckoo bird. He flitted around without even realizing it. He had minor errands to run—he had to bring a few pots of water from a well at a distance, he had to make sure that the little goat they had was tied up in a place with grass to graze, or collect some leaves to feed it. In the afternoon, the old lady cooked kali or ground maize and made a spicy stew to go with it. He had one more shell full of toddy and gobbled up two or three balls of kali. He had never eaten food as tasty as the old lady's. As far as she was concerned, making stew was hardly a chore. She whipped it up like magic. It appeared as though she was watching the mill, but she would be cooking within that timeframe.

Muthu received his lessons in the evenings.

As night fell, the old man's vision deteriorated. That's why he started while the sun was still hot. The first lesson he taught him was how to wear the rope around his body as a harness and around his feet. He taught him how it could be fatal if he didn't tie the harness around his body properly or tightly enough. The old man had countless stories of men who had died that way. Whenever he recounted a story, it went on and on. In the verve of his youth, he apparently had once climbed up a palm, sat amongst the tender fronds, untied and dusted a toddy collecting pot and kept drinking from it. The more the pot filled up, the more he drank. When he was beyond intoxicated and tried to climb down the palm, the rope around his feet slipped and he fell down. No matter how hard he tried, his feet kept splaying uncontrollably away from the trunk. He stayed

within his harness, slid all the way down and finally fell
to the ground below. 'It was but Mother Earth's grace,
she considered me her child and caught me. I broke my
foot and had to stay in bed for two months. That's when I
learned my lesson. That God does things like this for you
to learn your lesson, Ponnu,' he once said.

By his age, he had had so many experiences. They
constantly reappeared in his memory. And he flowed
from one into the other. Muthu found himself wondering
everyday if he went to sleep after the stories stopped, or if
the stories stopped after he went to sleep. He taught him
how to walk carrying the box on his hip, the harness on
his shoulder, the ladder and everything else, all at once. It
took him a few days to master the skill of climbing palms
in an instant using the harness rope. He had to push the
harness up first and then push his body up to its height. If
the harness rope came loose, it meant sliding all the way
down and starting all over again.

He knew how to climb a palm tree with his bare chest
and slice some palm fruit from the top. To climb a tree or
two, it worked. But if he had to climb fifty trees in a day,
it would be impossible without the harness. He had to be
careful not to let his body slip through the rope. He was
first taught to climb palms with young spathes. Gradually,
he was taught to handle spathes—it was not easy. If he
pressed the stick holding the spathe hard, it would wither
and die. The spathe had to be held carefully in such a
way that it got its nourishment as always. It was the art of
cheating the tree that needed mastering. Muthu felt the
thrill of learning how to cheat and rob from the tree. The

spathe had to be led to believe that it was nourishing its own when the sap was actually being robbed, spilling into the toddy pot. He used to feel bad for the palm.

In three months, he learnt to climb up and down palms and collect theluvu by himself. That had given him immense confidence at that age. He learned enough for the old man to remain in his hut and let him climb all the trees by himself sometimes. Not once did he get angry at him. If he ever drank beyond his limit, he groused about his sons, about how none of them paid any attention to him. 'Do you know how nice it would be for me if I had someone like you by my side?' he said. 'None of my grandsons even bother to come to see us.' The old man needed some sort of meat for dinner every night. He didn't eat without meat. He set a trap every day. Mostly it was squirrels that got trapped. If he placed the traps under the trees, he caught guinea pigs. He trapped quail fledglings too. Muthu had never eaten quails until then. Because he didn't want to expose his father's lie about him being the son of a tree climber, he ate whatever the old man brought without questioning. Quail tasted buttery and he ended up eating it a few times even though he didn't want to. Mynahs were tasty. They had no flesh. 'Bony birds,' the old man called them. But even sucking on their bones made for a delicious meal. Surprisingly, he even trapped Koel fledglings sometimes. If nothing, he found crow fledglings at the very least. Crows had a distinct taste. On days they trapped a bandicoot, it was equivalent to landing a goat. Muthu ate a variety of meats there. Along with learning how to climb trees, he learned to hunt as well.

Every step he took on the ladder wearing his harness, he felt as though he was climbing into the sky. He had never done any work so willingly before then. He knew all the nuances of farming but that was something he had learned instinctively. He was fully captivated by the art of climbing palms. The old lady cooked up arrack the same way she cooked food. She did not care for toddy. 'How long can you keep drinking padi after padi before getting anywhere with it,' she said, unlike arrack, where half a cup did the job. He did not go anywhere outside of that farm for those six months. He wasn't upset about that. The old man went to the market or to visit some place, once in a while. The old lady never went anywhere. She made palm jaggery so well that it melted in the mouth. All her time was spent making them and protecting them by spreading hay over them. So what if the place brimming with happiness is but a cocoon? One can simply remain inside it for as long as one pleases.

After the theluvu season ended and only a couple of palms were still oozing sap, the old man's workload expanded to include chopping off palm leaves and flattening and preparing them to be used as thatches for the hut. Muthu continued to help him with all that as well. On one such afternoon, Appa arrived. He ruffled Muthu's hair and gave him a hug with an affection like he had never displayed before. 'Who would give away a boy like this one? Please leave him here with me. I will take care of him as long as I'm around,' the old man said. Appa laughed and said, 'I would, if he weren't my son!' and broke the news to the old man. The old man's face shrank. The old lady remained seated in silence. Appa narrated the whole issue with the palm climbers at length.

'Not one climber wanted to come to my farm. That's when I thought to myself, "It's hardly a matter to climb trees. I don't need those fuckers. I have a son who can be trained". And I felt confident about it. At his age, he can be taught so many things. Just you watch, what havoc the palm climbers in my village are going to go through this year,' he rambled on. The old man's face did not brighten again. He took Muthu behind the hut.

'You didn't say a word about all this even once, Ponnu. I suppose you were bound to keep your father's word. Anyway, let all that be. This profession is my people's profession. No matter what, you must never take it up as yours. You will not forget what I taught you all your life. But I have just one ask. Stop at using this skill for your family and you. Don't ever take it up as your profession. If you all clamour for this job, what will we do? Consider this the fee you pay me, your teacher,' and he wept. 'Okay, *thatha*,' Muthu said. He placed his hand on top of the old man's to make his promise.

'The boy has learned everything very responsibly. That itself should have made me suspicious but I trusted what you said so much. Just don't let this boy climb trees for a living,' the old man said to Appa.

'Yes, but why has your face lost colour over this? My anger made me bring my son over. But he isn't going to do this for a living, don't worry. This boy will not climb anywhere other than on our land. Does that take care of your concern?'

The old lady held Muthu's face with the hands that made palm jaggery, and wept. Muthu cried too. Her words flowed out as tears. With a bag full of new karuppatti, Muthu reached home.

During the season that year, Muthu identified a solid, mature tree to climb first. In tree climbers' jargon, the first tree they climb is referred to as *seer*, or gift. Muthu too referred to it that way. The tree gave plenty of toddy and theluvu. His technique worked perfectly on it. However, other than Appa, no one else supported this. 'Did I sleep with a tree climber to bear this son of mine?' Amma asked. 'Who amongst you all is going to sell the toddy at the rock?' Periannan asked all the ladies in the house, mockingly. 'Why should we do that? Get him married to a tree climber's daughter. The two can frolic over and around the stone,' replied the eldest daughter-in-law.

'Should we set up and make jaggery over here?' Kaali asked his father with a straight face. 'Let's give up farming altogether and climb a few trees each,' Pongi joked. Not realizing the sarcasm in their comments, Muthu quickly tied pots at the knuckles of a handful of trees. The tree climbers were truly astonished. No one knew where the boy had learned to climb so well. If a few more of them began climbing trees like this, the whole community would have to leave the village and find some other place for survival.

Appa bragged about how he cut off the noses of the tree climbers. But Amma yelled at him. 'You have got your son trained to climb trees. Are you going to find him a girl to marry too? Will any warm-blooded farmer give his daughter's hand to our son? Stop all this now.' And it worked. It was decided that theluvu collection would be limited only to the family's consumption. Collection would stop after two pots from a tree with ample sap. He climbed much before the day broke. In the evenings, he climbed only after darkness began to set in. By and large, no one spotted him climbing the trees. Two years went by this way. After that, Chinna and Koyini came over, crying. They couldn't find another farm that had the same quality of trees anywhere else. Or fifty trees together like it. He had had to bear the ridicule of the people around, a beaten Chinna said. 'The devil got her tongue when she blabbered that night. For that, should we be punished so badly?' he asked. She cried nonstop. Appa instructed Chinnan to resume climbing trees. Muthu climbed a tree or two when they oozed sap off-season. Just to keep from forgetting what he had learned.

Muthu attended the funerals of the old man and the old lady who had taught him. He thought of them as another set of parents even now. He had mentioned to Pongi some time ago that the time when he was truly happy were during those six months. If they ever wanted to tease him, they called him the palm tree climber. And he would say, 'Better to be born a palm tree climber's son than a farmer's son.'

Muthu chuckled at the irony of how a skill he had learned to satisfy his father's ego was about to come in handy for him now.

25

He rinsed the rice and made kali with it. He then sprinkled water on the embers and extinguished the fire. There was no sign of Kuppan. The moon was fully visible from where he stretched himself over a rock. He suddenly sat up and counted the palm trees in the light of the moon. There were thirteen in all but he couldn't tell how many of them were male and how many female. He spotted a couple of small burnt ones. Even if he cut the branches off all of them, he would get two and a half, maybe three bundles of palm sheathe. How would that suffice? He could maybe erect a little enclosure for a kitchen. To build living quarters, he would need to buy sheaths of palm, worst case. Surely, there would be some way to source some. Once he returned from home, he should look into installing a temple for Karattusami. His reign over the entire land was vital.

Kuppan still hadn't returned. Perhaps he hadn't been able to find a shop in the darkness after all, or perhaps he had got into trouble there? He sat staring in the direction that Kuppan had left, for a while, in panic. Both the oxen were seated and had begun to chew cud. In the light of

the moon, Kuppan arrived like a moving shadow. He had
to go a bit far, he said, and it was only after a detailed
interrogation about them that they sold it to them. He told
them that they were staying at the naattamai's place. 'If we
hadn't gotten used to drinking this rubbish, you wouldn't
have had to roam around in the darkness, Kuppanna,'
Muthu said, concerned.

'Don't look at it that way, saami. How can we expect
everything we want to fall into our laps? We have travelled
so far to buy this land. If we have to go a little more to
find the arrack, that's not so bad, saami. You see, one more
thing got settled because I went there. They were tree
climbers. They say you could buy sheaths around there and
they could even cut up a few for us if we wanted,' replied
Kuppan. Muthu noticed that he too was proactively making
plans to help them settle in and he felt happy about that.

'If there are trees on our land, I can climb the trees and
cut up a few branches myself, Kuppanna. None of these
climbers are going to be as good as me,' he said.

'How did it even occur to your father to send you to
a tree climber to learn that skill? Quite fascinating,' said
Kuppan.

'What is so fascinating about that, Kuppanna? You
know the barber who comes to our home? It was from him
that Appa got this idea,' Muthu began telling Kuppan.
'I'm going to narrate a story now to you, for a change,' he
began.

Mani, the barber, came to the farm at least once a
week. There was always someone who needed a haircut or
a shave. If he didn't come, Appa yelled at him the next

time he saw him. And Muthu's brothers mocked him. 'We haven't seen you come by our farm, Mani. Getting very comfortable in life, are we?' they asked. One day, Muthu needed a haircut. The practice was to sit on a rock near the cowshed by the house. Muthu had already seated himself there. Mani opened his box to take out his knife, scissors, etc., when he exclaimed, 'Adadaa! I forgot to bring water, Muthu!' Mani had a cup made of iron, much like an oil cup, that he used for carrying water.

Muthu felt too lazy to get up after sitting on the rock. 'Just take the water from the reservoir yourself,' he said. 'If anyone sees me do that, they will say something. Won't you please get some for me, dear?' Mani asked again. 'No one is around, go fetch it yourself,' Muthu egged him on to help himself to the water reservoir. Just as Mani scooped some water from the reservoir, Appa passed by and saw him. 'So, you've become so great that you think you can take water from the reservoir with your cup?' he yelled. Even though Mani was petrified for a moment, he pulled himself together in the next instant and replied, 'We don't fall under the untouchable group, saami. We are the same blood as you. We touch you when we give you a shave. If any function were to take place in your family, you couldn't do it without us. Why is that? Many years ago, during my great great grandfather's time, many generations ago, we were children of your household, like Vaira, my ancestor. Didn't you know that?' he asked. Appa did not know anything about it so he asked Mani to explain himself.

During those times, farming was not practised in the region—it was a land covered with trees. People lived off fruits from the trees and tubers from under the soil. When they started farming little by little, an immigrant community who came from somewhere to settle down here showed them how to cut down trees to clear land for farming. On one side lived the hunters and on the other, the immigrants. For any other type of work, they could step in to help when there were no labourers available. But who else could step in to do theirs? There was a barber to shave a hunter's beard, but there were no one to shave the immigrant. So, they decided among themselves that the hunters would first get their shaves, and then the immigrants would follow.

One bright afternoon, a barber was giving an immigrant a shave on a rock at the village periphery. He had finished with one side of his face and was working on the other side. Just then, a hunter came by and called for him. 'Dei,' he said, 'I have a village dispute settlement to lead. Hurry, I'm in a rush. Give me a shave and then you can carry on.' The barber left the immigrant halfway to attend to the hunter. The rule was to put the hunters above the immigrants. He left even without confirming to the immigrant that he would complete his shave once he was done. The immigrant was livid. He felt belittled that he had been abandoned there with a half-shaved face. He decided that the immigrant community needed their own barbers.

He called his youngest son and told him, 'From now on, you are the barber for the immigrant community. I don't know where you will go or how you will learn the trade, but you ought to. Take your wife and your family along and live separately. I will give you land and property, but you must not do farming anymore. You will be a barber.' It was the descendants of that last son who continue to practise as barbers, Mani explained. But he didn't stop there. 'You see, we too have relatives like you. And our traditions match yours. Our women too wear white. So why are you stopping me from taking water from your reservoir when I have the right to be invited into your home for a meal?' and he began to lay more claims to his rights.

'Of course, you can even come seeking a girl in marriage,' Appa mocked him but what he heard Mani say had sowed a seed in his mind. If someone could send his own son to take up a profession such as a barber's, what could be the issue with his son taking up the profession of a tree climber? The palm trees were, after all, on their own land. Not only for the theluvu—the immigrant community was fully dependent on palm trees; they couldn't do anything without it, from building homes to performing last rites. The fronds, the sheaths, palm hearts, fruit and so much more came from them. And climbing trees was never considered as an act fit for untouchables. Unlike cutting hair, where one couldn't enter the house without first cleansing themselves with water and having his clothes washed separately, climbing trees was akin to driving oxen to plough land. 'And so, using this rationale, he sent his youngest son to learn tree climbing,' Muthu finished.

'Is there so much behind you learning to climb trees?' gasped Kuppan.

'Why, of course! Look Kuppana, I too have a story!' Muthu then went on to the next topic. He said he was going home for two days and that while he was away, all

Kuppan had to do was to make sure the oxen were well-fed. He then asked Kuppan if he had any message for Thangaa. 'It's not like we got married only three months ago, nga. What message am I going to send for her? Tell her I am well. Tell her she too can join us here in some time. That's enough.' He served Muthu the food on a plate and placed it before him with a glass of arrack.

Kuppan's breath seemed laced with arrack. Since Muthu had asked to buy only a small quantity, he probably had some at the shop itself. The man who was used to drinking every day hadn't touched alcohol for twelve days for Muthu's sake. Perhaps he had decided to drink at the shop and that's why he was late. But Muthu chose not to ask him about it. Kuppan measured out more for Muthu and poured himself a smaller quantity. 'The saaru is very tasty. I don't know how someone who cooks so well can eat my cooking,' Kuppan said as he ate. The arrack had no kick to it. Usually, it burned the throat as it made its way down. This one was not potent at all but went well with the cluster bean seed saaru he had made. All because of the water, he decided. The first fill from the well they had dug had served to quench the thirst of the oxen. Kuppan and Muthu had drunk as much as they could of that water and had bathed in it too. It was the same water used to cook and also to mix into the arrack. It was indeed a big windfall to find so much water on their first attempt. Muthu finished eating and lay down on his cart.

The moon was making its way to the horizon. In some time, the land would be fully dark. He wondered if he should light the lantern, but decided against it. The light would give them away. *No need to attract any attention.* Since the time when he was allocated that small sliver of his parental property, it was only today that his mind was at ease. He had his own land now. As much land as the four brothers had combined, all to himself. When he closed his eyes, various thoughts flashed in his mind. He fidgeted for sometime and then passed out, slipping into deep sleep. After several days, he fell into a sleep so deep that it was devoid of any thoughts.

He woke up when he heard what sounded like a loud howl from a dog. The gentle dew-filled air touched his skin and gave him goosebumps. Loud snores from Kuppan, who was sleeping under the cart, filled the air in intervals. He looked at the oxen. Their heads were turned towards the road—they were watching intently with their ears perked up. They had eaten every bit of their food. For a moment, everything appeared as if veiled by a thin film. His head was no longer foggy from the arrack. The sound he heard was a lie, it must have been his imagination, he thought as he climbed down and urinated. Suddenly, there was another very loud howl from the direction of the road. Immediately, a similar howl rose from somewhere in the field. In a flash, there were howls from all four directions. His body got chills as he tried to figure out what was going on. The oxen stood up quickly. Maybe there were foxes in this region. But if there were any, surely the naattamai would have mentioned it? The sound came individually from all directions at first and then in unison from all sides.

When he listened patiently, he realized that the howls were of men and not foxes. Meddlesome men who had heard that they were going to spend the night in the field had come to scare them away. He knew he couldn't trap them. But he could shoo them away with noises, he thought and sat up slowly. He suddenly let out a sound in response to the howls. He remembered watching people who became possessed by a spirit, took inspiration from the sounds they let out, and began with a low 'mmmm' sound that soon grew into a very loud 'aaaa' sound. He ran to different parts of the field and continued to make noise. He became so involved and grew so passionate that he couldn't get himself to stop.

The oxen saw this change in him and trembled with fear. He was dancing around making noises. As he moved about with his hair dishevelled and without any inhibitions, different noises arose from him. The howling from the other side stopped. He paused to make sure they had, in fact, stopped and continued. Screams for howls. Gods for ghosts. He thought to himself that he should keep a torch ready tomorrow. That way he could dance like a warrior with the torches lit in all four directions and no matter what sort of night it turned out to be, his performance would scare away even the scariest of ghosts. He kept making the 'aaaa' sounds long after the howling had stopped. Despite all this, there wasn't the slightest movement from Kuppan.

26

Three days after he had left, Muthu returned to the farm in the afternoon, as promised. Along came his second daughter Rosamma as well. They had taken a bus to Saethur. There, they had waited for another bus and got off at the Karunkaradu stop. It was a four-mile walk from the main road to reach the farm. The fatigue from the bus ride and the long walk showed on the poor child's face. She plopped herself down under the neem tree. She regained her energy only after drinking some of the kali mixed with water that Kuppan had made. They had brought with them two little white goat kids in a basket covered with jute sacks. Two large sacks that weighed quite a bit. The child was more exhausted from carrying the load than from walking the distance.

Yes, Muthu wouldn't let her be. 'How's the farm, Rosa?' he asked her. She didn't have a full grasp on the situation. What would a ten-year-old understand about all this land business, anyway? For a child who had seen farms with wells and lush green plantations, this appeared to be just a barren land. 'It is our land all the way to that low-lying area. You see the marker stones along the south? That is the end of our land on that side,' he explained to her. She seemed a little surprised at the expanse of the farm. 'Are you wondering why there's nothing growing here? We are only now going to start correcting the land to make it suitable for farming. There is a lot of work to be done but in a year's time, this place will become just like how you like it,' he said, patting her head.

After spending some time in the shade, he took his daughter to show her the water well they had dug. He still hadn't seen it by daylight. Kuppan had chopped off all the thorny bushes along the path to the well and made it wider. All around the water pit, a wide, strong mound had been built with rocks to prevent dug-out earth from sliding back into the pit. 'Kuppanna, you have accomplished a mammoth task,' a pleased Muthu said. The pit was deep enough to hold a man. Looked like Kuppan had dug a little deeper. The water was clear on top and sparkled in the afternoon sun. The water was surely at least knee-deep. 'This is a spring, Appa?' Rosamma asked as she peeked into the well standing across from him. Hearing those words brought a deep sense of contentment to Muthu.

'Kuppanna, did you hear what the girl said? Spring! This is a spring! And what did the two of us refer to it as? A water pit! How beautifully she has called it a spring. From now on, this shall be known as a spring,' he exclaimed.

'What is the use of having adults around? This is why we need little children around. Their words are the words of God,' Kuppan acknowledged. Muthu was opposed to bringing Rosamma with him at first. When he returned home and told Peruma the news, she welled up and cried. After waiting for him day and night for all those days, she broke down in delight. Slowly, he told her everything that had happened. All the people in that household sat down around him and listened in awe. No one from that region had ever left to buy land elsewhere. They found all this fascinating.

When he described the land, he set the expectations low and clearly described that it needed much rectification before they could start reaping its benefits. 'If the land was ready, you couldn't have bought it at such a price,' Veerannan commented. Muthu didn't mention anything about the three acres of poramboke land. He told Peruma alone about it. One month maybe, but in two months at most, they could all move there, he said. It took a lot of effort to convince Peruma, who insisted that she join him immediately. 'Men can live on rocks or under the open sky. But for women, you would need at least a small shed, wouldn't you? Can I have you live on open land? The elder one is on the verge of puberty. Let me set up a little and I will come with the cart to take you and our things,' he promised.

Peruma declared that he take Rosamma with him to help him. He had Veerannan go to his family temple to bring back blessings and holy ash for his new farm. Along with the holy ash came Pongi too. 'Won't you come by our village? Have you come to hate us so much?' he asked. Pongi was genuinely very sad. 'When it has been ascertained that not a cent of that land belongs to me, what right do I have to come?' Muthu asked.

'Blood is thicker than water, da. We are all still your brothers,' Pongi's voice softened. In a small bag was some soil from the temple and a rounded stone. Muthu didn't remember seeing any ironwood tree in or around Karunkaradu. For now, he would place the stone under a neem tree even though Karunchaami preferred the ironwood tree. He took a cluster of ironwood fruits that were fully ripe and on the verge of bursting open, and kept them in the bag. If they burst open, the seeds would fly all around the farm like wisps of cotton. He could plant them and they would grow tall enough to provide shade for Karupanaar in a few years.

Muthu wasn't planning to carry the two little white goat kids in a basket. He thought he would buy them near Karunkaradu. But, Peruma filled half the basket with their favourite leaves, placed them in the basket, covered them with a jute bag and tied the bag tightly all around and a little gap for air. Still, it turned out to be quite a burden to carry—they were so young and hadn't yet weaned off. They suddenly remembered their mother and started crying out for her in unison. The people in the bus turned around and stared at them every time it happened. But they were a good breed and each could bear five or six younglings. Where would he find such a breed in the new place?

For food, two bags, one with millet flour and one with rye flour, were packed for him to take with him. When he asked her if she thought he had ten hands to carry everything, she pushed Rosamma forward. When he asked her what he was going to do with a little girl in the middle of nowhere, she said, 'She is not suckling, she is going to become a young lady soon. She can accompany you and be of some help cooking for you and taking care of the young goats. Otherwise, she is just going to eat three meals and play around all day here,' Peruma said clearly. Rosamma and the little boy were the ones who always competed over everything. When she was getting ready to go with Muthu, the little boy wanted to go as well and created a ruckus. With no other way around, their father promised to take him along as well. Early next morning, when it was time to leave, he didn't wake up the boy. He was sure to have screamed loud enough for the whole village to hear whenever he woke up. Peruma would have smacked him right across his mouth and made him stop. There was no way he could have managed the little boy if he had brought him along.

Somehow, I should bring the whole family to the new place in a month. Now that there is a place of our own, why be dependent on someone else? If everything had to be set up for them before bringing them over, it will take very long. We can live here and set things up one by one. The two little goat kids saw the new place and bleated in fear. The leaves in the basket didn't seem like they had been touched at all. Rosa placed little ropes around their necks and tied them up. After crying for their mother for a day or two, they would learn to graze for food a bit at a time. They would anyway lose weight before gaining some. They were both female and, in a year, would be ready to bear kids. She held a few leaves on her palm and brought it close to them. She then forced a few leaves into each of their little mouths. They nibbled on them lightly.

She looked around the land to see if there were any other
leaves the goats might eat. There was a lone Vadhanaram
tree standing along a mud path. She got hold of one of
the branches with a curved end that Kuppan had chopped
down, and marched towards the tree. The two little goats
pranced behind her. The leaves were yellow and old. She
plucked some tender leaves from the tip of the branches
using the curved end of the branch she held, and collected
them in her lap. When there was enough, she sat down and
held her lap open before the goats. She remembered all the
instructions her mother had given her. She should never
waste time. She should not trouble her father. She should
take on the full responsibility of preparing their food. If she
found making kali hard, she could take her father's help.
She was responsible for the little goats and the oxen. She
had to cut grass to feed the oxen.

She felt very responsible, as if she was one of the
grownups. That feeling gave her joy. Her only wish was
that Ponnaiyan had come; then she could have played with
him. She didn't miss her older sister much. She needed her
little brother. Just one month and he will be here, she told
herself. The little goats chewed on the leaves but only a
little. She tied up the rest of the leaves and ran back to the
rock, the little goats following her. When she stopped, they
stopped. When she ran, they ran too. She felt content that
she had the little goats to play with. She emptied her skirt
into the basket and went to check on the vessels. There
was a ball of kali soaking in water in one pot. She placed
the ball on a plate and rinsed the pots that had the kali and
saaru. There was a circle of char on the underside of both

pots. She broke off a cluster of the Matura flowers and used that to scrub the pots with some ash. Clearly, they had only washed the insides of the pots to cook kali and saaru every day. She cleaned and washed the dried crumbs off the rims of the plates, too. She should find some coconut husk, she thought to herself. After washing all the vessels, she took the bunch of flowers and went into the farm.

She dug out the tall, overgrown grasses and stacked them into piles. The little goats stayed close to her. She enjoyed running around, engaging them. Muthu observed how quickly his daughter took to the land and beamed with pride. It was good that Peruma had sent the child with him. She knew so many things. Muthu kept an eye on Rosa as he continued to do his work. His first task was to find a spot for the Karunjaami. There were plenty of favourable spots in the field. In a field full of mini knolls and rocks, there was hardly a scarcity for the perfect spot. But the ideal one would be where no one troubled him and he troubled no one. Once he decided where the shed was going to be, he could place the altar based on that.

Kuppan and he surveyed the entire land and stopped at the southwestern corner. There, above the poramboke land and the rivulet but within the legal boundaries of his land was a tiny knoll that was four steps tall. It sloped gently downwards and after a stretch, ended in a little well, like a tail. Around the top of the knoll were a few kiluva, neem and black babool trees; several vines of veldt grape vines spread across them. The top rock was wide enough for a fully grown man to lie down with his hands and legs outstretched. Muthu felt that it was the ideal spot for Karunchaami. There was a similar black mound in the middle of the land too. Four or five other spots had even smaller boulders. It wasn't that the god demanded a hill or a mountain on which to sit. He would be happy even if he was set on the soil in a corner. But since this field offered so many raised spots, Muthu thought it would be nice to place him in a clean and comfortable place.

If he placed him on the land, he would have to dedicate a stretch to him. Wherever he was placed, he needed a tree. Whether it was neem or ironwood, once they grow taller, they would spread their shade and that portion would no longer be suitable for farming. In the rocky region, that wouldn't be a problem. This spot was particularly unique. There would be any hurdle for movement. If the women were having their menses, they wouldn't have to cross him during those days. The knoll was suitable for making pongal or for sacrificing hens too. Muthu looked at Kuppan. Maybe he had a different thought. 'Let's place the temple here, saami . . . the neighbouring boundary runs adjacent to this end. Even if they are tempted to do mischief, their minds may change upon seeing him. This may even keep that troublesome Mookan from meddling with us,' Kuppan agreed. This added convenience that the spot offered left Muthu more satisfied with his decision.

27

They decided to install Karunchaami on that spot and began cleaning the area. Black thorns were spread everywhere, wild like the locks of a mad woman. This tree was the top enemy to farming here. The neem was not very tall. It had grown through the gaps in the broad shoulder of the black thorn tree and had begun to spread over it like an umbrella. But that is the neem's nature—it grows between the gaps of something, spreads its canopy and then destroys everything in its shade. The girth was as wide as a hand. Abutting it was a kiluva tree. The kiluva didn't need to be cut from the bottom. If the top was chopped off, the goats would prop themselves against the tree and eat any new leaves, since kiluva leaves were their favourite. If they thinned down the overgrowth, they could offer their prayers and light lamps without concern. It was an hour's worth of work. They could set up the God in his abode before sunset.

Even the God must have been tired from travelling by bus the last couple of days. When Kuppan cleared the path to the little well that they had created, he used a few staffs with pointed tips on one end that he had cut up to

dig the earth. Just as Muthu moved to gather them and
the machetes, Kuppan clutched Muthu's arm and signalled
him to be quiet by putting a finger over his lips: 'Shhhh.'
Assuming it was a snake he had spotted, Muthu looked
in the direction that Kuppan was pointing. There, amidst
the overgrowth, was a rabbit lying down close to a rock
on the grass. It looked like a white bud bulging distinctly
from the red rock. Its eyes alone remained alert, attentive
to all directions. The two of them moved a bit away from
the spot. If a rabbit heard the slightest rustle of a snake,
it would hop away. It could cross a couple of farms in the
blink of an eye before pausing to turn and look around.
Rabbit hunting was hard. The only way to nab them was
by setting up nets. Still, it was the first sign of life they
had seen as soon as Karunchaami had stepped into their
farm. Maybe he wanted to establish his consecration with a
sacrifice. *Why not give it a try?* Muthu thought.

He gestured to Kuppan to stay where he was and
hurried to the cart noiselessly. He took the spears. 'What
are you doing, Appa?' Rosamma, who was trimming grass
nearby, ran towards him. 'A rabbit, dear.' When she started
following him, the two little goats began to follow them
too. She quickly gathered them, placed them in a basket
and rushed back. She saw that her father held two spears
in his hand. She got another one from the cart and ran
towards the rabbit. The spear was made of split bamboo
stalk and a very sharp iron tip. It was impossible for a
creature to survive an attack with that spear. The rabbit
now had turned towards the north and was lying down
calmly, its eyes getting heavier.

From where they were, it was difficult to jump over the knoll; it was too high. Of the other three sides, the north side was open and was conducive for the hunt. Kuppan stood on that side. Rosa stood on the southern side. If they attacked from the east side, the rabbit would be trapped. But the slightest movement and the creature would become alert. Muthu had gone hunting at night in the past, but never had he tried attacking a rabbit directly like this. His hands trembled with nervousness and trepidation. His sweat drenched the spear. Kuppan, understanding his hesitation, gestured him to come over to his side noiselessly and went towards the rabbit himself. Muthu and Rosa stood ready holding their spears in their hands. 'Swish!' A sound pierced the air around. The spear that went flying from Kuppan's hand landed on the neck of the rabbit. After the rabbit stopped struggling, he picked up his spear along with it. It was a medium-sized rabbit. If Muthu had tried to get to it, it would have fled. He had intended to go as close to the rabbit as possible and then pierce it with the spear in his hand. The spear that Kuppan hurled from where they stood had landed perfectly on its target.

He did everything he could to keep from lifting Kuppan up with joy. Rosa was still full of excitement at catching the rabbit, if only it had come towards her. Her face reflected the disappointment at it not having turned out that way. As soon as they decided on a spot for the God, he accepted a sacrifice. This felt like a good omen too, just like how they felt when the oxen had stopped on the road as soon as they had arrived at this village. They decided to complete the task of creating space for the idol. The rabbit could wait—nothing would happen to it in an hour. They gave it to Rosa and told her to store it properly, and got on with trimming the overgrowth. Once they got through the thorny trees, the rest would be easy. As one held the branches taut with a forked staff, the other chopped them off. The seemai karuvela was poisonous. The slightest jab was enough for it to show its prowess. Goats eat their fruits eagerly and then spread them everywhere around the farm through their dung. If they didn't attend to them right away, their roots quickly penetrated deep into the soil, making it very difficult to pull them out. Once the outer growth was removed, Kuppan severed off the main trunk. He sorted the cut branches into two piles, one of the thorny stalks and another of twigs. There was enough collected to serve as firewood.

The tree base had to be removed for it not to regrow. They loosened the soil all around the base and tugged it out. The kiluva tree was left alone. They could cut off a few branches every day for the goats. If they cut too much of it at once, the tree would die. Muthu cut off the vines of veldt grape. Rosa carefully collected the tender stalks of the veldt grape vines to make kaduppaan, a savoury powder, with them. Muthu left enough for the vine to regrow. A couple of varieties of grass had grown densely around the rocks. They pulled out as much as they could, dug out the rest and collected a large bundle for the oxen. It was only because the grass was so dense that the rabbit had come over to cool off in the heat.

The neem tree alone stood tall, its canopy lending shade to the God's abode. They looked for clayey soil and

brought a basketful to spread over the knoll. They then
went to bring some water. Until then, neither had spoken
much. Muthu seldom spoke while working. When he
did, it was only a word or two. 'How much he talks while
driving the cart. But when he unloads or loads the bags,
he does not utter a word,' they said about him at the rice
mandi. He called out loudly for Rosamma to join them. 'By
the way, Kuppanna . . . any news from the village during
the two days I was away?' Muthu started. Kuppan liked to
talk while working. He struggled to stay silent like Muthu.
As soon as the question was asked, words gushed out of
him like goats rushing out when the pen gates open.

He had spent the two nights at the village choultry.
The men there hadn't let him sleep for a long time. They
couldn't get over how Muthu and Kuppan had spent an
entire night on the field—evidently, it was a source of
unending fascination. They prodded him about Muthu and
his family. Kuppan got the impression that if they had been
ready to give one or two rupees more, there would have
been several others interested in selling their land to them.
Better land than what they had bought. It was a surprise
to them that the land he had bought had so much value.
'Let us make some money first, Kuppanna . . . We will
see about buying more land after that. It is only because
we bought this land that the rest have gained value. We'll
see . . .' Muthu told him.

About staying in the field, apparently one of the
men said, 'You can handle ghosts and spirits, insects and
animals. Just wait until Subbukodukkan returns. He hasn't
been seen around here recently. Maybe he is in jail. But

it won't be that easy for the police to capture him again. Maybe he has found greener pastures and gone elsewhere. His wife would have found out about these people staying in the field by now and would have sent him word of it. Just wait till he shows up. I'm sure you'll scuttle to move into the village.'

The naattamai had come to the choultry and chatted with Kuppan too. Everyone feared Subbukodukkan and a lot of stories about him were passed around. Ostensibly, he was very skilled at stealing cows and goats. He never went to a place where the cows and goats were kept tethered. He would see them when they were grazing and cast a spell on the goat he liked. While all the other goats returned to the pen, that goat alone would go seeking him instead. They even knew of cows that broke the long ropes they were tied up with, to run to him. He came to this region two or three times a year. When he did, they all went to him one by one and requested him to not harm their possessions. 'Please keep this chicken as a token,' they would say and offer him one. His favourite were full-grown roosters. He targeted the possessions of those who did not come to him.

He lived in a hut by a lake a couple of villages away with his wife and children. He was always travelling but his wife did not do any work. She cooked, ate and sat watching the path by the lake shore. If she wasn't found sitting there, it meant he was around. The children usually played around noisily. They raised a drove of pigs that loitered around there as well. It seemed that lately, he had been taking their eldest son along as well. That boy, lanky and tall like a palm tree, could not be spotted amongst the other children.

He did not limit himself to stealing cows and goats. If someone paid him to do something, like setting a farm or a stack of fodder on fire—and these were the simpler tasks—he would do so. Rumour had it that he had committed murders too, but those hadn't been ascertained.

'We should be very careful, Kuppanna. We should meet with the registrar, get the paperwork done and clear up the entire poramboke land. Right now, a whole band of thieves can hide there and we would never know,' Muthu said.

'We will clear up the portion that's in front of our land, saami . . . this section goes on and on a long way, doesn't it?'

'What can we do about that? We can fix our end of things. Maybe the other landowners will follow our lead and take care of theirs.'

The whole conversation about Subbukodukkan stirred several thoughts in Muthu's mind. He poured water over himself from head to foot, changed his komanam, and collected all the items for the altar mechanically, fully lost in thought, until he reached the rock. Kuppan was chatting with Rosamma and sharing a laugh.

What does Kuppan have to worry about? He works all the time. He never shrugs away from any sort of work. But, he does not bear any responsibility of rectifying this field or dealing with Subbukodukkan. He does all the work that Muthu does. He eats what Muthu eats. There is no difference between the two. Yet, Muthu is perpetually worried and Kuppan is never worried. Even while hunting the rabbit, Muthu was worried if they were going to be successful or not. Kuppan had no such thoughts. And he executed the task perfectly. Muthu felt he was carrying a big burden that was weighing him down. Maybe once he rectified the land and got the farming going, his burden would lessen.

Peruma had placed Karunchaami in a little onion basket, just large enough to hold about three kilograms of onions, with a lid. Inside the basket, wrapped within a plastic packaging for puffed rice, were some soil, the stone idol, camphor, incense sticks, *sambraani* or fragrant benzoin resin and a foot-long spear. There were three clay lamps in there too. He placed the stone idol carefully on the soil they had poured over the rock. He then placed tiny stones all around the deity to hold him in place even if the soil was washed away in a downpour. It was a smooth stone. Pongi had clearly looked for a good stone around the field and selected it. He planted the spear in front of the deity. Where would Peruma have bought such a small spear from? He bathed the deity with the water he brought in a pot and lit the sambraani in front of it. Rosa poured some oil in the clay lamps and added wicks to them so they could be lit. Since they didn't have a lamp protector, Kuppan created a tiny niche with large stones to protect the flame. A little bell was in there too, to be tied around a goat's neck. Muthu covered his mouth with a towel and began the ceremony. It was a very simple ceremony but Karunchaami would have surely descended into the stone. Why else would he have wanted the rabbit sacrificed?

Two lamps were placed in front of the deity. One sat in the niche. The three of them prayed together.

Oh Karunchaami of our land . . . please come and live here—all of this land is yours. You have to guide us and help us transform this land into all that I have imagined. Please protect us from theft and sickness. You are responsible for whatever happens within the boundaries of this land, your land. These people are scaring me with stories of Subbukodukkan. I hope to get through all perils with your support. Muthu prayed in his mind for a long time.

He then said to Rosa, 'Pray to Karunchaami. Say "My father has brought me to this forsaken land. Please bring my amma, akka and my little thambi so I can play with him soon. May the goats and the cows multiply, and my father send me and my sister away after marriage with abundant gifts".'

Rosa murmured the words as she prayed. Kuppan prostrated flat over the rock.

'Even if I forget, you must not forget, Rosa. Light a lamp and prostrate every evening.'

She nodded her head. He felt a relief that comes from accomplishing a task of great significance. *Let Subbukodukkan show up, I will teach him a lesson or two*, he thought and felt a strength from within. Early dusk started to set in. Muthu saw the bundle of grass that was cut from around the rock and a basketful that Rosa had cut. 'The oxen don't have to worry about their food today, Kuppanna!' he exclaimed.

'The child has cut so much grass. She is very smart indeed,' said Kuppan. 'This is all her mother's training.'

If they all saw a task each to completion, they could make the land healthy again soon. Muthu began to roast the rabbit over the fire. Kuppan helped Rosa light the stove. By the mercy of God, they were going to eat delicious food. Kuppan had kept a handy stock of arrack in the cart. He would tell Muthu about it after the meat was on the stove. He may hesitate because the little girl was around but there was enough only to wet their throats. Still, Kuppan was a little apprehensive.

If they could grind a paste for the saaru, they could eat to their stomach's fill. There was plenty of meat. The saaru would last the next morning, too. They could also make a dry roast with some chopped chillies, that could be tasty too. Suddenly, Muthu burst out, as though something just came to his mind. 'Kuppanna . . . you were narrating the story of Subbukodukkan, that he would come to rob us if we lived on our own in our farm. But he seems to steal things from the village too. What do they say about that? Why do they each give him a chicken then? An entire village fears a single man. I think these fellows are but a bunch of cowards,' he said.

'Yes, saami. What they mean is that if one lives within the village, there is safety in numbers. Say, if someone was to be beaten up brutally in the middle of a farmland, no one would be around to intervene. But we cannot have these people as our neighbours, saami. They are either at home or around where they live all the time. Only one or two heads can be spotted busily working in the fields. The rest are but homebodies— there is no dearth of enjoyment, entertainment and being in everyone's business all the time, just like my people, saami . . .' Kuppan chuckled.

Rosa, who joined them after putting a pot with water to boil, asked Kuppan, 'What is that, Thatha, the story of Subbukodukkan?'

'My goodness, you are indeed my young master's daughter, Aaya! How can you address me as thatha? Please call me Kuppaa.'

'How can I call you Kuppaa? It has to be thatha. But you must not address me as aaya.'

They all laughed at what Rosa said.

'How well you talk! Where did you learn to speak like this, Aaya?'

'See, you called me aaya again,' she said, annoyed.

'No saami, no saami . . . from now on, I won't use that word ever again. I will refer to you as saami. If your father is around, I will change it to chinna saami, my little master,' he said and Rosa laughed.

'You have to tell me the story of Subbukodukkan,' she insisted.

'Not at night, saami. I will tell you in the afternoon tomorrow,' he said to her politely.

Once the rabbit meat was seasoned and put to boil, they placed two more stones next to that stove and created another one on which they started cooking the kali. Rosa didn't have much to do. She didn't know enough to be able to cook rabbit meat. Muthu let her cook the kali and kept an eye on the rabbit meat. In between, Kuppan took Muthu to the cart and handed the bottle to him. Muthu said, 'Not bad, Kuppanna, you did a good thing' and then called out to Rosa. 'Rosa, bring the meat, dear,' he said. 'Why are you rushing, Appa? It needs to cook for a little

longer. Also needs some salt. Come, check for yourself,'
she replied.

How could he have let the arrack in his hand make
him suddenly so desperate for the meat? He thought as
he regained control of himself. He sent Kuppan to check.
Kuppan had her mix in a little more salt. He then had her
put four pieces of meat on a plate to check the toughness
of the meat. He took the plate to Muthu. 'Check the meat,
saami,' he said as he walked over.

Those pieces of meat were sufficient for them to finish
up their arrack. No matter how much it was cooked, rabbit
meat remained a little tough. They finished cooking it and
ate the meat sitting on the rock. It tasted really good with
the kali. It was their tradition to not leave any leftovers
from Karunchaami's sacrifice. So the three of them finished
the rabbit meat as if on a mission. Some kali alone was left
unfinished. They closed it with a lid and placed it carefully
on the cart with plans to dilute it with water and drink it
for breakfast the next day.

They spread out the gunny bags and bedsheets over
the rock to sleep on, when suddenly Muthu started crying.
'What happened, what happened, Appa?' Rosa panicked.
'Saami?' called out Kuppan . He too could not figure out
what was going on.

'Rosa darling, I'm making you sleep on a rock like this,
my dear,' Muthu wept louder.

'Tsk,' she muttered as she realized that her father was
inebriated. 'Just sleep, don't say anything,' she ordered just
like her mother would, then turned away from him and
went to sleep. Kuppan laughed quietly.

'Peruma, I have left you in my father-in-law's house. I've made my darling baby sleep on a rock here. When am I going to gather you all and treat you well?' Muthu continued grumbling. Rosa and Kuppan went to sleep on the other side from him. Neither intended to respond to Muthu's jabber.

'Kuppanna has left all his relatives to come here and be with me. At least half an acre will be yours for sure, Kuppanna. I will get that done next week. You don't worry. You are sleeping on a rock now but I will make sure you sleep in comfort soon. And Rosu, you are sleeping out in the open right now but soon I will make you sleep in a palace, just you watch,' Muthu continued on and then started laughing.

'Appa, are you not going to shut up and sleep? I will run away right now, otherwise,' threatened Rosa as she sat up.

'I won't anymore. You sleep, my dear,' mumbled Muthu as he put his head down. He passed out cold within seconds. It was the fatigue from working the minute he had returned from the trip.

28

It was a Thursday. Mattur, a village close by, had its market day on Thursdays. *Just like Karattur. It is easy to remember when the market was open.* Muthu woke up Kuppan while it was still dark and sent him to the market to buy hens and chicken. The man lying on the rock all night, hadn't slept a wink. He had watched the half moon go in and out of clouds until it went down the horizon, but hadn't registered any of it. His mind was brimming with thoughts of Subbukodukkan. *As soon as I mentioned to the naattamai that we were going to live on our land, the naattamai had immediately warned me about Subbukodukkan. Was he really all that these people made him out to be? If something were to happen after I moved Peruma and the children over to this place, how will I handle that? If there were going to be losses, will I be able to make up for them in this lifetime? I can correct the land, start farming, set up some security in place and then bring the family over. Then I won't have to struggle with protecting them in the middle of a farm with no relative to help in the vicinity. But if I propose this idea, would Peruma accept it? What can I say to convince her?*

On one side, Rosa was curled up in deep sleep. Her legs were bent like the little goat kids'. And then there was Kuppan, what a blessed man he was! He would go into blissful sleep the second his head touched the ground. And if he had a sip of arrack or toddy, he snored a cacophony of noises, like bandicoots fighting with each other. He didn't even spread a sack before lying down on top of the rock. 'The unevenness of the rock feels like a massage for my body, saami,' he said. Muthu stayed watching the two of them sleep and switch between sitting up and lying down all night. He hadn't been able to come to any conclusions. His eyes were burning as though he had consumed the extract of raw green chillies. The moonlight was gone but he could still see well, since the land was mostly barren. He served the rest of the grass that was in the basket to the oxen when they stood up on seeing him. He patted their backs affectionately. They gently grabbed some of the grass. He collected their dung and tossed it into a waste pit. This pit, almost as deep as a man is tall, must have been dug a while ago. The soil from that pit was sitting in a mound nearby. *That should be sufficient to start building walls for the house*, he thought.

He walked to the spring and brought back some water. The water in it was enough for a small pot to be immersed fully. Every time he saw the spring, he felt optimistic, that things would fall into place, just like the spring itself had. He drew out a couple of pots full of water and drenched himself with them from top to bottom. The water felt cool and comforting, even better than the evenings. It had been only about ten days, yet he felt a connection with the land as though he had been there for a long time. He was now familiar with its nooks and crannies. He felt a closeness to the land—enough to be able to walk on it freely, even in the dark. He had become aware of the bond one shared with land, the one on which he was born and grew up, only after he has to part with it. But this was different. This was like the bond that one felt and cherished with one's mind and body within an instant, like marriage.

He dried his hair and walked into the field as he squeezed out the water from his komanam. It was only when he reached Karunchaami's altar that he realized he was fully naked. He wrapped the towel around his waist and prayed to Karunchaami. He felt he spoke a whole lot to the God without actually uttering a word. Even though he didn't get any clarity, he felt assured that all will be well. He returned to the rock and sat there. A cluster of blackbirds began to chirp from one of the palm tree tops. Maybe they too suffer from sleeplessness, waiting all night for it to be time for them to start singing again. What work did they need to wake up so early for? The old man from Pattoor who had taught him to climb, used to say that God gave the blackbird a blessing that it would be the one to wake up all the creatures every morning.

There was still time until dawn. But if he woke up Kuppan, the skies would become bright by the time he would reach the market. 'Saami, did you not sleep?' asked Kuppan.

'Someone else asked for my gift of being able to sleep like you today. That's why my sleep went to someone else. It will return. Either tomorrow or the day after. Or a month or even a year from now, but it will return to me,' Muthu replied and smiled.

'Saami, don't be this way and not sleep. Only if you close your eyes for a little while, you can take the world, the people, the problems and the pain off your mind. Try not to give so much room to your thoughts,' said Kuppan.

'What can I do, Kuppanna, it is thinking that provides a living, and it is thinking that destroys a living too,' said Muthu.

An item he had to buy at the market was paddy rice—two measures of it. If there was something similar to a rabbit available, they could cook some rice with it. Then there were eatables such as puffed rice, pears and kacchaayam for Rosa. They needed rope to keep the oxen tied while they grazed. Rosa wanted rope for the little goats too. Muthu went through the list of all that was needed with Kuppan, and sent him off. Even though he wasn't used to going to markets, Kuppan always enquired in detail before buying anything. There was no rush anyway, he could take his time. Muthu had planned a lot of work for him to complete.

Once Kuppan left, Muthu grabbed the harness rope and his ladder from the cart and headed towards the palm trees. He was used to climbing trees before the break of dawn. He secured the harness around him, venerated the tree and began climbing. It had been a while since he had climbed one but how could he forget a skill he had worked so hard to acquire? He trimmed away the dried fronds that hung like matted hair. He worked his way through the dense overgrowth of sheaths and fronds. Many a times, mice built their nests in such overgrowth. And that attracted snakes to climb to the top of the tree as well. He needed to be extra vigilant. The spathes had collected over two years and dried in place. On the female palms, the fruits had scattered, exposing the completely dried-up toothless seeds. He didn't trim them back to the trunks but left a portion of the leaves.

On trees that had spathes, he trimmed away all of them. A couple of days of this and he would know which ones were worthy of tapping. By the time he finished all the trees, the sun was high up in the sky. He climbed down and drank some plain water. It was very messy around the trees with the spathes and leaves scattered everywhere, like a floor covered with discarded clothes. The leaves had to be dried and flattened, but he decided to do that work in the evening and hung his harness on the ladder which stood against one of the palms. The palms finally looked as though they had their hair cut. He then went to the spring and washed up. When he returned to the rock, Rosa had diluted the kali with water, ready for him to drink.

She had begun the task of preparing food when she saw her dad descend from the last tree. He took the lid on which she had served the kali and the plate with peeled onions from her, and paused to look at his daughter. She was but a child. Still in a skirt and blouse. Never mind that the full length skirt was already up to her knees. He could have asked Kuppan to buy a skirt and blouse for her. Maybe next week. In fact, he could take her along and have her choose one she liked. He was also very low on money. He had no income, nor the means for one yet. Moreover, he didn't know how much the land revenue official would charge for the deeds. He planned to update his accounts and take stock of the rest of the money. Rosa also drank some kali. The poor child had stayed on an empty stomach all morning.

In his enthusiasm to finish up the palm tree work, he had forgotten to pay attention to his child. She had found a good spot for the oxen to graze and had tied them up suitably. She carried water to the rock and washed all the vessels. She had cut grass and collected almost half a basket of it. He was so proud to see her work. He still carried the image of her grabbing a spear and covering one end of the rabbit hunt in his mind's eye. If everyone worked as diligently as Rosa, fixing the land was going to be easy. 'Is it hard without your little brother around, *kannu*?' he asked her. 'I have the little goats, Appa,' she giggled. It would be too much for her to work all the time. She needed someone her age to play with and have fun.

He drank the kali and lay down for a few minutes on the mat. The neem adjacent to the rock provided dense shade. There were so many boulders on the land. *Let's build the shed to cook and sleep in over this rock. The tract is also at an easy distance from here. Yes, this rock is best suited for it. It is directly across the place where the track becomes a two-lane road. People going in either direction can easily be seen from here. During the summer months, no one really uses the road. Once the farming season starts, people will start using the road actively. The path appeared clayey, likely from several years of carts moving on it. Should be able to see the people on the path clearly from the backyard. If anyone stepped into the farm or tried to harm the land, they can be spotted immediately. A fence should be raised around the property after a while. But until then, what was going to happen?*

There is no need to worry about people breaking into the house because of the mound. Planting a few more trees all around the rock like the neem that grew on one side, can turn this into a usable yard. The mound is spread over half an acre. It can be used even as a threshing ground. But then, everyone who passed by would be able to see it. Instead, the boulder located further inwards can be made a threshing ground. If one other mound can be used for piling hay and food for the animals, then there won't be a need to build a separate structure to store all that. All the rocky portions in the property probably adds up to about two acres, but they are needed too. The man who lay thinking about all this with his eyes shut, got up. If he whiled away time taking naps during the day, how would any work get done?

Rosa was collecting grass. 'Take a short break, won't you?' he told her. 'The little kids are missing me, Appa!' she giggled. 'Have they already forgotten their mother? Look how quickly they forgot her. That is the difference between animals and human beings. Are you giving them any water?' he asked. '*Mpakk*, mpakk . . .' he called out to them. They went running to him, thinking it was their mother calling them, and began to suck on his fingers. Just then, he heard the sound of a bullock cart pull into the farm. *Peruma has sent her brother over. Even though she was physically away, her mind and soul are very much here.* Rosa immediately recognized the sound of her uncle's cart. Behind Veerannan was a figure clad in a white sari, but he couldn't recognize her. He felt a fondness for Veerannan for finding his way over correctly. He wasn't expecting him—he assumed nobody was going to come by to help them for some time.

'Maama!' Rosa called out as she ran towards him. The goat kids too ran after her.

29

Thannaya *paati*'s sleep usually disappeared right as the blackbirds began to sing. She remained lying down, listening to their screeching voices. In all her years, she had never heard their voices from this close, as though they were singing into her ears. For the first few days that she had slept on the rock, she hadn't paid much attention to them. But when she started lending her ears to them, she felt that there was a discipline in their singing. Sometimes only one bird sang. When that bird stopped, the next one started to sing. Sometimes the two sang together without a pause. She felt there was a meaning to all that and began to try to decipher their sounds.

The first gruff voice that was loud must be a male bird, she decided. The voice that was soft and subtle was a female's. Every morning, they would discuss their agenda for the day. 'You go in this direction looking for food, I will go in the other direction. Before the heat rises, you must bring back a bug or worm or a piece of corn. We will meet up later. Shall we wager on who is going to bring more food? Until I return, you must remain in the nest. You can go after me. I will then take care of our things . . .' That was what paati imagined their conversations to be like.

At an early hour, when darkness still hadn't given way to light, no work could be done. If she tried to get down from the rock and hurt herself, it wouldn't bode well. Instead of being useful to her granddaughter's family, she'd have become a burden. Not only that. She would be branded as having travelled so far only to break her hip or leg. Was that necessary? She simply wanted to be of some use in the last few years of her life. So she didn't get up. Instead, she lay waiting and listening to the birds, letting her imagination take over. She even imagined the male bird to be her husband, Chinnaan. '*Edae* Chinnaan,' she called out one day and blushed coyly.

That was how she called him during their intimate moments when he was still alive. But other than that, she didn't ever call him by his name. If he was far, she would yell, 'oh *payaa*, payaa!' as though she were calling out to her son. He knew it was for him. Everyone in the village knew as well. When she referred to him in conversations with others, she'd say, 'my son's father'. It had been more than ten years since he had died. Still, thoughts about him came up every now and then. Somehow, listening to the bird's voice was like listening to him talk. Paati tried responding to the birds too. That turned out to be an interesting and convenient way to kill time during those sleepless hours. Otherwise who was she going to talk to on that rock in the middle of nowhere? Even back home, there wasn't anyone she could chat with at that hour.

Paati had a portion designated just for her, back home. She cooked separately for herself, too. 'Till there is strength left in my arms and legs, it is better to cook for myself. Why be a hassle to someone else? When we get hungry, they may be in the middle of some work. When they invite us to eat, we may not be hungry. If we make ourselves our own coffee or tea, we can eat and drink at the time we desire. We can even skip eating if that's what we want. When I'm bedridden, we will reassess things. Until then, everything will be separate,' she had said. She had no assigned work. She had no dearth of people around her—she had her son, daughter-in-law and grandchildren. She could do whatever she wanted to stay busy. She could tether the oxen, collect their dung. Once when she tried to tether a calf, she gave in to its pull and fell down. Her son chided her. 'Who asked you to do all this? Why can't you simply eat and stay put in the house?' No one ever asked her to do any work.

Instead of sitting around and being of no use at home, she decided to come here where she could be of some help to someone. Peruma was her granddaughter through her first son. 'Ammayi, Ammayi!' Peruma used to call her when she was little and wanted to be with Thannaya paati all the time. She lived in the same house as the one in which Peruma grew up. In fact, it was Thannaya paati who had practically brought her up, carrying her on her back and in her heart. Any time Peruma visited her hometown, she never missed paying a visit to her grandmother. She'd exchange a few words with her mother and then scurry over to see her grandmother. It was that intent—to be useful in her last years to a granddaughter she so cherished—that brought her here.

Ever since Muthu left with Rosa, Peruma had stayed watching the road. Muthu returned once more but said he couldn't take anyone back with him just yet. He told her about Subbukodukkan and said, 'Let me find out more about all that, give me a few more days. I will come back and take you all after that.' Peruma didn't like it one bit. But Muthu was firm about it. What could she do? Just how long could she stay on and eat at her mother's house? So she started cooking for herself in a separate shack. Unable to bear seeing her sitting around the rest of the time disengaged, Veerannan decided to head over to where Muthu was.

He had found out the way to Muthu's farm in his conversations with him. And he knew he could always ask around. Paati also got ready to leave with him. 'If he, as a man, has forbidden you to come over, there must be a thousand reasons for that, dear. Your daughter is on the verge of becoming a young woman, your son is still very young. He must have thought about all that. I am just an old bag of bones. I will go check on everything and spend some time there. You don't worry, take good care of your children,' paati said to Peruma.

Paati woke up as the skies lit up just enough to see one's face. It was the time when the sounds of different birds could be heard from all directions. The little girl Rosa was still asleep. Such a young girl. She was just like how Peruma used to be at her age. She occasionally wondered if she hadn't simply returned to her past. If she had to raise

Peruma once again, she would be younger too. This is Peruma's daughter, she reminded herself and a deep sigh calmed her just as she started to feel like everything was over. Looking at how deeply Rosa slept, she could never get herself to wake her up. It was only at this age that she could sleep until the sun soaked her in its light. Later, even if she wanted to sleep in, she wouldn't be able to. The pot that was atop the rock was always full of water. Every time Rosa or Muthu went by the spring, they brought back some water to refill the pot. Observing her granddaughter's husband up close gave paati much satisfaction. Not only did he not shy away from hard work, but he carried out every task with great commitment.

When she splashed her face with the water from the pot, the coolness spread all over her body. After she rinsed her mouth, she drank about half a small vessel full of the water that the kali was left to soak in. This had been a habit of hers for long. No feast could match kali water. If it was water mixed with pearl millet kali, all the better! It was like drinking sugarcane juice. It cooled her body and sometimes kept her feeling full even until midday. Once she took the palm spathes that were cut up like a broom and entered the farm, everything else faded away. From that point, until Rosa summoned her to eat lunch, it was only rocks with which she spoke.

When she first arrived here, she did not know what work she could take on. She thought she would simply be a guardian to Rosa who had got used to being here and kept herself busy by cooking food, cutting grass to feed the oxen and keeping company with the little goats. That first night when everyone was lying down on their mats in all directions, Muthu said to her very sincerely, 'it is our fate that we have to live like this, without a roof over our heads. Why do you, who have lived in comfort in a house with a generous front yard and a front plinth large enough for people to sit with their legs stretched out, want to live with us here on this rock? Even vagabonds live with a tent over their heads. We are lying here with nothing to protect us. You don't need to go through this. I will drop you back home tomorrow itself. I don't want to carry the blame of burdening you.' Paati simply laughed at what he said.

'Thambi, I have seen it all. My work is here, on this barren rock. What do I care for a land without rocks? They build homes, paint them with a mixture of plaster and eggs, but can all that compare to this rock, thambi? This rock comes directly from God to man. Sleep on this and it is most comfortable for your back; it feels as though someone was giving you a good arm and leg massage,' she replied. Kuppan, who was lying on a spread-out gunny bag, chuckled. 'You don't know her, saami. Her paternal home is in Sakoor. When she came to our village, it was as though Lady Prosperity herself had come over,' he said and began to narrate the story of Thannaya paati. Rosa, who loved listening to stories, got up from where she was lying down and scuttled over to sit next to Kuppan. 'Little saami loves stories,' Kuppan quipped.

The year Thannaya paati came into the village after being married into the family, they had harvested bountiful raagi. The water levels in the wells did not dip at all. With the abundance of moisture, the raagi plants grew as wide as outstretched arms. Not a single plant withered. The grains were big as pearls. She took the ears, cleaned them up and made tea for her mother-in-law. Even raw grains tasted sweet. Adding country jaggery to it made it all the more tasty. When the corns began to show signs of readiness, they fixed the date for harvest and sent word to the labourers. They had planted raagi on all four acres of their land. They needed a lot of help in harvesting it. Thannaya's mother-in-law sent announcements to all the labour settlements before the 9 p.m. horn sounded.

There usually was no dearth of help to harvest the ears. The farm got filled up with tottering oldies to children half their heights, each holding a basket tucked under their arms and a knife to cut the cobs. When the labourers were busy collecting the cobs, only their heads could be seen, looking like an army of ants, along with their moving knives. After harvest, it used to feel odd to see the plants with just leaves and no cobs as though bugs overran the land and collected all the cobs. Later, the land owner put some cobs back into every labourer's basket, proportionate to the number of cobs they had collected, as payment. For collecting cobs alone, the payment was not in the form of cash, it was only what the owner tossed back into the basket, no questions asked.

Thannaya's mother-in-law had invited all the labour communities. Everyone had seen the heads of the raagi plantations ripe and ready for harvest, and she knew that the crowds would come. So she got to the farms early with a few large baskets and pots of water and the entire family. But when the day broke, only ten people showed up at the farm. Out of them, five were women from their extended family and a few more were helpers from the landlord's house. That was it. At first, they did not understand why no one had showed up. It was only after one woman who had come to help explained that it became clear to them what had happened. The year before then, Thannaya's mother-in-law had given the labourers only a handful of cobs in return. The ladies who had worked all day had felt cheated because after the cobs had been dried and threshed, they could collect not even half a measure of grains from them.

This was the problem year after year. Thannaya's mother-in-law could simply not be generous. And the previous year had been especially bad. 'How could a woman be like this?' The entire village was saying. 'Her words are sweet but her actions are sour,' they said. That was why no one had showed much interest in helping with the harvest this year. 'Instead of spending the whole day in her farm and coming back empty-handed, we can do something useful around the house,' they said. 'If we aren't going to be paid well for our labour, then why bother when we can pass our time chit-chatting sitting under a tree instead? That is much easier than breaking our backs in the scorching heat for nothing,' said the oldies. The whole village stood them up as though they had ganged up against them. No one showed up from the Aalkudi labour community either. Thannaya's father-in-law's anger grew into fury and he began to chase the mother-in-law around the farm, beating her. People who were around had to intervene and stop him.

That day, aside from the ten who had come to assist them, Thannaya's mother-in-law, her husband's grandmother and she herself had gone to the farm as well. After they finished one section, they decided to stop and continue the next day. Since only the women of the landlord's house could pay the people who laboured on the farm, the father-in-law asked Thannaya to do so. She, who was still a new bride with her hair full of kanakambaram flowers and wrists full of bangles that jingled as she moved, dropped three generous handfuls of cobs into the labourers' baskets and filled them up to the brim. 'The landlord's house is blessed by the goddess of wealth in the form of a daughter-in-law! How she smiled as she filled our baskets. The wages didn't come from her hands, they came from her heart,' the women sang her praises all around the village.

The next day, the labourers arrived at the farm even before daybreak. Even before the labour siren was sounded at 10 a.m. at Karattur, the work was completed. That day, too, Thannaya gave away cobs for wages generously and from her heart. The labourers too carried their filled-up baskets on their heads with a satisfied smile and words of praise on their lips. Every year after that was the same. Kuppan continued, 'You see, to date, there is no one who comes even close to matching her generosity.' Since Peruma called Thannaya 'ammayi', her children called her that too.

'Ammayi . . . if you give away all the cobs to the labourers, then what will the land owners be left with?' asked Rosa.

'She's so little but look how inquisitive she is!' praised Thannaya paati before continuing to explain. 'The wages are always proportionate to the harvest, dear. By giving to the ones who do the work, we are not going to have any less. When they are happy, they speak words of joy, you see, which turns into better yield in the following year. When labourers are filled with satisfaction, our lands are filled with yield.' Rosa listened intently.

Now, Kuppan could not let a conversation come to an end so easily. 'It was only after she came to the family that the farm grew into something of consequence. She singlehandedly rectified four acres of land on the west end. No matter what time of the day, she was on the farm collecting rocks. In four or five years, the soil became perfect, you see,' he added. Muthu found that surprising. 'Could you just collect stones from the soil like that?' he asked.

'Yes, thambi, it is possible. You leave a stone, you lose a plant. Imagine how much you would lose if you had a land full of rocks. Let's say we clean up one portion of land this year. When we plough the land and loosen the soil, the rocks will come to the top of the soil. We take the rocks out. Next year, we till the soil and there will be more rocks. We will collect them again. And we repeat this over and over again. In about three or four years, the land will be ready. You won't find a stone even to pelt a goat or a cow with. The soil should be smooth, like the ash you smear on your forehead. That's when you can farm on it. If you leave the stones around and plant amidst them, no matter how great the soil, your yield will be less than desirable,' she explained.

'There are stones everywhere in this field,' Muthu said.

'I noticed that too, thambi. I was wondering what sort of work I could help with when I was on my way here. This work is mine now. My life cannot end before I gather all the stones from this land. That's why our God has sent me here. I saw you have cut up a heap of palm fronds. Pick ten or fifteen good ones from among them and slice them in a way that I can use them to gather stones, thambi. I can get started this morning. My granddaughter is my life. But just saying that doesn't mean anything. I need to do something like this,' she replied. Muthu sliced a few palm fronds for her that morning itself, even before the sun rose. Because he wouldn't have been able to rectify all of the land himself, Muthu had decided that he would focus on three or four acres of land and start small. Those acres were located right in the middle of the field. That way, they could keep working all around and the tilled lands would remain protected too. He pointed out that region to her first.

The whole field was divided into very small portions. He planned to combine a few of them to make a larger portion so it was easier to bring water, as well as to plough the land. Paati got started right there. She turned towards the direction of the temple and prayed. 'Ayya . . . please help me finish this task fully. I promise to come to your temple and fall at your feet,' she prayed. Muthu heard the sound of the palm fronds scraping against the ground. He didn't believe that the stones could be gathered by sweeping. One can sweep the front porch clean, or a workshop or even a threshing ground. But a field? Paati wrapped the loose end of her sari over her head and settled herself in one of the smaller portions. The sound of her drawing the frond over the field could be heard constantly.

Muthu watched her for a little while and then went on to take care of his work. Kuppan was clearing the dangerous thorny bushes. Muthu's focus on that day was to get the palm fronds ready. He had enough to get at least 300 of those, he estimated. He needed them to build a hut on the rock. Then the grandmother and the great granddaughter can sleep there comfortably. The men can sleep anywhere. When the sun started shining bright, he decided to take a break and check on paati's progress. He peeped from a distance, not wanting to be seen by her. He first noticed that she hadn't changed her position since he had last seen her. He also spotted a few small gatherings of stones here and there. *Alright, let her do what she wants*, he thought to himself and went back to his work.

Paati continued to gather the stones with the palm broom. She drew a circle as far as she could reach and gathered the stones within that circle in one neat heap. That portion had plenty of lime chalk stones that were easy to collect. Pregnant women liked to nibble on these stones as they had a sweetish taste to them. They could also be used to create the landing in front of the house. First, these stones must be spread out and packed in place. Then, they would have to be covered with dirt. If built properly, the chalk stone would hold the dirt together in a way such that no amount of rain could dissolve the assembly. Such a landing built with chalk stone could also be used to dry the portion of produce that would be given to labourers for their efforts. Paati took a small, fully formed stone and popped it into her mouth. Not just to pregnant women, the stone tasted sweet to anyone. She made a mental note that she must have them gathered and heaped separately.

The stones gathered from one circle added up to a small basketful. That was quite a bit. By the time the whole portion was swept for stones, they would have cartloads. When she finished about half of that portion, she felt her stomach twist with hunger. She needed to eat something. Her hips and back hurt. She couldn't bend to work for long like she used to be able to. Her legs were stiff and she found it difficult to stand up again. She got up and walked slowly, shaking her legs loose. She then got out of that portion and looked at the portion standing on the divider. The area she had worked on looked like a front porch that had been swept by a child. Tiny stones still remained in plenty. One more sweep and she would be able to get them out too.

After she reached the rock, she drank the mixture of kali and water and slept for a long while under the neem tree. It was only after Rosa woke her up to drink kali for lunch that she realized where she was. Two pieces of shallots to accompany the watered-down kali. After she ate, she didn't feel sleepy again. But it was too hot to go back to work on the land. She had Rosa hand her two measures of pearl millet from the sack, sat herself down in the shade of the tree and began to winnow the chaff from the grains. She could have Kuppan pound them later. She would cook it in the morning and everyone could eat it with relish. They could have kali one day and cooked pearl millet the next. There needed to be enough food to feed two men who spent all day working hard in the fields. The pearl millet could be served with cluster bean stew. She finished winnowing and lay down under the tree again. When the sun began to descend, she got up and picked up her broom. As she made her way back to the portion where she was working earlier, she called out to Kuppan, who was still cutting away the thorny shrubs and said, 'Come over there later with the hand spade and basket.'

She continued to sweep the rest of that portion. She was so focused on her work that all she saw was the movement of her broom as it rolled the stones over to gather them in a pile. The more she swept, the more stones seemed to surface. She flipped over a rather flat, palm-sized stone carefully. About four or five baby scorpions began to scatter, running in all directions. She crushed them all using the same stone. She became a bit concerned that something like this happened as the evening rolled in. At the same time, she remembered that wherever scorpions live, the soils tend to be very good. That thought made her happy. When only a corner about the size of a sari was still left to be swept, Kuppan came by. 'Kuppa, this portion is full of lime. It could come in handy to build a porch tomorrow. Collect this and store it separately, maybe by that boulder there,' she said and continued to sweep the leftover portion. When she was done with this portion, she would call it a day. 'Saami . . . when they lay scattered they were barely noticeable. This is excellent lime. If our men saw this, they would take all of it to make lime plaster,' he said as he gathered all the lime in the basket, carried it over to one side of the rock and poured it all out.

There, by that boulder was a smaller boulder, barely visible with most of it hidden under the soil. Add a forearm's length of soil over it and that could be used to farm as well. The plaster collected in a tiny little mound over that rock.

The next day, she gathered together little rocks in the same portion of land. It is easy to collect rocks big enough to roll. The ones that were finer had to be gathered by running the broom very close to the dirt in a way that the mud got left out but the tiny rocks didn't. It took a lot longer that day. She had Kuppan gather the fine gravel into a separate pile. When Muthu saw all this, he was truly astounded.

In ten days, there was a large pile each of lime, fine rock and brick stone. Muthu realized that paati was no ordinary woman and he believed she could sweep the whole field and get it prepared for farming. 'There are scorpions scattered about across the land, thambi. Their presence only means that this land is gold. You won't find scorpions in untreatable land,' paati said to him. That made him feel even more assured. If she swept all of the land, they would collect an enormous pile of rocks. What was he going to do with all of it? After the first rain, they will be able to find out where the rainwater drains from and where the soil gets eroded. Once he knows that, he can pile the rocks up to bolster that side of the bank so that the water stays contained. While Muthu stood gazing at the skies wondering when the next rainfall was going to be, paati continued on without a thought in her mind.

30

It was peak afternoon. Muthu was lying on a cot under the neem tree. Waves of heat from the sun forced his eyes shut. It was Chitthirai, the onset of summer. Once the sun came up in the sky, it was impossible to do any work in the field. By now, almost all of the thorns and shrubs had been cut away. Except for the two vellaivela trees by the perimeter, they had cut down everything to their roots. The two goat kids chomped on the leaves of the vela trees all the time. A few of the neem trees also were spared; they could remain until the sowing begins. They could cultivate most of the land this year. The neem trees in areas left uncultivated could be left alone. They came in handy for tethering cattle to and for their shade. After all, the shade of the neem tree is unparalleled. There were tree stumps visible here and there, drying in the heat. The stalks lay strewn all around the field. Once they were dry enough, they could be collected and bundled up to be taken and sold to Saethur's firewood seller. They must add up to about three cartloads. The wood they got from the thorny bushes was sufficient for their cooking.

Whenever Rosa had some time, she shaved the thorns off the stalks of the black seemai karuvela, trimmed the long ones to stalks of similar lengths and made small bundles of them. She chose a rock at the edge of the low-lying area and continued to stack the bundles over that rock. Small bundles that were easy enough for her to carry. It was mesmerizing to watch the way her hands moved when she shaved the thorns off the stalk. There were enough bundles to last them for a whole year. This particular thorny bush was bad for the soil—it was detrimental to farming. In Aattur, they would pluck this shrub as soon as they spotted it, even if it was barely a sprout. But not here. These shrubs could be seen everywhere. The firewood would fetch at least twenty or thirty rupees. The money could be used to invest more in the farming efforts. It would still take several days to clear all of the dense growth. Just cleaning one spot took a whole day. They left the aavaarai tree as it was. Rosa kept staring at it and remained fascinated by it. Apparently paati used to be fascinated by the tree the same way too.

Food was not an issue. The gunny bags of rice that Veerannan had brought with him would last for another month or two. Should Muthu want more, he would bring more, enough to last a whole year. He had brought paati to give Rosa company. But paati was really so helpful herself. The work she did and the way she did it with so much patience! No one could match her. In these times of despair, it had been the family that he married into that had come forward to help. His own kith and kin were nowhere in sight. If he prospered, perhaps his family would line up to move close by. Apparently Pongi had sent word to find some land for him too and that he would move there as well. But why could he not have come by once to check on him? Veerannan had already come by twice in the past two months. Every time he came, he brought along all sorts of things in his cart. Seeing Muthu feel awkward, Veerannan said, 'Why not, Maama? We only have each other to help. If I was in need, won't you have come forward to help me?'

When Muthu got married to Peruma, Veerannan was a little boy. At the time, during the ceremony, when he had to put on a ring, Veerannan was nowhere to be found. They looked all over for him for so long that Peruma and her mother began to cry. Veerannan was barely aware of what was going on. He saw the crowd and all the din and had got scared. But how could they have someone else play that role when Peruma had a brother of her own? In the end, they finally had to drag him by his hands through the crowd, his nose runny and face teary, and sit him down for the ceremony. Now, he was grown enough to provide support to Muthu.

Even the cot that he lay on had been brought by Veerannan. He had dismantled the legs and the frame, tied them up and rolled up the rope separately. He brought two cots. Kuppan and he had spent half a day setting them up and weaving the rope. The pattern they had made with two bonds leading to a square in the middle had turned out quite nice. Rosa's eyes had been transfixed on them when they were weaving the cots. Once they were finished, she jumped on to one and tried different sleeping postures. He stayed for two nights and a whole day. In that time, whatever work he did stood there reminding them of

him long after he had left. His idea for determining the
location for a well, turned out to be very useful. After they
finished the rest of the work and after the first showers,
they could finish sowing seeds and then begin digging
the well. When they started that work, he said he would
bring four or five men from their village for help. After
the sowing season was over, there won't be much work
to do back home anyway. A thirty-feet deep well had a
good chance of striking groundwater. He could not leave
everything as it was and go home, even though Peruma
was most certainly waiting for him every minute of the day.
He sent word through Veerannan that she wait for three
more months. He needed to make a larger shelter for them.
He also wanted to size up the problem of Subbukodukkan
before he brought Peruma over.

Even though he was lying down, he wasn't really
sleeping that afternoon. As he rolled over, he saw four or
five hazy men walking towards him from a distance. He
watched them without fully opening his eyes, wondering
who would come there at that time. But as soon as he could
hear the voices, he sat up. A few men were approaching
him, along with the naattamai. *If they are coming here in
this heat, this must surely be about the incident from two days
ago*, he thought to himself. He quickly rehearsed some
responses in his mind anticipating their questions.

On the way to the low-lying area over to the west of
the property was a small section of land that was verdant
and lush, covered with a variety of grasses and climbers.
It was an idea that Muthu had implemented for this
piece of land to be green even in this season. At the end

of each day, Muthu bathed after work. He drew four or five pots full of water from the spring and bathed as much as he wanted. 'I can keep bathing in this water endlessly, Kuppanna,' he said. Until Muthu felt the coolness of the water within him, Kuppanna kept drawing water for him. He had worried that the spring may dry up in the summer heat but nothing of the sort had happened thus far. There was enough water to meet all their needs. Muthu then drew water for Kuppan, despite his protests. 'Why are you drawing water for me, nga? What will the people who see this say? What will paati say? If I go into the village tomorrow, they are all going to mock me by saying you bathe me,' he tried pushing back. But Muthu wasn't bothered by that. 'Let anyone say what they want. You enjoy your bath, Kuppanna,' he responded. So as not to trouble him more, Kupanna protested the whole time. 'Enough saami, enough saami.'

'More water, Kuppanna, cool yourself down with this spring water, Kuppanna. More water from our own spring, Kuppanna,' Muthu said.

'You are young blood, I, on the other hand, am bent out of shape with fatigue. Any more of that spring water and I will die of cold. Just because a needle is made of gold, one should not poke one's throat with it, you see.'

'Who is bent out of shape, you? Judging by how you work, you are in good enough shape to take another wife,' Muthu replied, poking fun at him.

'Sure, why don't you look for a bride from this area. She can be of help at the farm along with everything else,' Kuppan chuckled.

'We can find one, no problem. But what if she ends up having a child or two?'

'So what if she does? How does it matter how many there are? It matters only if there is property, land or house to worry about. They will fly away like little fledglings spreading their little wings as soon as they learn to fend for themselves. No harm there, saami.'

Bantering like that the made the whole act of bathing seem so joyful. Even jumping into the well and resurfacing from the deep waters back home didn't equal this feeling in the body and mind. The work he did in his twenties was but a ritual. Working to create something new was euphoric. He was so engrossed in every task he did that he became oblivious to everything else around him. And no matter how much he worked, he never felt tired. He was able to feel that joy of taking a bath in that spring at the end of each day. On the days when the moon was up, bright in the sky, he felt like going back to work after his bath. It was paati who stopped him. 'There are many red scorpions here, thambi. What if something untoward were to happen in the night? You can continue in the morning.' He didn't feel like disobeying paati. He told himself that the least he could do for that old woman who had come so far to be of help to him, was to give her the satisfaction of being listened to.

Sometimes Rosa would come to the spring at dusk to take a bath. His little girl. An age where she should be jumping into wells and swimming till her eyes turned red. Boys could do that at any age. Girls, if they missed that narrow window of time, would lose the pleasure forever.

Whenever she went to the well, she never wanted to get out. Peruma used to pelt her with stones from the top and force her to climb out. 'If a girl enjoys so much, she will not be able to give up pleasure. Stay under control. You aren't a boy who can do anything you want,' she warned her. 'Go away, Amma!' Rosa would climb out with a shrunken face, disappointed. For such a child, how was bathing from a pot going to be enough? No matter how many pots of water were emptied on her, she would plead for more. 'I'm not able to draw enough to sate little saami,' Kuppan would have to declare. In those moments alone, Muthu had nothing to say.

The cold water did not suit paati. At the onset of darkness, she would heat up a pot for herself. She set up a stove just to heat her water. She collected a stash of dried palm fronds and other barks and branches for that sole purpose. She didn't spare anything in the forest that could be burned. When she lit the stove, tongues of fire had to engulf the pot on all sides. She would warm her hands in that glow as the water boiled. At the tea stand, a curious few had asked Muthu, 'How come you have such a big fire every day on your land?'

'That is to drive away spirits,' Muthu responded with a smile.

The water paati used for her bath had to be hot. Indeed, she liked it piping hot. 'Ammayi, if you bathe in such hot water, won't your skin burn?' Rosa asked her. 'Your mother also asked me the same question. I'm used to this, my dear. You too bathe in hot water, your dark skin will become lighter,' paati replied with a laugh.

'Look, Daddy, ammayi is making fun of my dark skin,' Rosa whined to her father.

'Don't worry about all that, my dear. A mirror for the one with dark skin, a slap for the one with light skin,' Muthu replied. Paati had a wheatish complexion.

'Looks like the two of you are going to land some blows on me,' she said and cackled, showing her toothless mouth. Muthu had noticed that paati enjoyed such conversations. So he indulged in them often.

It was Muthu who changed where they bathed. He placed a large vessel that he bought at the Mattur market and set it in a divided portion by the low-lying area. One of them had to keep filling it up while another bathed from it. He moved the vessel a little every day around that portion of land. Just as Muthu expected, by the eighth day, he saw grass sprout up in that area. Because he kept moving it, the whole portion of land got water and began to sprout. In a fortnight, the whole portion was fully covered with grass. He trimmed them every two days to feed the oxen, who, in turn, thoroughly enjoyed it. They literally devoured it within the bat of an eyelid! 'Did you really feed them just now?' paati would ask Muthu. Thereafter, because they wanted to make sure that the grass got enough water, they all bathed more than usual.

When so much effort went into growing the grass, how could they be quiet if someone else cut their grass and took it away? One afternoon, when everyone was resting after lunch, paati felt a rumbling in her stomach. 'With an arsehole like mine, why do I need to go to shit in this bright afternoon,' she mumbled as she made her way to the low-lying area. In what seemed like a scene from a movie, she saw someone cutting the grass from that portion. She saw the movements of a sari. She immediately raised her voice. 'Who the hell is this who thinks she can steal from our farm in the middle of the day? Who thinks she can use anyone's fence to scratch her itch? We work our backs off to get the grass going and you think you can just come by and take it all?' She yelled without a pause, as she would have back in her village.

The woman who was cutting the grass must have been less than thirty. As she stood up, her nose ring flashed in the sunlight. She had collected half a basket of grass already. 'Ey, one with the nose ring, don't you try your tricks here. I will chop that bun off your head, better watch yourself. Now, drop that basket and scamper,' paati barked as she gestured a punch. She then rushed towards her, grabbed the woman's basket, dumped all the cut grass on the ground and flung the basket back at her. It had been quite a while since she had had a fight like this. It was rare to see people around here. Paati exchanged a word or two with the women who passed by the farm. This woman, however, didn't get even a second to respond to paati. Only after paati had hit the basket a couple of times and tossed it into the next portion of land did she open her mouth. 'You come to my village and you think you can get away talking to me like that, you old bitch? Just wait and see what I do to you,' she shouted back while grabbing her basket and walking away briskly. Only after she heard the woman say 'my village' did paati realize that she was in another village, not her own.

The way that woman walked away seemed like she was
going to bring big trouble. *Why did I speak like I would at
home? I came here to be of help at my granddaughter's and here
I am causing trouble instead*, paati grew frightened. She had
seen how Muthu always addressed the locals with caution
and politeness. He even warned Kuppan to not get into
any situation 'with these people'. He hadn't explicitly said
anything of the sort to paati or Rosa. Maybe because they
don't go out or because he didn't think they could cause any
trouble, but it never occurred to him to tell them. But now
that the trouble had come through paati, what was Muthu
going to do? Paati felt a burden weighing her stomach
down. She quickly relieved herself, washed up with the
water in the pot and rushed to the tree under which Muthu
was taking a nap.

When Muthu saw paati rushing over to him, crying,
'Thambi . . . look what happened when I went to the patch
at this hour,' he panicked, thinking that maybe she was
bitten by a snake or such.

'Where, where?' he asked. Kuppan and Rosa came
running too.

'Not that, thambi. An unknown woman adorned with
a single stone nose ring was cutting the grass from our
portion of the land. Without finding out why she did that,
I simply yelled at her. For a second then, I forgot that we
are in a different village. She left angrily. Not sure what she
is going to do, thambi,' paati explained. That made Muthu
calm down a little. Had she been bitten by a snake or some
other creature, he would have had to carry the blame of

abandoning her in an unknown place. He was relieved that it was not that sort of issue.

'Is that all? I thought you got bitten by something and I panicked. Let them come. Let any number of them come. We can take care of that,' he said to comfort her. His eyes scanned all four corners of the land, went back in the direction of the village and held still.

31

The recipient of paati's scolding was not going to let matters be, she was going to march over to the village and bring people—or so Muthu had anticipated. But nothing of that sort occurred. The afternoon heat burned his head. It had rained only once since he had moved here. Just enough to till the land once. They had tilled the two portions of land from which paati had removed all the rocks and pebbles. But one round of tilling wasn't sufficient. The land had hardened from neglect. The plough didn't go through the soil. It felt like splitting rock. He tilled it a second time. This time, paati sowed half a measure of green gram. However, there was no rain after that to raise the crops that broke through the land like palms brought together in veneration. The goats nibbled on the crops. The heat didn't abate one bit. He feared that every year would turn out to be this way. If there was no rain, did it matter how good the land was? He was certain that the month of Vaikasi would bring some rain. That seemed to be the view at the tea stall, too. The groundnut seeds and corn that Veerannan brought were stored carefully in the hut.

It occurred to him that the people would come over when the sun was making its descent. The people of this place loved comfort. They would not give it up for anything, no matter how important. *Would be better if they came during sundown*, he thought. The issue would also cool down and so would the urge to retaliate. Their ears would be more open to listening. 'Saami, don't utter a word to them. You can touch burning cinders, but you can't take back words that have been spoken,' Kuppan cautioned him. 'May my mouth rot. What is the point of growing old?' paati reproached herself constantly. Muthu's mind was filled with thoughts about how many people might show up, what kind of questions they might ask, and what his responses should be. If no one appeared, then he planned to go into the village and talk to the naattamai himself. Or, early in the morning, when the naattamai came to the tea stall at the bottom of the hill. It may be better to talk to him there instead of going to the village at night. If he spoke to him calmly, he would take care to not let this grow into a problem. Many older men who were now familiar with him could potentially help him too. But he had to be cautious, for regardless of how familiar they may be with him, they would definitely side with their own over an outsider.

Muthu went to the tea stall once every week or ten days. After he woke up early in the morning to feed the cows, he couldn't go back to sleep. Instead of tossing and turning in his cot, if he went over there, at least he could keep himself updated on any news from the village. While he was in that area, he ascended the knoll and went to the temple too. It was nice to climb the knoll before sunrise. The hill had no steps; the path appeared like a slide, made of just lumps of soil and rocks. At Karattur, the knoll had steps. A healthy person could quickly climb all the way to the top without stopping. The older folks had shelters for rest, mandapams, as they made their way up. But this knoll wasn't for older people. The mud path would be too slippery, even with a stick to support them. The only steps were the few closer to the temple at the top. Many people from all villages around the region came to the tea stall.

Those who seemed new at first had slowly become more and more familiar. Among them was a trustee of the temple. On the first day of their introduction itself, Muthu mentioned to him, 'I come once every five days to see the God and offer my salutations, nga, regardless of whether the priest is there or not.'

'They told me at the tea stall that you go up to the temple. Somehow God manages to include even those new to the town,' said the trustee.

'God always includes, nga, it is the people who find it hard to,' replied Muthu.

The trustee's face shrank a little. 'What makes you say that? Tell me if you have any problem with anyone.'

'Aiyo, don't read between the lines, nga. I was only saying that generally,' Muthu responded and began to talk about the steps leading to the temple.

He said, 'This is the God who pointed me to this land. I noticed during the Maasi festival that throngs of people come here. So, as my contribution, I will build ten steps. Not this year, let one more year pass. Once I reap my crops and see some money, I will inform you. Please enquire around and let me know if anyone else wants to contribute as well. We can build it together. If we build about twenty or thirty steps, it will make it easier for people to reach the temple.' The trustee was very pleased. He mentioned this to several people after that. This man from the west was talked about so much that everyone in the neighbouring region had come to know of him. 'This is all our God's handiwork,' Muthu told Kuppan.

The naattamai never missed visiting the tea stall. Muthu had planned to meet him there to have the conversation. But before he talked to him, ten men showed up at his farm that afternoon. It was clear from their faces that they planned to fight. But they came with empty hands. 'If a woman shows up alone, you think you can say whatever you want to her?' one of them asked. 'Show us the prowess that you showed to that woman,' said another.

'Please don't yell unnecessarily without knowing what transpired,' Muthu replied. By then, Kuppan, paati and Rosa came to stand by him. He had already instructed them that no matter who came and what they said, only he would do the talking.

'Sure, why don't you put up a dais and describe in detail,' responded another.

Muthu had seen some of them at the tea stall and on the pathways by the farm. But he had never been introduced to any of them. They had begun their interaction by casting the aspersion that they had manhandled a woman. *I should not go too easy on them*, he thought. Each one had come charged and was saying whatever came to his mind. Paati came forward. 'I was the one who picked up a fight with that woman. Don't we have cattle and goats that need to graze on the grass that we have grown on our land? Does this look like a land just lying around? We have paid a full 200 for it and are toiling on it daily. If someone saunters over and takes what is ours, why would we be quiet? Look at the group that has come to talk about fairness. Send that woman over, this should be settled between her and me. Why are you all getting involved in a dispute involving women?' she shouted at them. It wasn't clear if they understood even half of what she said. But in that moment, even if they picked up only a word or two, the message should have reached them.

'You think you can use an old woman to hit us,' said one man as he leaped forward and put his hand on Muthu's chest and shoved him.

It was clear that they had come to exacerbate the situation and draw Muthu into a physical altercation. Even though he knew that if this ended up at the panchayat tomorrow, there would be no one to take his side, he didn't want to hold back out of fear. He instantly yelled to Kuppan, 'Pull out the arivaal, Kuppanna. Doesn't matter if I die in the process but I'm not going down before chopping off a few heads,' all the while looking at the man. Kuppan rushed to grab the arivaal. The man who had shoved Muthu was not very strong and was much like a dried castor stalk. His hand had felt mushy on his chest. He noticed everyone was like that. When they saw Kuppan turn up with the arivaal, they were frightened. Still, they didn't want to appear to be.

A middle-aged man stepped forward and said, 'You are rushing into things. Watch yourself. If you raise your arivaal like this, how will you survive here?'

'Agreed, anna. If I am spoken to the way you are speaking to me now, why would I touch the arivaal? If you talk to me as though I grabbed that woman's hand, how will I not get angry? On top of that, if I placed my hand on your chest in the middle of a conversation, would you stay quiet? My hands and legs are strong too. I'm not going to simply sit there and bear the insult. Sometime or the other, death is certain anyway. At least this way, I would be known for dying fighting,' Muthu exploded.

That man immediately turned around to the rest and said, 'Scram now, stop messing with this man.' He turned to face Muthu again and said, 'Don't you take all this seriously, *mekaarare*, the man from the west . . . apparently, when her basket was tossed, it broke to the point of being useless. When a woman comes over crying, who will not get angry? That too when her husband came over to us, angry. We thought we should confront you. What are you going to do about the basket now?'

'What you say makes sense. I can maybe buy her a basket. That's all. But going forward, there should be no business of trying to take this and that from our land,' Muthu replied, calming down. He was certain that the group would leave.

'Okay . . . just give the money for the basket to her husband. We will leave,' said the man.

There was a lot of murmuring amongst themselves. A discussion about how much money to ask for. He figured out that they were making plans to spend the money on toddy. 'I will buy a basket from the market. Ask that lady to come by and pick it up,' Muthu announced.

Immediately, one of the men said aloud, 'No way. Give us the money. As though you know what kind of basket she will want.' They finally managed to collect a rupee from him and left the place. He knew that the rupee was way more than the cost of a basket and that he could have sent them back without any money. But the men wouldn't have left without taking anything. He had to pay them something for the sake of maintaining peace.

Muthu assumed that it was to discuss this incident that the naattamai and the rest of the men were now coming over.

32

The man who had sat up from lying on his cot did not stand up until the approaching men got much closer. In a flash, he walked a few feet forward and welcomed them with his hands joined. They were not used to that but they still managed to return the greetings by barely putting their hands together. He waved to a few to sit on the cot under the neem tree. A few more sat on the smaller rocks that lay there. 'I don't even have enough seats to seat you all. You could have sent word and I would have come to see you. You wouldn't have had to come to this barren land,' he said.

'Not a problem, mekaarare. Moreover, if it is our issue, we should be the one to come to you,' replied the naattamai. Muthu did not know what he was referring to. He began to doubt again if this was about the basket lady.

One of the men said, 'We are organizing a feast at the temple.' Muthu felt relieved.

'I'll be right back,' he said entering into the little hut on the rock to find paati. He said to her, 'They have come here about a feast for the temple. Nothing else.' Paati's face relaxed too, after hearing that. She picked up the palm comb and left to continue collecting more rocks. Kuppan was in the middle of tethering the oxen. Muthu filled a large sombu with water and served the men. He instructed Rosa to bring more water from the spring. After drinking the water, the naattamai said, 'The water from your well is sweeter than the water we get in the village.' Muthu pointed upwards and said, 'Don't know what I did to deserve such a spring,' and continued on to ask them, 'What should I contribute to this festival, please tell me.' The men looked at each other's faces.

It was the naattamai who broke the silence. 'The incident that occurred the other day reached my ears, mekaarare. Whether we should take money from you for the temple or not has led to a huge fight. Whatever said and done, you should have not picked up the arivaal. This is a place where my people live. If you had a problem, you could have come to me. I would have shaken some sense into those useless fellows. Because of that, we have a few people refusing to let you be a part of the festivities. They say, "If he has already dared to pick up the arivaal, this stranger would claim more authority if we let him pay for the temple." Some of us think you should pay your dues to the temple. But then, beyond praying there and making offerings, you must not claim any other rights. What do you say?' he stopped. Muthu felt this was a good opportunity to show camaraderie to the villagers.

He replied quickly. 'I will act as you direct. I will pay my dues. I will make my offering. That is enough for me. What do I need beyond that? If you let me, I will come to your temple. If you don't want me to, I won't. The other day, one of them placed his hand on my chest as I was talking and shoved me forcefully. That is why I got angry. If he hadn't first shoved me, why would I grab my arivaal? That too, I only asked Kuppan to bring the arivaal to me, I didn't actually take one in my hand,' he said.

'See! I told you he will comply with what we say,' the naattamai said cheerfully, looking at the others. He turned to Muthu and said, 'The tax is two rupees per household. We start the *koya nombu*, the official kick off, next week. You can pay after that.'

'I will pay then. If you are planning to include *karakaatam* or any other entertainment, I will pay five to help a little towards that expense as well. Two will go towards the temple and please take three for the dance. On one of the festival days, we will serve country palm jaggery tea to everyone who comes to the temple.'

The men were satisfied. Their faces were clear and fresh and they were all smiling as they left. Muthu accompanied them to the road. They told him that after the temple festival in the month of Chitthirai, this region gets two or three showers. That's when they prepare the land. Sowing in this region was done only in the month of Aadi, two months later. To grow groundnuts, Vaikasi would be the right time. Groundnuts were not grown in this region, typically. Most likely, Muthu would be the first one to grow them. Maybe a few more may try sowing groundnuts in Vaikasi next year.

Once they reached the cart road, they stopped and chatted with him for a little longer. One of them said,

'They say Subbukodukkan is on the prowl in this area these days. Stay alert.'

'You have your cattle, poultry, goats, everything with you and you live on your farm. He is one wily thief who will not hesitate even to commit murder. These days, his wife and children are happily roaming about in the lake area. Usually that means that the man is somewhere in this region. By now, he would have heard about you. If we who live in the village together are so frightened, what will become of you who lives by yourself? Be careful. Or I will find a house in the village for you. Move there,' the naattamai advised Muthu.

'I will be careful and live here,' Muthu replied with a laugh.

'You don't listen to us no matter what we say. It is we who fear for you. Just last year, the police arrived here looking for Subbukodukkan in relation to a murder somewhere. They took his wife and children to interrogate. Even then they could not nab him. Last year too, a few goats and a dozen or so chickens were stolen,' another man said.

They told him more and more about Subbukodukkan before they finally left. Once in a while, the men from the village stopped by. They were curious as to what these people who lived on the farm by themselves were up to. 'Why have you cut this up like this?' they asked. 'Can you actually sweep rocks and segregate them? I can barely sweep my front yard. If the whole farm has to be swept for rocks, how many years will that take?' A few more showed up when they knew he had slit some palm for toddy, demanding they be given some too. It became a routine chore to give an answer to each of them and send them back. It meant they had to stop working and sit down to entertain their queries. 'Why stop working, saami? Our hands can continue working while our lips talk. They will notice that and leave on their own after some time,' Kuppan said. 'If we do that, I'm afraid we might hurt their feelings, Kuppanna,' replied Muthu. But they had to resort to that strategy eventually.

He responded to the questions of the visitors with a word or two, and did not stop working. He never shared with anyone his full intent for his land. It was the people who came seeking toddy that were difficult to handle. They could not be turned away no matter how much he explained to them that it wasn't for sale. 'Let me give you some sunnambu theluvu,' he would offer. But they didn't want that. He climbed the trees before dawn in fear of these men. He didn't tap all the palms, just four of them. Two of those were for theluvu. Only Muthu knew which two, though. When it was still dark, he collected them and keep them hidden in the altar. He and Kuppan went over to drink from it periodically. The job of boiling the palm water and pouring into wooden moulds to let them crystallize into palm jaggery, was done in the afternoon. Every day, they had at least two or three moulds of palm jaggery. Rosa made herself coriander tea with the palm jaggery. Paati enjoyed the tea too. Eating the jaggery by itself also made for a tasty treat.

Angry that he didn't give them any toddy, some of the men would threaten to call the police. Once, Muthu turned to them and said, 'Call as many police as you want. I will show the collection pots to them all. This is sunnambu theluvu. If they find toddy in any of the pots, they can arrest me and take me away.' Because he had said it so confidently, no one thought he had toddy. But Muthu continued to be careful. He hid the toddy collection pots in places as carefully as possible—amidst the dense foliage of the bomma tree; the toddy collection pot would sit surrounded by other collection pots in such a way that no one looking up the tree from the ground could ever tell that toddy was being collected. Even if someone demanded that a pot be brought down, he could simply pour sunnambu theluvu from an adjacent pot into it before bringing it down. These were tricks he had learned from the old man in Pattoor.

So far, the police had never come to the village to arrest anyone for tapping or drinking toddy. If they did show up, he would figure it out then. The police came at least once a month to Aattur because it was so close to the Karattur town that they always kept an eye on them. When the police arrived, every man scampered to find a place to hide. The police wouldn't relent either; they would nab five or so men and take them away. If they were tappers, the police made them climb the trees and show the contents of the collection pots. If they were drinkers, they checked their breaths. Muthu had found the perfect spot to hide from the police. He would climb high up on the alunji tree and sit crouched within its dense foliage. From there, he had a clear view of the men running and the police chasing them. He struggled to suppress his laughter sitting at the top. It didn't seem like the police had ever been to this village at all. If they did, it must have been to inquire about Subbukodukkan. People here seemed to be more frightened of Subbukodukkan than the police!

Muthu was filled with thoughts about him. Was he really such a big thief? He decided he shouldn't sleep even for a second at night. He could not control Kuppan's sleep. When he was in the market, he picked up a stray puppy and brought it back with him to the farm. The puppy was grown enough to eat rice. It was female, though. No one let a male puppy out on the streets. But it was good to bring a female dog over to the farm first—they were loud barkers. For the first year, there shouldn't be any problems. By next Purattasi, the farm would be teeming with male ones.

A dog was a necessity for the farm at the moment. With its ears perking up, dogs react to the smallest sound. Its bark is also loud enough to be heard from quite a distance away. This dog would give him company when he stayed up at night as well. When he ran chartered loads in the past, he became used to sleeping during the day and staying awake at night. *From now on, that is what I shall do. I can cut up some sticks like spears and keep them handy. I can also keep the arivaal sharpened. No matter what kind of person he is, he is still only human.*

As he walked into the farm with these thoughts in his mind, he heard Rosa scream out to him. 'Aiyo! Appa, come here!' He immediately ran towards the direction of her voice. There was anxiety in her voice. At this hour, the problem was likely to be related to a snake or something like that. He sped up wondering what the issue was. In four leaps, he was near the voice.

Paati was seated holding her hands. Through her toothless mouth, she was hissing, biting her gums. In front of her lay a wounded red scorpion. Paati had been bitten by it. He examined the bitten finger. The pincer hadn't got stuck in the sting but the sting was clearly visible. He held her and brought her carefully to the rock. 'Thambi, the pain is unbearable,' paati said. Even though she bore the pain with great difficulty, tears still rolled down her cheek on their own.

Kuppan, who was trimming the bushes, came running too and learned what had happened. 'Big saami, you should not be afraid. This won't do anything to you. The sting of the red scorpion will hurt for a whole day but after that, the pain will vanish without a trace. Little saami, please bring some tamarind. There is nothing that tamarind cannot cure when it comes to scorpion stings,' he said. Rosa returned with some tamarind. Muthu carefully applied it around the sting. By now, the sting had become clearer. 'Tamarind can take care of stings even from buffalo scorpions. Don't be afraid. It will throb until this time tomorrow but after that you will be left wondering where it vanished,' Kuppan reassured paati.

Grabbing a bunch of neem leaves from nearby, Kuppan then performed a *paadam*, an aura cleanser, for paati. 'Do you know how to peform a paadam too, Kuppanna? We can put some fear into the villagers then! You never mentioned it to me until now. What all paadams do you know to perform? Tell me, I myself will spread this news around,' Muthu said.

'I know a few, nga. For trance, spider bites, poisonous bites, hexes cast on children. Usually there will be a person or two in the village who would do just this. So I don't do it usually; only in emergencies,' he replied. The throbbing pain in Paati's hand subsided a little. Muthu wondered if he should stop all the efforts to remove stones. 'This red scorpion, the damned thing, looks exactly like the red earth. Sometimes you can't spot it even if it is right under your nose. Only when it moves and sparkles like a red stone as it catches the light, can you even tell,' Kuppan continued to chatter.

Rosa hadn't let go of paati's hand from the time she had held her in fear. Paati's body was still shaking. Kuppan asked her for a flask of water and walked over the temple for Karunchaami. Muthu sat next to paati, who now sat up on the cot. He caressed her hand calmingly. The scorpion had stung her at the tip of her middle finger. The tip must have touched the ground as she gathered the stones into the palm sweep. When the scorpion was ready to attack, bothered by the sweeping action, the middle finger must have appeared right in front of it. Muthu took a neem leaf and gently brushed that over her arm. He could see the pain in paati's face. In the past couple of weeks, ever since she got here, he had never seen her in so much discomfort. Her face always bore a smile, bright as a blossom. The face that was otherwise wrinkled shone with beauty when she smiled. Making her laugh was something Muthu enjoyed a lot. He addressed her as 'aaya'. She too treated him like a grandson and duly called him 'thambi'. What would he do if something were to happen to her?

Kuppan instructed her to place the flask of water in front of Karunchaami. They lit up the lamp and prayed. Kuppan then tossed a fistful of holy ash into the water. He asked

Rosa to bring the water carefully and walked up to paati.
Rosa carried the pot back deferentially. He had Rosa pour
some water in his palm and slapped the water on paati's
face. Shocked, paati's face distorted and began to shake.
After he did that three times, he had her drink from the
flask. Paati drank two mouthfuls and said, 'This is bitter!'

'That's it! if you can taste the bitterness, you are going
to be fine,' Kuppan said reassuringly. After that, paati
spoke, feeling much calmer.

'I have myself told so many people that getting stung
by a scorpion can hardly do any harm. Only now that I got
stung, do I see what it really means. Anyhow, if I live a little
longer, I will sweep up the whole farm. Then, one day you
will reminisce about how I gathered all the stones before I
passed on. This land is going to turn into a paddy farm, for
sure. I hope to live to see that happen. But if that doesn't
happen, then let me die today and let things carry on, that's
all. You don't need to take me back home. You can keep me
for a couple of days for the people from home to come over
here to pay their respects and then bury me in this land. As
a fertilizer for this land, I will come back as crops and plants
every year and take care of you all,' she said tenderly.

Rosa couldn't help her tears. She began to cry loudly.
Where were we born and where do we die? Muthu's eyes too
began to well up with tears the more he looked at the old
woman who wanted to become nourishment for his land.
To hide his tears, he consoled Rosa, 'Don't cry, darling.
Nothing will happen to ammayi.' His voice wavered and
his tongue remained caught in his throat. Ostensibly, he
was reassuring himself.